I0727849

Necessary Evil

of

Nathan Miller

DEMELZA CARLTON

DEDICATION

*This book is dedicated to all those whose names
I've borrowed for characters along the way.*

*I'm not entirely sure how your namesake developed into
a vengeful, sadistic, psychopathic dominatrix or a brutal,
callous, murdering rapist as the story progressed...*

*You never know what's hiding under the
safe-looking surface until it's too late.*

Nathan thought Caitlin was a little angel, too.

ONE

Don't get into cars with strangers.

So stupid to think I was strong enough to resist.

But I never dreamed it would happen to me.

Dashing through traffic in daylight. A tingling instant preceded my sneeze. Desperately scrabbling for a tissue before the explosion. Sneezing, blowing, blech... I wanted to wash my hands, but there was nowhere on the Terrace to do that. I looked up, wondering where I could.

My search met her stare, through the open window of her Mercedes. I knew my sneeze couldn't inspire such fascination, so I looked behind me. Her laughter dragged my eyes from the ordinary street scene back to her. Apprehensive, I started to walk towards her, because my path lay past her.

She stepped out of her car, continuing to stare at me. I tried to look anywhere but at her. She had a nice car – a shiny red Mercedes with even shinier mag wheels, but not the newest model. I'd seen the newest ones in the doctors' car park at the hospital. Yet there was something in the lines of this one...

"Now that's a nice car," I couldn't stop myself from saying.

She smiled and motioned for me to come closer. Her hair was a short, dark bob that shone in the sun, her lips a glistening bright red that matched the car.

"My friend wants to ask you something," she said. Cracking open the car's back door, she jerked her head in the direction of the car's interior.

I leaned on the door frame and stuck my head inside with considerable curiosity. My eyes took a moment to adjust from the bright sunlight outside to the tinted gloom.

There were two guys in there - one in the passenger seat and another in the back. The one in the back was breathing heavily, like he'd just finished a long sprint... or he was making an obscene call. I could barely see his face, just his eyes. His eyes were on me, wide as saucers.

Pervert. I tried to back away, but the bitch behind me didn't let me. She hit my diaphragm with the heel of her hand, forcing my breath out in a huff. Unable to breathe, the street stood still in my mind as I stared around, desperately hoping for someone to see - someone who'd help me. Did eyes meet mine? Did I imagine understanding? If it was, it came too late. The burning flare that was my need to breathe exploded and she shoved me into the car. I fell on flesh encased in fabric as I gasped for breath, a flailing fish in the pervert's lap as I lay across the back seat. I dimly heard the doors and windows shut. The

motor hummed as the car accelerated away -
before I had enough air to scream.

3

motor hummed as the car accelerated away -
before I had enough air to scream.

TWO

"And now in breaking news, Caitlin Lockyer has been found. In the early hours of this morning, a man discovered her body dumped on a south-west beach. Sources say that she was left on the beach to die, but she was found in time and moved to hospital in Perth, where she remains in a critical condition.

"A police spokesperson would not confirm whether the girl known as the Absent Angel is alive or dead. . ."

Let me know when you work it out, won't you? I don't feel dead. . .

"Oh, turn that down. She's waking up. . . Get a dressing over that one and we can make a start on these ulcers. . ."

Unfamiliar hands touched me. Unfamiliar voices talked about my injuries as dispassionately as a GPS giving directions.

Was it safe to open my eyes? Were they helping me, or did I need to fight my way free? My head felt full of thick fog, so the thoughts were slow to surface.

Pain made the decision for me – twin pains. A sharp pull on my hair as someone tore the skin from my back. I cried out, so I didn't hear what the low voices murmured. Cold metal touched the side of my neck.

Going to cut me again. Going to hurt worse. . .

"No!" I shouted, or tried to. My voice rasped in my throat.

I couldn't feel my hands, but I still tried to use them to push myself upright to a sitting position. The moment I put weight on them, feeling returned. Pain shot up every one of my fingers, through my wrists and up my arms, like electrodes attached to every nerve. My scream sounded squeaky and weak, which is why I heard the snip of the scissors.

I opened my eyes to see bright light, briefly blocked by what was unmistakably my hair.

The scissors cut my hair, I realised. Taking everything away from me, even my hair. Bastards.

"You promised!" I sobbed out. "You promised you wouldn't let them hurt me again. Please, come back!"

He was shot. You saw the blood. If he wasn't here, was he even alive? Did they kill him?

I shook my head, trying not to see the picture in my memory: his shock at the spreading patch of red on his shirt, over his chest.

I focussed on the grinning pictures on the ceiling above me. Winnie the Pooh, Eeyore, Mickey Mouse, Minnie Mouse. . .

Eeyore I liked. He looked sympathetic. I wanted to scream at the rest of them or scratch their eyes out. Stop grinning at me like my pain is funny!

A concerned face came into view. "She's awake. Honey, can you hear me?"

"Yes," I told her impatiently. "Where is he?"

"Who, honey? They can't hurt you any more," she said soothingly. Dropping her voice lower, she murmured, "We need to give her more pain relief. This isn't enough."

They could hurt me and he'd promised to protect me. But he couldn't if he was dead and I couldn't sleep until I knew where he was. I didn't even know his name.

I ignored the soothing woman, who didn't know what she was on about. "Where are you? Please, come back. You promised."

Carefully, I pushed with my elbows and not my hands this time. I struggled to sit up and see where I was. Where he was.

Gloved hands weighed on my shoulders, pushing me down. I took a swipe at the hands, growling, "Don't touch me!" as I collapsed on the bed again.

I turned my head as a shoe squeaked on the vinyl floor. The soothing woman now had a syringe.

She was going to give me something that would make me sleep. They'd kill me in my sleep and I'd never wake up!

I struggled to rise and this time they didn't stop me. Every head was turned away from me to the door of what I recognised as a hospital room in an Emergency Department.

Hey, the news got something right. I was in hospital. But which one?

I heard his voice. I finally saw his face clearly as he pushed past an orderly to enter the room. The face of the man who killed another in an effort to protect me, before the police shot him. . . Fuck. Focus. Memories could wait.

"Don't let them hurt me again!" I shouted at him as I lunged for the syringe with my uncooperative fingers, before my arms gave out and I was lying flat on the bed again. I couldn't feel if I'd managed to snatch the syringe or just knock it out of her hands. I didn't have the energy to lift my arm to check, either.

My eyes didn't leave him. His face looked pale and a bit scared, though he tried to keep his voice calm. He had no shirt on and a white dressing, spotted with a little fresh blood, looked like a misplaced breast pocket on his bare chest. He said something about being in hospital, but I didn't catch the words.

"I'm so tired, but I'm scared to sleep," I told him, my voice starting to give out as my eyes filled with tears. "What if, when I wake up, you're gone and I'm still there with them? Please. . ." I didn't know what to ask him for. Please don't be dead?

He promised he'd be here, again.

I could feel my mind going under. Like drowning in a warm bath, only I could still breathe. He promised. Even if he was dead, he was shot trying to help me.

"Thank you." I tried to say the words, but I wasn't sure if they came out right. Even the ghost of someone killed trying to help me deserved my thanks.

Is he a ghost or is he real? I thought but was too tired to give voice to it any more. As a ghost he couldn't protect me. Directly above me, all I could see was a blurry yellow bear.

If this kills me, Winnie the Pooh, I'm taking you and your smug smiling face with me to hell. This last thought followed me down into a spiral of darkness.

THREE

The sibilance of sound as his voice spoke in endless waves. Sentences ebbed and flowed in the dark – always the same ones with slight variations.

Sssssorry. . .

"Caitlin, I'm sorry I didn't help you sooner."

"Stole a shirt from a corpse. Stuck it on you. Sorry. . ."

"So sorry. . ."

"Sorry I didn't. . ."

Sssssafe. . .

"It's okay, angel, you're safe."

"Safe in hospital, where you belong."

"You're safe now. They can't hurt you."

"I'll keep you safe, Caitlin. I swear. . ."

"Shh, it's okay, you're safe now."

Sssssshe. . .

"She's the same age as you. I couldn't let them. . ."

"She said she knew who'd killed her."

"She's all I have left. Please. . ."

"After a few drinks, she wanted to leave, so we made it to the back seat of my car before she. . ."

"She was my twin. . ."

"She must've spiked my drink. . ."

Ssssssssister. . .

"My twin sister. . ."

"The only sister I have left. . ."

"Said, 'Are you sure you didn't get the sister instead? We'll call him Chris, just in case. . . '"

"Please, wake up and help me save my sister."

"Said it'd remind me of the sister I didn't want them to take. You or her, he said. . ."

"Do you know what it's like to lose a sister?"

Sssssshhhhhould've. . .

"I should've tried to help you sooner. . ."

"Should've known she seemed strange. . ."

"Should've grabbed you before she did and run. . ."

"Should've known. . ."

Ssssorry. . .

"Sorry. Caitlin, I'm so sorry."

Surfacing to sound, before submerging in darkness once more. Sorry. Slipping. . . sinking. . . from safety to screaming nightmares.

Shit.

FOUR

Mercedes – Red – Chris – Her – Mike – Sorry – Pervert

Saucer Eyes looked like he was going to cry. I was going to make him cry if he so much as touched me. "How c-"

"Shut up!" said the one in the passenger seat.

Saucer Eyes wasn't much older than me. His breathing slowed, but it felt forced, the muscles in his legs tense beneath my back. Thighs as taut as a fully laden clothes line. One hand clutched the door handle, but the door didn't open, no matter how hard he pulled on that handle. His other hand mashed down the window button, which wasn't opening, either. Held prisoner by the car's child lock. No one trusts a pervert, not even his peers.

He wouldn't look at me as he mumbled something, half under his breath, that sounded like, "Sorry," before he turned away to stare out the window.

I dragged air in through my nose, inflating

my burning lungs like brand-new balloons. I wanted to kill the bitch and her two blokes, too. But first...

"Let me go, you bastard!" I blared, feeling satisfaction as Saucer Eyes' hands shot up in scared surrender.

You can wait, pervert. The big bastard gets his balls ripped off first. Besides, the only way out is through his door, if the back doors are child-locked shut.

The big, chunky bastard in the passenger seat just laughed.

I tensed, testing each muscle for readiness as I prayed I could do enough damage to make him let me go.

I launched my body at him, clawed fingers first, reaching for his face. I wanted to scratch his eyes out, but his fist to my jaw jerked my head up so hard I saw stars as I landed in Saucer Eyes' lap, stunned. I sucked in a sobbing breath, not game to give in to the blokes who could kill me. Fight them 'til I fucking killed them, for I'd never let them win as long as I drew breath. One more breath and I'd be up, ready to rip out an eye.

Chunky twisted in his seat, telling Saucer Eyes, "Chris, hold her still," but he wouldn't touch me. Still surrendering, Chris was saucer-eyed and shaking, set against a background of the dark car ceiling. Chunky caressed the forming bruise on my face with a satisfied smile, saying, "Beautiful," before he clamped a cloth over my face, crushing me down onto Saucer Eyes. Chris.

I remember gasping for breath, fighting what I knew was sweet, cloying chloroform, but I couldn't. All I could see was Saucer Eyes' face, his anguished look as his lips formed the

words I couldn't hear, "Oh God, I'm so sorry,"
before it all vanished in a dark haze.
    It's all dark after that.

FIVE

The first unfamiliar voice I heard was male. I struggled to focus, but it was like my body was too heavy to move, from my eyelids to my toes. Even the voice sounded like it was far away or a TV with the volume on low.

"Guards. . . no one. . . we need her to stay safe. . ." I heard the unfamiliar voice say.

The reply came with words I couldn't hear, but my heart relaxed at the sound. I didn't know his name, but I knew his voice meant safety.

The unfamiliar man heard him, though, and he responded, ". . . get them before the local police do. . . be her fucking best mate. . ."

It's his job to guard me. He's not police, but he's here. He's going to stay and keep me safe. And he has orders to get them before the police do. Shit, not before I get there first. I want to kill them all for what they did to me. Maybe he'll help me. . . my best mate, all right.

They kept talking while my thoughts drifted in the dark.

Some of the words penetrated the fog in my head. "Let me know what you find out. And don't let anyone fucking kill her." The unfamiliar voice faded, as if he was walking away from me.

That's right. Don't let anyone fuck or kill me. Not even in self-defence.

Drifting. . .

SIX

I heard voices as I floated in the dark, mostly his but sometimes others. Sometimes I could discern a few words, but they seemed too far away to focus on. The only concept I seemed to be able to hold onto was whenever I heard his voice, there was no pain and I thought, It's okay. I'm safe. In between those times, I fought them in the dark, over and over again.

I couldn't open my eyes to see if any of them – him or them – were real. I was too tired, my eyes too heavy. Or my eyes were open and it was so dark that I couldn't see, just like before. This felt different, somehow. It was warmer here.

I heard his voice as a wordless hum and relaxed in the sensation of safety it brought. Through the contentment in my head, I heard him clearly say, "Alana."

That's my name! My middle name, anyway. I struggled to focus on what he said next. Something about his sister.

". . . Never stopped fighting, never let them win. So they

broke her and they killed her. How could anyone do that to her?"

How could anyone do that to me?

"I wanted to hunt them down and hurt them for what they did to her. But the police didn't arrest anyone and they could still do it again, to someone else!"

Hunt them down and kill them. Then they'll never do it again.

"I'm sorry, Caitlin. I never wanted to see you hurt. Not like this. I should have helped you sooner. . ."

It's not too late. Help me hunt them down and kill them. Then maybe I'll forgive you for what you did. . .

I felt the fury bubble up inside me, but all it did was exhaust me, pushing me deeper into the dark where I couldn't make out what he was saying.

SEVEN

Dark — Chris — Mike — Awake — Card

Angry voices in the dark. No... one angry voice, one petulant one.

The angry one shouted commands. "You're not to talk to her, except to give orders or ask questions." Even at a distance, the bastard's voice hurt my pounding head.

The petulant one sounded almost whiny. "Mike, she'll be scared and not feeling well, with the aftereffects of the drugs. I want her lying down..."

You can want me all you like. Get close to me and I'll kick your balls backwards through your teeth.

"Of course you do. It's easier to fuck her lying down than standing up."

My blood ran cold and I missed whatever the angry prick said next.

"But she's not a threat," the petulant voice whined.

Sure, mate, you believe that until I get close enough to bite something off.

"You don't need to have her tied up like this," he continued.

Fucking right you don't.

I twisted my wrists within the rope - it was a little loose. Not loose enough to pull out of, but I could still move my hands a bit. The rope didn't restrict my circulation. I shifted, rolling on the concrete like an overturned turtle. I still had my clothes, but no shoes. More rope on my ankles.

I had to get rid of the rope. I needed to find a sharp edge to cut it, so I could get free. I squirmed, wondering what in hell was in my jeans pocket. It felt like a really thick credit card.

"Please. I don't think I can..." the petulant voice begged.

Mike said, "Sure you can. Nothing to it. She's tied up so she can't escape. You don't need to say a word to her. If you're lucky, she might still be unconscious. You can stick it in and be done before she wakes up to think about fighting you. Easiest lay of your life."

I heard the smack of flesh on flesh. Did Mike slap Chris on the back? Or did Chris slap Mike for saying what he did? Shit, who cared?

I managed to get two fingers into my pocket, almost dislocating my shoulder in the process. Wincing, I pinched the strange card between my fingers. Slowly, I edged it out, wishing my hands weren't tied behind my back. I wasn't sure how to bring it to my face so I could see it. I explored the edges with my fingers, trying to work out what it was.

I heard something scrape across concrete.

"What the hell is that for?" Mike sneered.

It was the Swiss Card I'd bought Jason for his birthday. This was in my bag - one of them must have stuck it in my pocket. Someone was trying to help me.

"In case I get hungry or thirsty. You said she's mine all night." Chris sounded uncertain.

Mike laughed. "Yeah, you would need a snack to keep your stamina up for more than a minute. Have fun with her. Tell me about it tomorrow."

I heard heavy footsteps leaving.

I desperately tried to pull a blade out of the card, but I couldn't seem to find one. Oh shit, oh shit...

EIGHT

Strange hands touched me again. This didn't hurt yet, but I called for him in panic.

I heard his voice clearly this time. "It's okay, Caitlin. You've been hurt and we're trying to help you get better."

A woman's voice, closer than his. It must've been her hands on me. "You're in hospital as a patient now and all of us on the clinical team here are doing our best to help you get better." She knew me. She knew I wasn't usually a patient in hospital. "Your roommate's sleazy and, if I were you, I'd wake up fast so you can ask for a room transfer."

Inwardly, I laughed. No matter how sleazy, there was no way I'd give in to anyone's amorous advances for a very long time. Mr Sleazy Roommate would give up long before that.

I could smell disinfectant now. Faint, but it was there. They were both quiet, so I heard the crackle of ripping paper and plastic, interspersed with the feeling of tugging on my skin, then something soft being smoothed back over it. Changing my dressings? I was aware of the edge of pain now, as feeling returned to my body.

The woman's voice was low and kind. "I'll get you some more medicine for the pain. That'll help." Another crackle nearby, but I couldn't feel anything touch me. "There, all done. Sleep well."

I felt my body fade away until I was just a consciousness in the dark again. Then even that slipped away as I fell asleep once more.

NINE

"Pregnant."

"Rape."

I heard the words and struggled to focus. I could feel my body faintly, so I tried to move my fingers, but it was too much for me yet.

The calm voice sighed, sounding sad. "If she was awake, I could ask her. But she's a seventeen-year-old girl who's been through hell and a lot of pain, given how long she was missing and the state she's in now."

I found I could hold my breath. A seventeen-year-old girl who'd been through hell. That was me, all right. But pregnant? NO!

"I've left a note in her file and I'm leaving it at that. There's no need to ask her, or even mention it. She's definitely not pregnant."

I let out my held breath in a sigh of relief, but it was only loud in my ears. Too intent on their own conversation, they didn't hear me.

The second voice belonged to a young woman, who sounded very serious. "I'd ask, Dr Lannon, just to be thorough. What if. . ."

I stopped trying to move and stayed as still as I could. Even knowing the man was Dr Lannon didn't reassure me.

I'm not awake. Don't ask me. I don't want to tell you.

His normally calm and patient voice sounded irritated, louder than before. "Did you see her when she came in? Have you been here when she has nightmares?"

"No, I've just read her file because she was on my patient list today."

"This girl was beaten and raped repeatedly for weeks then left on a beach to die. It's been all over the news. Do you want to be the one to remind her and make her relive all the gory details?"

I could hear footsteps leaving – her reply sounded further away. "No."

Their conversation drifted away as they left, my thoughts stirring sluggishly.

Beaten. Raped. Left on a beach to die. I remembered pain. I remembered sand. Left to die?

No. My death was meant to be sudden and witnessed. Never alone.

My body slipped away again – did that mean they'd given me more pain medication? I struggled to hold onto my thoughts of sand. . . beach. . . as I sank into oblivion and what I can only describe as the arms of a nightmare.

TEN

Dark – Chris – Awake – Card – Headache – Stab – Free

The door cracked open, without a clichéd creak. Dim light spilled into the room. Feverishly, I kept digging my nails into the card, trying to find something to cut my bonds. I closed my eyes, trying to visualise the card I held.

"Hey." His voice was barely above a whisper. "Are you awake yet?"

No. I'm busy sleeping, so fuck off, I thought but didn't say.

I found the scissors. Trying not to move too much, I dug the blades into the rope.

"Awake?" he said again. He shone a torch into my face.

I opened my eyes slowly. My head ached horribly and I couldn't see clearly. He loomed like a blurry shadow above me, between me and my escape.

Chris held up his hands, surrendering – just like he had in the car.

I wondered if he knew what I held in my hands.

He shook his head convulsively. "I'm not going to hurt you." He sounded like he was begging, but that made no sense. Begging me to believe him, maybe. "How are you feeling?"

I tried to talk but nothing came out. I sawed furiously at the rope.

He crouched on the floor near me, but not near enough to touch me. "Would you like some Panadol for the headache?" He sounded kind. Perhaps he could see my panic and mistook it for fear.

I remember he waited a moment, like he wanted to say something else, but he seemed to change his mind. He moved from a crouch to his full height, leaving the room as quickly as he'd come.

I felt something snap and kept slicing at that rope, desperately trying to free myself before he returned.

The rope gave, loosening around my wrists. Carefully, I tried to pull my hand out.

Yes!

Feverishly, I untied my legs. I tried to find a knife in the card - something, anything I could threaten Chris with to make him let me go. I pulled it out a tiny bit, so I'd be able to find it again when I needed it, and stuck the card back in my pocket.

My feet tingled as I wiggled my toes, trying to relieve the numbness. Whoever had tied my feet had done a better job than they had with the restraints around my wrists.

Cautiously, I stood up, my toes curling and refusing to cooperate as circulation returned. I tried to take a shuffling step, but the whirling dizziness in my head almost made me fall.

I had to get to the door so I could get out. Hide somewhere so I could get between him and the door when he came in. Shut him in here and run.

I couldn't see, but I continued to drag my feet across the floor until my outstretched fingers touched the wall. I almost cried as I slumped against it.

No. Couldn't cry. No matter how scared, I had to keep it inside if I wanted to escape and live. Couldn't hesitate.

"You can do this. You can do this," I heard Chris's voice murmur from the other side of the door.

You can do what? Rape me? FUCK YOU. I pulled the card out of my pocket and extracted the knife.

The door started to open. Chris had his back to it, shouldering his way into the room, carrying something.

He was going to see me as soon as he got the door open far enough. I needed to get the knife to his throat while his hands were full.

I straightened up, trying to ignore the blinding pain in my head, as I threw myself forward, blade out.

I felt it sink in, with a strange ease. Not like cutting up meat. Baked potato, maybe.

Blackness descended.

ELEVEN

When I was aware of my surroundings again, I found I couldn't hear anything. It was too quiet. I opened my eyes in shock, blinking to make sure I'd really, finally opened them.

I looked up at a white ceiling with an institutional fluorescent light. The light was dim, leaving shadows on the ceiling, but it felt too bright to me after so much darkness.

Focussing on trying to keep my eyes open, I experimented with moving my toes, then my fingers. My toes moved fine, but my fingers felt like they were tangled in the sheet. I could certainly feel them, but they barely moved through the resistance of whatever wrapped them.

I tried to lift my arms so that I could see my hands. I managed to bring them into my field of vision, before I tried to move my fingers again. It took me a few moments to realise that the white swathing my hands wasn't a pair of weird, white gloves. They'd bandaged my hands and all of my fingers. No wonder I couldn't move them.

It occurred to me that I was pretty useless with my hands disabled.

I shouldn't be alone. He promised he'd be here. Did that mean they killed him?

I called for him, irritated that I didn't know his name.

I tried to sit up, but I was afraid to put any weight on my evidently injured hands. Crunches were never my strong point, but this was the first time I'd regretted avoiding them. Everyone should do daily crunches, just in case their hands are disabled and they need those tummy muscles to sit up.

I heard his voice nearby and I struggled to focus on his words before I saw his face above me, looking exhausted. He wore a shirt now and he looked fine, as if he'd never been shot.

He touched his fingers to mine and I felt the heat of his hand through the bandage before he ripped his hand away as if he'd been burned.

I didn't feel burned. I couldn't feel any pain in my hands or anywhere else. Stunned, I tried to process this and came up with two options – either we were both dead and he'd waited for me in the afterlife, or I'd been given so much pain medication I just felt like I was made of cloud.

I hesitated, feeling it would be rude to ask if he was dead. He didn't look it. "I'm not dead, am I?" I asked instead, wishing to be right. My voice felt weak from lack of use and my throat was dry, so the words were much quieter than I expected.

He smiled broadly, his eyes laughing.

Was it funny because the answer was no or yes? Worried, my eyes fixed on his face. Please, don't let me be dead!

I sighed in relief as he told me I was in hospital and on strong pain medication.

Medication I didn't remember being given. "What happened?" I demanded in my weak voice.

He looked bewildered. "You were hurt." I don't think he wanted to explain how badly I'd been hurt – thought the strong drugs were a pretty good indication. As for how I'd been hurt. . . shit, even I didn't want to think about that.

I tried to explain to him what I remembered of the last things I'd seen, before waking up here. Nurses and scissors, syringes and simpering cartoon characters. How do I describe there's a huge gaping hole in my memory and I'm asking him to fill it? How do you describe a huge gaping hole, except that it's dark? I shook my head, trying not to think of the dark again. I swallowed. "What happened?" I asked him again, my voice louder this time.

His words came out in a rush. "You fought the nurses. You were so scared. I think they gave you something to make you sleep – you've been asleep for a while."

I'd fought the nurses? Why? All I'd wanted to do was find out if he was okay. Haltingly, I told him what I remembered – trying to get up and not being able to – but he interrupted me.

He sounded horrified. "You did too much as it was – if you'd done any more, we might have lost you. You came so close, Caitlin. . . hell, I was scared." His eyes held mine for a second before he looked away.

I almost died? When I find out who's responsible, I'm going to hunt them down and kill them slowly. Why didn't I remember? I came that close to death and I didn't even know? My eyes filled with tears that I couldn't wipe away with my useless hands. I tried furiously to blink them away, but what he said next turned the waterworks tap on full.

"It's over."

The shock, the relief, all of it just gushed out of me as I bawled. His hands hesitantly patted my back as he helped me cry into his shirt.

It felt like the tears would never end, but they did. Realisation came that if he was telling the truth and I'd nearly died, I owed him.

I chose my words carefully. "Thank you. I think. . . you saved my life." I tried to find a nice way to phrase what I wanted to ask next, but I just couldn't. "Who are you? I barely know you."

"My name is Nathan Miller. I found you lying on the beach. I just brought you in to the hospital," he rattled off, as if by rote.

So that was his story. And he was Nathan Miller. His sister was Alanna Miller. He'd be a prime candidate for Mr Sleazy Roommate. I found I was looking at my hands, now sedately placed in my lap. For the first time, I noticed the IV line into my right hand and the pain relief mystery was solved.

Focus.

"Nathan Miller," I repeated carefully, as I tried to find the words to express what I was thinking.

Nervously, I licked my dry, cracked lips and made an effort to smile, though my cheeks felt too heavy to do it. "Thank you. You chose to keep your promise. . . Nathan."

I watched him carefully for his reaction. First he opened his mouth, as if he had a burning question to ask, but his mouth stayed open as he stared at me. He looked wistful.

I dropped my gaze to my lap, counting the seconds slowly before lifting my eyes to meet his again. Contact made. Nathan began to apologise.

I started to say that he hadn't hurt me, when I remembered that he'd been hurt. The blood on his shirt and the dressing on his chest. The memory on the dark road was slow to surface. "You were shot," I said slowly, reaching up to place my hand over where I remembered the blood, the dressing. I could feel a dressing there still, or at least the roughness of fabric sliding over gauze instead of skin under his shirt. He jumped at my touch, as if even the light contact from my hand hurt him. I drew my hand back.

His answer shocked me. "Yes. So were you."

I was shot? That's how I nearly died? My thoughts whirled in my head, water down a plughole, taking me with them.

I could hear his voice continue, but I couldn't make out the words any more. I tried to open my mouth to ask one of the million swirling questions and choked, coughing so hard I couldn't get a word out.

Worn out with coughing, I fought to keep my eyes open. Would he stay, to make sure I woke up again?

Somehow he understood. "I'll be here," he promised, a reassuring smile on his face.

I floated away again.

TWELVE

When I awoke next, it was daylight. Last night's dark window showed sunlight and blue sky. I stretched and saw the IV was no longer connected to my arm, though the needle was still taped to my hand.

Time for a walk, I thought. Let's see which hospital this is and what ward. Is there a guard outside my room or is Nathan all the protection I have? If he is and they come looking for me. . . I'm going to die.

Carefully, I sat up and dangled my legs off the side of the bed nearest the door, too high up for my feet to reach the floor. I looked for the buttons to control the bed so that I could move it lower, then realised that I couldn't press them.

I poised myself on the edge, hesitating a second because of the half-metre drop. I almost put my hands on the mattress beside me to take my weight as I slid off the bed, but then I remembered that my hands were damaged. So, with my hands up as if to demonstrate how defenceless I was, I gave a little jump and my feet hit the floor. The impact set my legs on fire, the muscles turned from ordinary tissue to white-hot, molten metal.

Blinded by pain, I swore through gritted teeth as I felt myself falling forward with fuck-all I could do about it. I instinctively stuck my hands out to break my fall. The bones in my hands caught the same agonising fire before the rest of my body hit the floor heavily. Tears sprang to my eyes, but they burned away on my hot cheeks.

Fucking perverted bastards. Bloody legs that wouldn't fucking work.

I reached up to the bed, to try and pull myself up again, before I realised that my useless hands couldn't grab anything.

Damn bed too bloody high up. Fucking linen. Bloody broken fingers. . .

I didn't realise I was swearing out loud until Nathan appeared in front of me, asking what was wrong.

What wasn't wrong, I thought bitterly, as I added to the list of things to swear about. "I can't fucking walk and I can't fucking get up." I felt like biting his toes off to quell my frustration.

"Here, let me help you." His words were gentle.

"It's either that or stay here on the fucking floor all day," I muttered.

His arms closed around me, cradling me to his chest, so I could both hear and feel his laughter at my reply.

Instinctively, I wanted to shrink away from his touch, from anyone and everyone else, yet at the same time I relaxed, telling myself, You're safe. This is Nathan. He won't hurt you.

Nathan let out a small grunt of pain as he lifted me up. I wondered whether his wound had healed enough for him to be lifting anything, but he didn't make another sound as he carefully put me back into bed, pulling the sheets up to cover me again. He rubbed his shoulder, almost unconsciously, as he sat in the chair beside my bed.

Belatedly, I thanked him.

"What happened?" he asked, echoing my words from the day before.

What to tell him? I was useless, I couldn't walk and my hands and legs didn't work. I was a sitting target for anyone. And I didn't know if I could trust him to protect me.

I tried to be vague. "I got out of bed, tried to take a step and it hurt. Then I fell." Tell him. He'd find out anyway. At least now I'd see his reaction – I'd know if I couldn't trust him. "I can't walk if it hurts that much," I admitted grudgingly.

He told me to stay in bed and rest, smiling kindly.

"I needed. . ." I wondered if there was a nice way to tell him I didn't believe he could protect me. If he was as useless as my legs at present, they'd find me and hurt me again. . . I looked away from him as I tried not to cry. My eyes lighted on the door beside the one leading out of the room. "I was trying to get to the bathroom." Well, with all the IV fluid they'd pumped into me as I slept, I did want to make use of the facilities in the ensuite. Second to my desire to live was the pressing need to go to the loo.

Nathan didn't hesitate – he offered to carry me.

I wanted to ask if it would hurt him, but I fought the urge. He knew his own limitations – I wasn't even sure of mine yet. I felt like an overfilled water balloon, so my only reply was to thank him as he carried me to the toilet.

The feeling of his skin against mine made me self-conscious about the hospital gown I wore and how little it covered, though Nathan didn't seem to be fazed about it. He lifted me up deftly, carried me to the bathroom quickly and put me down gently, as if this were something he did every day as part of his job.

A bathrobe would be nice, I thought. I decided to buy one when I could go shopping, just in case I was ever stuck in hospital wearing one of these again.

Nathan's back blocked the doorway and he didn't say anything for a few minutes, until he burst out, "If you want, I could ask my sister to drop by your house the next time she comes in to see me. She could pick up some of your own clothes for you to wear."

Mortified, I realised he was just as aware of my near-nakedness as I was. I choked back the horrified reply I wanted to make so I could politely refuse his offer as coherently as possible.

I reached for the toilet paper and it started to dawn on me how useless my hands were. First one hand, then the other – no, I couldn't even grasp it. But with two hands together. . . I could hold something between them if I concentrated.

Right. Play it out, carefully. With one bandaged hand, I pushed the roll of toilet paper, making it unroll slowly. Okay, faster now.

"Let me know when you're done and need my help again."

His voice made me jump and knock the toilet roll back the other way.

"I. . . I'm not done, but I may need your help in a minute." My throat was dry and my voice failed somewhere in the middle. Don't turn around. Don't look yet, I begged him silently, as I tried to unroll the toilet paper again. The only thing worse than having to plan every step to wipe your own bum is knowing someone else watched you do it. Please, don't look.

Too late. Nathan leaned over me, deft hands grabbing the toilet paper I wanted, before he gave it to me. Helping me. Then he called me a kitten, wearing a worried smile. My eyes locked on his as I used the toilet paper as quickly as I could.

Kitten? Meow. I struggled to understand the comparison. Something to do with pawing the toilet paper? I lifted my useless hands up and they did resemble white paws, a little. Why try to hide it from him? He knew how disabled I was. I looked up to meet his concerned gaze. For the first time, I saw the dark circles beneath his eyes. He lost sleep over me? He genuinely seemed to want to help me.

I made an effort to try to smile, though my cheeks still felt too stiff and heavy to do it properly. "Meow. I feel about as weak as a kitten, so the comparison is probably right." I let out a breath I hadn't been aware I was holding. "Now, I would appreciate your help one more time, because I think you're right. I need to rest in bed a bit longer."

"At your service." His arms closed around me again, carrying me back to bed, where he covered me with the sheet, as clinical as any nurse.

As if he'd read my mind, Nathan reminded me that

while I was in hospital I could ask the nurses for help.

Didn't he realise that I couldn't press the nurse call button? I kept my eyes down, hoping he wouldn't read that thought, too. Then inspiration hit, as I thought of something true that wouldn't sound like an excuse. I told him I didn't like strangers touching me. Too many strangers had touched me, hurt me. . . I felt myself shudder at the memories that threatened to pull me back down into despair. I tried to focus on what he was saying, his words a lifeline out of the dark.

"And the last time you asked a random stranger for help, you ended up in hospital with him and now you can't get rid of him – he even followed you into the bathroom."

That was a joke, I told myself. He was trying to be funny. But I'd never asked him for help, yet he kept helping me. I looked down at my lap, where his warm hand covered both of mine. The contact didn't make me shudder – in fact, it felt comforting. I looked up again to meet his worried eyes and wistful smile. I want to trust you, I thought.

"After you saved my life, got shot and even helped me wipe my. . ." I tried to put it into words, but failed. I started again. "I don't think you qualify as a random stranger any more. I would like to think you're a very good friend, even if I don't know you very well." Will you be my friend, Nathan, or are you going to join the list of bastards I want to kill?

He made a weak joke in reply, but the real answer was in his expression. For the first time, his smile reached his eyes, which didn't look worried. Just relieved.

THIRTEEN

Dark - Chris - Falling - Card - Headache

"Oh shit! You're better than I thought."

I felt my body falling - but I didn't hit the ground. His arms tightened around my back, pressing my face against something soft. The knife slipped from my fingers as I tried to stop him from smothering me.

The impact with the floor jolted me, but it was softer than I expected. The restraining arm released me.

I squeezed my eyes shut, willing the dizziness to fade. I needed to fight. I knew what I was lying on and it wasn't good.

I almost whimpered in fright as I felt the foam mattress depress beneath his weight, not far from me. I slid my hand carefully into my pocket for the card, desperate for another blade to replace the one I'd stabbed into the mattress instead of him.

One hand at my shoulder, another on my thigh stopped me dead. I froze in fear.

"One, two..." he murmured.

What about three? What happens on three? I wanted to scream, biting down so I didn't make a sound.

With an ease that suggested plenty of practise moving unconscious people, he rolled me over onto my back. I shoved my hand deeper into my pocket, fishing for a weapon.

If only I could see to use it.

My head pounded its own rhythm as his fingers crept beneath my neck. I could feel the heat of him close beside me, leaning over me. The ache intensified as he lifted my head.

I couldn't see, but I sure could spit. "If you're going to try to force me to give you a blow job, I'll bite your chipolata of a cock right off." I had the card out of my pocket and I was ready to stab him with the corkscrew if I could pull it out.

He moved away, to my considerable satisfaction. I felt his weight ease off the mattress and breathed again. I'd found the edge of the scissors.

He laughed softly as his hand closed over both my fingers and the Swiss Card. "Fair warning. You won't need that against me. Put it away. You might need it later."

He clicked on a torch, searching for something. I blinked, trying to focus. My heart sank as I realised he'd shut the door behind him. I prayed it wasn't locked.

"Here. Don't lose this." He took the card from my hand and slid the knife back in. "Good thing you stabbed the mattress and not me."

"Why?" I spat back, shoving the card back in my pocket.

"I can't help you if I'm dead or dying. Here. It's juice." He pushed a plastic bottle into my hand.

I opened the bottle, turning my head to the side to drink so I didn't bring on the dizziness again. My mouth tasted horrible and I tried to swish away all traces of drugs or blood before I swallowed.

Silently, he waited.

When I'd lubricated my throat enough, I interrupted his reverie. "Why would you help me?" I struggled to sit up.

He dropped the torch on the floor, lifting both hands to my chest, stopping just before he touched me. Like he wanted to push me down again, but he didn't dare. "No hurry. Lie down as long as you need to, until you recover. He gave you a second dose of chloroform in the car, so you were under for a while."

"You want me lying down so you can rape me. I heard you talking." I glared at him, hoping he could see my malice in the dim light. "You stay away from me or I'll use the knife on you."

FOURTEEN

"I heard you were awake, hon." A motherly-looking woman in a hospital uniform smiled at me, giving me a quick wink as she placed a tray on the table over my bed. "I wasn't sure what you'd like, so I picked out the best of this morning's breakfast menu for you. I'll give you your menu, too, so you can order what you like for tomorrow." She poured me a glass of orange juice.

"Thank you," I replied in a hushed voice.

She smiled in reply, before she left through the open door. I could see the hospital corridor outside my room, with the food trolley full of breakfast trays.

I glanced over at Nathan, who was very focussed on his food, his mouth already full.

I guess it wasn't poisoned, then. I looked down at my tray. A covered plate, a glass of orange juice, a box of cereal in a bowl with packaged milk and a small bowl of diced fruit. It wouldn't have looked out of place on an aeroplane.

I couldn't remember the last time I'd had anything to eat

or drink. I wasn't sure how my stomach would cope.

I stretched one hand out for the orange juice, then realised I'd need both hands for this. I cradled the glass in between the bandages, like a hot drink on a cold day, and took a cautious sip before putting the glass down again. I'd wait a few minutes, then see if I should have anything else. What was the last thing I had? Oh, that Coke. A warm can Nathan'd had in his pocket on the beach. He'd cracked it open, drunk a little to show me it was okay, then he'd helped me drink it. Giving me the energy to do something stupid that got him shot. NO. . . don't think about that now. I forced myself to concentrate on the orange juice, the fruit and the covered plate. Don't look at the bowl with the milk.

I focussed so hard on the tray I wasn't aware of Nathan getting out of bed until he came between me and my breakfast, leaning over me to press the button to call a nurse. I exclaimed in surprise – I'm sure I swore.

He pretended he hadn't heard. "You need someone to help you with your breakfast," he said.

Don't need help yet. Right now I just needed to decide whether I'd keep the orange juice down. One more sip. I reached for the juice carefully, concentrating so hard my teeth ground together. "I was managing fine," I told him.

Then I wasn't. Something went wrong and the orange juice tipped off the tray onto the bed.

Between my damaged hands and useless legs, the most I could do to get away from the mess was to swing my legs off the side of the bed, shuffling toward the pillows. Now what? I wanted to get up and rip the damp sheets off the bed, bundle them into a washing machine and get fresh ones. But I couldn't.

Nathan stood frozen with his mouth open, just staring at me.

I looked back at the juice, running across the top of the sheets toward the bed's lowest point. Of course, this was the bit bearing the most weight – compressed under my backside. Orange juice in open wounds, soaking into my dressings. Torture. I could avoid this.

This will hurt, too, I told myself, but it's only a few steps. I fixed my eyes on the chair by my bed and took a deep breath.

Warm and gentle, Nathan's arms lifted me off my bed. My head against his chest, I could both hear and feel the rumble of his voice as he said quietly, "Please, let me help."

Surprise. Relief. Comfort. I realised I felt safe. Tears of gratitude sprang to my eyes and I struggled not to shed them. Distracted, I barely noticed as he bypassed the chair to lay me carefully in his bed. He turned away from me almost immediately, shifting the breakfast trays around until they were side by side on a table in front of me, blurring as my tears multiplied.

I reached for a tissue automatically, but his hand was there first. I'm here to help, his eyes said, though he didn't say a word.

I expected him to give me the tissue, but I was stunned as he touched the tissue to my eyes, my cheeks and my nose, wiping my face carefully as if he did this every day. It wasn't until he turned away, crossing the room to drop the tissue in the bin, that I found my voice.

It took two tries to get the words out and even then my voice was so quiet I don't think he heard me over the running water as he washed his hands. "Thank you."

When Nathan returned, he sat beside me and started to help me with my breakfast. A waft of steam, sulphur and salt as he lifted the cover – those eggs smelled good.

He opened the butter and began spreading it across my toast.

He was going to help me. Maybe even feed me.

He lifted up the box of cereal, pouring cornflakes into the bowl. Dark thoughts stirred, a memory of stale, dry cereal in the dark, choking it down as unseen hands fed me. Even the thought of being fed like a baby again makes me lose my appetite. My throat contracted at the memory. Desperately, I tried to force it away.

He said something that I didn't catch as he started cutting my eggs into small pieces. He loaded a piece onto the fork and held it out for me. Not like feeding a baby – more like holding a carrot out to tempt a horse.

I closed my eyes and ate even that small bite carefully. How long since I'd last had solid food? Could my stomach handle it?

I realised that I couldn't make it to the toilet to throw up. I'd be sick on the floor, or in Nathan's bed. Either way, he'd see me do it and that's a horrible thing to do to someone.

But I'm not going to be sick, I told myself. I was hungry, not nauseous.

I opened my eyes to meet his.

"More?" he asked, already loading up the fork again.

"Please." I tried to respond with a smile of my own, but my face still felt too heavy.

Not once did he make a belittling comment. He offered

me every bite, as courteous as a waiter proffering a tray of finger food. Two bites into the toast and I was full, my stomach shrunken after so much time eating so little.

"More toast?" he asked, holding up the barely touched slice. "Or some cereal?" He reached for the spoon.

I shook my head as emphatically as I could, trying to keep my eyes on the toast and the toast inside my stomach. I forced myself to swallow.

My mouth was dry. Now I could have done with the spilled orange juice. My eyes strayed to my bed, where the orange had soaked into the sheets like dye.

He's kind, I told myself. He even tried to save me from humiliating myself, which is far more than he promised.

He reached for something on his tray as I put my arms around him, holding him close so that he'd hear me thank him this time.

Too late I realised that he'd picked up his own juice, which he now held precariously in his hand. As the juice in the glass slopped dangerously I pulled back from him, not wanting to spill this one, too. Embarrassed, I looked down at my hands.

The nurse's voice startled me. "She shouldn't be out of her bed."

Nathan explained to her how my bed needed fresh sheets because of spilled orange juice. He loaded the explanation with innuendo, reinforced with a charming smile, until the nurse blushed and stumbled over her words.

Hello, Mr Sleazy Roommate, I thought, turning away to hide my smile. I wondered why he hadn't turned on the charm for me yet. Maybe he liked tall, blonde girls with bigger boobs than mine.

His knuckles were white as he gripped the glass of orange juice, its contents still not quite steady. He set it down on the tray, focussing on flirting with the nurse.

So I didn't imagine it, the way he'd jumped when I touched him, I thought. I hadn't hurt him this time – I'd been careful not to touch where he'd been shot. I made this charming man nervous and unsettled.

The thought cheered me even more and I felt a smile on my lips that was lighter than before.

His eyes were on the nurse changing my bed linen, so he didn't see me smile. Nor did he notice me stealing the remainder of his orange juice.

FIFTEEN

"Are you sure you'll be okay?" Nathan asked, looking worried. I surveyed the remains of my breakfast tray. Only the cereal was untouched, just like yesterday.

He'd switched the TV on and there was a movie on that I hadn't seen yet. He seemed antsy to leave, so I did my best to look capable as I replied, "Sure. I'll survive 'til you come back to feed me my next meal."

If I could have crossed my fingers, I would have. I felt a peculiar sense of panic that he was deserting me so soon — only a day after I was fully awake. I needed to know that he'd be back.

Nathan smiled. "I wouldn't miss it."

My heart relaxed. "See you when you get back, then," I said lightly, forcing my eyes to the TV screen.

Nathan said some form of goodbye and left, looking as reluctant as I felt.

He'd been gone for maybe two minutes before a nurse came in. "Hi," she said. "I don't know if you remember me

– I'm Judith. We worked together a little when you were on prac."

I looked at her and she did look vaguely familiar, but I couldn't remember much about her. "Were you the one who told me about the food in the dining room?" I guessed.

Judith smiled. "Recommending you try the day's curry and avoid the fish and chips? That sounds like me." She held up a piece of paper. "Your friend wanted me to ask you to ring her, whenever your sleazy roommate was out. Now your guard is phoning in his daily report, he won't hear me."

I brightened. "I have a guard? Nathan didn't just leave me here alone."

She laughed. "No, he has a host of his muscly mates standing guard in the corridor, watching everyone like bouncers do." She cleared her throat, offering the paper to me.

I leaned over to read the writing. I recognised Jo's name and number. I looked up at Judith. "She wants to come and visit?"

She winked. "Yes, but when he's not around. I'll help you dial."

She pressed the buttons and helped me cradle the receiver between my cheek and my shoulder. "I'll be in and out, making your bed and changing your linen, so I'll be back in a minute, okay?" she said and I nodded, the phone ringing in my ear.

"Mmm, hello?" Jo yawned.

"Good morning," I replied.

"OH! You're up! I'll be right there! Oh. . . wait. . . here's Jason. He can keep you company on the phone 'til I get there." The phone crackled as the receiver was passed over.

"Good morning, beautiful," Jason teased. I looked around. Judith must have gone to get fresh sheets.

"Shut up, Jason. I definitely don't feel it today."

"Ah, you're always beautiful, no matter what you're wearing. Is it one of those skimpy hospital gowns that show off your arse?" he said lazily, in the voice that made other girls pat their hair and check to see they were showing enough cleavage.

My response was a little different. "Fuck off. My arse is none of your business, nor is what I'm wearing. They've got me wrapped up like a mummy, for reasons I have yet to find out. You should stay away from the hospital or I'll set the nurses on you. They've already decided they don't like my roommate. They'd probably stake you outside for the bandicoots."

Jason laughed. He never did believe me. An endless bloody optimist toward relationships, he was the biggest pessimist when it came to music, work or anything else. "Not even for your birthday?"

I realised I didn't know what day it was. "How long 'til my birthday?"

He laughed again. "They must be giving you some really good drugs at the hospital. Your birthday's next week. I was going to give you the best present ever – me in my birthday suit."

I suppressed the thought of him naked. Once I might have thought of him in the way he wanted, but that was when I was much younger. "Cool, you do that. I could do with a laugh. Bring a magnifying glass with you – I need a new practice dummy for tae kwan do."

I waited for that to sink in. I'd used him as a punching bag once when I was still at school and I hoped he remembered. I'd had a couple of drinks of vodka at his birthday party and decided to give him a birthday kiss. He'd stuck his clumsy tongue in my mouth, his groping hand up my shirt and his horny hips against mine. I hoped he still hurt from my drunken self-defence. I'd kneed him so hard I think I'd have broken his boner, if it'd had bones in more than name.

His next laugh sounded forced. "Okay, maybe a different present, then, but not as good."

"Yeah, whatever," I replied, losing interest. I wondered when Judith would be back to help me end the call.

"So, when do you think you'll be ready to play again?" Jason blurted out, as if that's what he really wanted to ask.

I looked at my gauzy hands. "A month," I decided. It'd take a fair few finger exercises to get my hands back to normal after they'd healed, but I could get by with just a keyboard for most gigs, if we stayed away from the songs where I had to pick up a guitar.

"Fuck! A whole month?"

"I hurt my hands. They need to heal. In a month I'll probably have a few new songs for you to learn, too. That'll take you a while," I replied.

"New ones? Ah, I got us a gig playing in one of the pubs in Freo — regular Saturday nights. As soon as you're old enough, you can be in, too," he said, sounding generous.

I snorted. "As soon as I'm eighteen, I'll be telling you where we have our gigs, as well as what to play. It's my band, Jason, even if I can't play in pubs 'til after next week. Don't you forget it. Or you'll have pleckies where your nipples should be."

I forgot Jason liked kinky stuff. "Any time you like, baby."

Fuck. "Call me baby one more time and I'll shove your guitar up your arse." I felt my body shudder as the shadow of a dark dream crossed my mind. A throwaway statement now held horrible memories. I forced myself to focus on the phone conversation and nothing else.

"And on that note, I'll leave you to think about my tight arse. . . and see you later!" He hung up.

Fucking Jason. He was a decent singer and a good guitarist, but a hellishly horny human being. The day I got with him would be the day before I killed myself, and the day after all of hell's demons had a career change selling ice cream, fresh from the ice caves of hell. He might be Jo's brother, but I thought he'd sing better if he didn't think with his balls.

Judith came in maybe a moment later. "All done?" She smiled. "I brought you a fresh nightie. Let's get you changed before Mr Sleazy gets back."

I knew she was talking about Nathan, but if she'd met Jason, she wouldn't have worried.

SIXTEEN

Dark – Chris – Angel – Baby – Apple

He swallowed, sounding nervous. "If I... stay where you can see me but I can't touch you, will you lie down? You need to recover. You'll need your strength." He moved a few metres away, sitting cross-legged on the concrete with his torch on me.

I lay down again, my eyes never leaving him. "Why would you help me?" I demanded again.

"Because I didn't ask to do this. None of this was my idea. I woke up in the back of that car maybe half an hour before you came by."

"But you're going along with it. Bondage, like out of some stupid erotica book," I responded furiously.

"I tied you loosely and took the card from your bag. I slipped it into your pocket, before they made me throw the bag out the window." His voice dropped lower. "Your name's Caitlin, right?"

I started at the sound of my name. "How'd you know?"

"Your driver's licence, Caitlin."

I stayed silent for a moment, but the urge to speak won. "Don't. My name is for my friends. You're not my friend. You're someone I'm going to kill."

"I have to call you something. Baby?"

The laughter in his voice set my teeth on edge. "Fuck you. Call me that and I'll strangle you with my bare hands."

"Angel? It's written on the front of your shirt."

My shirt says I'm no angel, stupid. I didn't say it. "Fine," I said instead.

"Do you want some Panadol for your headache, angel?"

It sounded like a caress or an endearment, the way he said it. Sleazy bastard. "Yes," I admitted.

He stretched out his arm and placed an open plastic box in the torch beam beside me. "It's fruit. Eat something first." He dropped two pills on the plastic lid, sticking it on the floor next to the box.

I ate a couple of pieces of apple before I washed the pills down with my last mouthful of juice.

He said nothing.

I broke the silence. "Why am I here? What do you want from me?"

I could hear the fear in his voice. "I don't know."

SEVENTEEN

The knock at the door surprised me. I looked up, expecting to see Judith.

"Good morning. Are you decent?" Jo's voice startled me, as she peered around the door with a smile.

Probably not, but there's not much I can do about it, I thought. Instead, I tried to smile and told her to come in.

She came straight to the bed and gave me a one-armed hug, a plastic bag in her other hand. Then she perched on the bed near my feet and said conspiratorially, "I brought presents!" as she dumped the bag in front of me.

"Oooh, what?" I asked, curious. Please don't let it be a bottle of Passion Pop.

She started pulling things out of the bag. "Chocolate, those sherbet things you like. . . I wasn't sure if you'd get any of your stuff from home, with your Dad still up north for a few more weeks, so I picked up a few things from the shop that I thought you'd need. Pyjamas and some underwear." She pulled out a pair of satin pyjamas and a couple of pairs of knickers, all with the tags still on. She laid them on the bed. "A brush and some bathroom stuff. Including *this*." She held out an electric toothbrush, still in the packaging, looking triumphant.

I stared at the pink electric toothbrush, its handle in the shape of a Disney princess, trying not to remember my last attempt to brush my teeth. I'd managed to get the brush into my mouth, but that was about it. Asking Nathan for help had proved even more disastrous – after the first time he'd almost choked me, he hadn't been game to help me brush more than my front teeth. With an electric toothbrush, I might be able to brush my own teeth.

I looked up at her again, more grateful than I could say. "Thank you."

She smiled nervously at my strange tone. "They only had kids' battery toothbrushes, so it was Disney princesses or Dora the Explorer. I thought you'd prefer a princess one. This one's Aurora, Sleeping Beauty." It came out all in a rush.

I laughed weakly. "Yep, I guess that's me. It's a wonder I woke up at all." With that sobering thought, all hope of laughter died.

"At least you're looking better," Jo said quickly, with a forced smile. "Where's your gallant hero this morning? Off polishing his sword?" Her face was set, so I knew she was going to rant. "Oh, come on. The half-crazed look in his eyes, full of guilt for what he did to you, and the anguish he's causing you now by sticking around? You're barely a shadow of yourself – what did he do to you?"

Nothing. He did nothing. I didn't bother opening my mouth – once she got into stride, she'd keep going 'til she ran out of breath. I waited, my eyes on the earrings she'd put in – one upside down, one sideways. She must have left home in a hurry.

"Caitlin, please! You cry at the drop of a hat, and there he is, saying nonsensical things like, 'It's all over now,' when it never will be, not until you get rid of him." She paused again. "The bruises on your face are fading. You're starting to look almost normal now. At least he isn't hitting you any more."

I let the words wash over me without really hearing them, but she knew me too well to let me get away with it for long. She brought her face so close to mine I couldn't focus on it. "It's lucky that he found you when he did."

When I met her eyes, she continued, "It's incredibly lucky that he was walking on that bit of beach just after you were dumped there. It couldn't be a coincidence – he knew you'd be dumped there, didn't he? He was one of *them*."

I sighed. I had to say something. "I was lucky he was there."

"It's all right, you can tell me. I know he was one of *them*." She looked feverishly eager.

Was she talking aliens and conspiracy theories? "One of them?"

"One of the ones who hurt you," she said slowly. She looked expectant.

Now I could say something. Now she'd hear me. "Nathan never hurt me."

She snorted. "What, you're telling me none of this hurt when he did it?" She pointed at my hands and the dressings on my wrists. "When he cut you, when he tied you up, when he broke your fingers, when he raped you. . ."

The tears started, part anger and part pain. My anger packed more power into my voice than I'd intended. "No! He never did anything like that. He couldn't do that to me. He would never. . ."

"You didn't always see the face of the man who was hurting you, did you?" Jo demanded.

My voice died to a whisper. "I don't have to see his face or know his name to know who he is, Jo. He's not one of the men who hurt me."

Nathan advanced into the room, as if he'd been listening outside and couldn't stay out any longer. I found I felt grateful for his presence.

He said something to her, but I didn't hear it.

She opened her mouth to deliver an angry reply. I shook my head slightly, lifting my hand to wave goodbye. She returned the wave and left without another word.

I settled into Nathan's comforting embrace and let the tears flow until they ran dry. Anger and pain drained out of me with the salt water, leaving a contemplative calm.

I lifted my head from his chest to help him wipe my face and a flash of pink caught my eye. The electric toothbrush. I could have clean teeth again! I smiled through my tears.

EIGHTEEN

Carol bustled in with an armload of dressing packs. "Time to change your dressings. Let's see how you're healing up!" She smiled for all she was worth, but her eyes told me she was putting a positive spin on something she liked as little as I did. She didn't want to see my wounds, either.

I felt sorry for her, but I was happy to see her. It was a relief to know both the ward and the hospital I'd been sent to, not to mention see a familiar face in uniform. "Hi, Carol. Of all the wards to bring me to, I ended up in yours."

Her cheery smile didn't reach her eyes. She was trying to tell me something without words. "Of course. St Elsie's is the best hospital and we're its best ward. We had to fight for you, but we traded a couple of sporting injury patients to the other wards to keep you."

Sporting injury patients went to the day surgery. In and out in a day, such patients were rarely sent to a ward at all. Fight for me? Oh. . . perhaps she meant they'd fight for me if they had to. It was a sweet thought, but I couldn't allow any of the capable nurses on this ward to stand in the way of a bastard who wanted to kill me.

What if one of them killed him before I could?

I forced a laugh. "You just wanted fewer names to learn at handover."

Carol laughed easily as if my joke had been funny. "You know it. Actually, while you were asleep there have been some very interesting men in the ward keeping guard over you. I almost thought about asking them to pull out their weapons. . ." I saw her eyes drift in Nathan's direction before coming back to me. Mr Sleazy Roommate had been busy, charming the nurses in the ward while I slept, and she was trying to warn me.

Nathan looked worried. I realised there was something he didn't want me to know, so I feigned ignorance. "I have guards?"

"Sure, a different police officer every day, like some sort of desk calendar. They make sure you don't have any unwelcome visitors. Plus. . ." This time her glance at Nathan was more obvious. Had he told the staff that he was my boyfriend, so that they'd let him stay?

I stared at him, wondering if he'd really done something so silly. There was more he wasn't telling me. As he averted his eyes, I wondered how much of it I already knew.

I remembered something and tried not to smile as I spoke. "I thought you had a new man – Scott. How does he stack up against the desk calendar guys, or is he out of the picture now?"

"I'm still with Scott, but that doesn't mean I can't look." Carol drifted off and so did my thoughts.

She broke my reverie. "So, where do we start?" She had

a hand on the curtain and another question in her eyes. She wanted to know whether I wanted the curtain pulled across, so Nathan didn't see.

I gave a slight shake of my head and shrugged. "What does it matter? I guess it's time for me to see what they've done to me," I replied, too tired to keep up the cheerful tone.

My eyes met Carol's as her hands hovered over me, staying close to my thigh. I nodded, knowing she'd deal with the worst wound first. I braced myself as she ripped the dressing off as carefully as she could. I wasn't prepared for what I saw.

"Fuck, that looks bad!" I burst out.

There was a deep hole in my leg. The nasty, gaping wound had been sliced open further with a scalpel and then stitched closed, before it had started to heal, but the scar was going to show for the rest of my life. No bloody wonder it hurt to walk. I shouldn't be on that until the stitches were out.

Carol's eyes met mine, hurting for me.

"A skin graft over that would help hide the scar," she said reassuringly, as if I didn't already know that. I wondered why it hadn't already been done.

The truth dawned on me as I looked at the gauze shroud I'd been enveloped in. "But where would you take the graft from? Everywhere is. . ."

A shroud I could still be buried in. . . Oh shit.

Tears formed and fell, as if I had no control over my own bloody body any more.

"Hey, that's the worst of your wounds. The rest are healing up nicely. You'll see." Ever the professional, Carol tried to reassure me as she continued. She smoothed the new dressing down and moved to the next one. I barely felt the rip, making me wonder if my pain relief dose was still high. I watched as she worked, counting the wounds hidden under the white.

"Oh God." Nathan stood beside me and I hadn't noticed him move.

Carol quickly shifted the sheet so it covered more of me, but his eyes were fixed on the soft flesh of my inner thigh. The horror in his expression told me he wasn't perving on me in any normal sense of the word. He looked like he was going to cry.

It was instinctive, my stupid desire to hug a grown man as if he was a child who could be comforted. But he accepted it, hugging me tightly as if he'd been the one hurt. Somehow, despite how strange it seemed, I felt comforted by the contact.

Whatever his motives were, at least he made me feel better. Or he would, if. . . I winced as Carol ripped off another dressing. She was right to keep going without hesitation. The faster she changed my dressings, the sooner she'd be done with them. And the less I had to see of the messy red, white and blue-grey mosaic my body had become.

NINETEEN

Dark – Mike – Chris – Kiss – No

"So you fucked her, then untied her and dressed her again?" Mike sounded incredulous.

"Well... it was cold and she wanted to put her clothes back on. So... yeah."

If he'd said it was dark at night the way he said that, I wouldn't have believed him.

"Bullshit." This sounded closer. I kept my eyes tightly closed, hoping that he'd go away if I was asleep.

No, that only works for children's nightmares. Not real ones.

"Get her up and on her feet." The foot that kicked my leg could only have been Mike's.

"But she's still not well after the drugs you gave her..." Chris hedged.

"Then she'll be easier to control. Get her up and hold her for me."

A light hand touched my shoulder. "C'mon, wake up," Chris murmured.

Chris was on my left. Mike was down near my feet.

I rolled to my right, praying the dizziness had dissipated. If it hadn't, I knew how this would end. I shifted into a crouch, ready to defend myself but not knowing how. "No!" I shouted.

"Fuck. Hold her still." Mike edged closer.

I backed away from them as Chris started to approach me, too.

My back touched something. Desperately, I turned to see I'd backed into a corner. No!

Swallowing hard, I turned back to face my captors, hands up in what I remembered was a basic block from my self-defence classes. Now I wished I'd taken more classes. "Don't you fucking touch me."

Mike sounded completely unfazed. "There's nothing you can do to stop me."

Fuck, but he was fast. He grabbed my arms and stomped his boot down on both of my bare feet. I tried to pull free, but he knew what he was doing. He twisted my arms up behind me and held them with one hand. The other he plunged into my hair, grabbing a handful and twisting that, too. I couldn't move my head without ripping out my hair. I swallowed a scream.

"Now kiss me, bitch." He smiled.

"Why?" I spat.

"Because you can. You may as well enjoy the last man you ever have."

"Fuck you!"

Shouldn't have opened my mouth. He tasted of ash, stale beer and worse. I retched as he shoved his tongue halfway down my throat, but his body pinning mine to the wall kept me upright. Worse, he enjoyed it. I could feel him hardening against my tummy. I'd have bitten his tongue off if I could've stopped choking.

If one horrible kiss was such a violation,

how much worse could rape be? Oh God, I didn't want to find out. He'd hurt me.

Mike broke his lip-lock and grinned. "You will, little bitch. You'll fuck me more than you can handle."

"Don't you fucking touch me!" I shouted again, trying to squirm away from him.

"She's mine!" Chris protested. "You promised!" He sounded five years old, instead of a bloke bigger than me.

Mike swung me around by my twisted arms, my muscles screaming in pain, slamming my body into Chris's. "The little bitch is all yours if you fuck her right here and now."

I spun around to face Chris. My voice came out as a whisper. "No..."

TWENTY

Nathan's voice told me I was okay. I relaxed, ready to go from dark nightmare to peaceful sleep once more, but I realised that the arms holding me tightly were anything but okay. Then they were gone.

I could hear footsteps and breathing in the dark, but no one touched me. "Nathan?" I asked quietly, hoping it was his breathing I'd heard.

Someone touched me again and my reaction was automatic and unexpected. Instead of wanting to claw his eyes out, I found myself relaxing into his embrace. This was not fucking okay. What if it had been someone else, someone I couldn't trust?

I shoved at him and he let go of me. I tried to ignore the hurt look on his face as I demanded, "What are you doing? Why were you touching me when I woke up?"

His expression went from hurt to horrified and he didn't know how to explain. "You've been having a lot of really bad nightmares and you wouldn't wake up. You. . . were screaming. Screaming for me to help you. You. . . didn't scream as much if I. . . hugged you."

It started to dawn on me that I had no idea just how much he'd done while I was asleep. I was sure I'd heard his voice while I slept and I needed to know if what I remembered was real or just part of one of my many fucked-up dreams.

"How often have you. . . hugged me?" I asked carefully.

If I'd dragged the answer out of him with pliers, it wouldn't have come any easier. "Whenever you had nightmares, until you stopped screaming."

I held his gaze, trying to be sure he was telling the truth. He'd been here for every nightmare, every scream. My first thought was to wonder why he'd bothered, but I wasn't ready to ask him that yet.

He started to elaborate without a word from me. "I did it because I couldn't wake you up. I promised. . . I promised I wouldn't let them hurt you and they were hurting you in your dreams. I couldn't just sit by and do nothing." He looked scared.

Somehow, I decided that he was telling the truth. It had been his voice I'd heard, telling me to keep fighting, through all the bad dreams and hellish nightmares.

He kept going, his voice climbing higher in his desperation to make me believe him, but I wasn't paying attention to his words any more in his rising panic.

I cut in as he paused for breath. "That explains. . . some things," I finished, not willing to tell him how many times his voice had broken into my nightmares, nor that I felt comfortable in his arms. I couldn't afford to be comfortable in anyone's arms, not yet. For my own safety, I had to do this. "Nathan, could you do me a favour?"

"Sure," he replied without hesitation.

I breathed a sigh of relief, careful not to let it show. "Next time I have a bad dream, can you please wake me up first?" My eyes held his to demand his answer.

His smile looked relieved. "Sure, with pleasure." His eyes held a glint that I didn't trust.

I pulled away from him even further. I didn't care if he'd just made an innocent comment. I couldn't give in to anyone, not yet. So I tried to clarify it, to make sure he understood. "But please don't touch me."

The light in his eyes died. I'd guessed correctly – the innuendo was in there for a reason. He didn't look at me or say anything else as he wandered back to his bed.

I relaxed in mine, wishing this whole mess could be over. That I could consider giving in to Mr Sleazy Roommate, if only for a moment. But that was out of the question now.

I heard Nathan sigh as if he agreed with me. Of course he did.

TWENTY ONE

"Bye, Dad," I said softly and batted the button to end the call. I heard a few seconds of dial tone before I managed to silence it.

I lay back and sighed. Part of me wished to have a hero for a father, who'd have come charging in the day those bastards took me, before they could do any damage. But my dad wasn't like that. He had too many of his own fears to face up to.

He and I both knew he couldn't stand to see me hurt. It'd remind him of losing my mother. I wasn't surprised that he'd been away the whole time I'd been gone and he was planning a longer stint – even the faint possibility of losing me would've turned him into a bigger workaholic than before. One day I'd have to sit him down properly and get him to tell me what had really happened to her. But not before he'd worked off his present panic at nearly losing me.

I breathed a sigh of relief that he wouldn't be back soon

— that'd give me the time and space to finish this without placing him in danger, too. I wouldn't be out of danger until they were gone.

I'm sorry, Dad, if it costs me my life to end this, but I can't move on unless I know they can never hurt me again. And for that, I'll need to see them safely to hell. Even if it means escorting those bastards there personally.

"Evening meds!" Carol sang out, rattling the pill cup.

I smiled and opened my eyes. "Can I have some milk with that today? I'd like to sleep early."

"Hot or cold?" she asked.

"Cold," I replied instantly.

She returned perhaps a minute later with a mug I recognised from the handover room. She helped me tip the cup of pills into my mouth and held the mug while I sipped the milk.

"Are you okay? Do you need more pain medication?" she asked, looking concerned.

I smiled. "No, I'm sure you're giving me too many already. I can't feel any pain right now."

She hesitated. "It's just that you've been crying. Did your roommate say something he shouldn't have? Or is he too professional, pretending he doesn't care about you? You know he's barely left your side since you arrived. I even caught him cuddling up to you in bed a couple of times." She looked at me in alarm. "Nothing sleazy. He wrapped you in your bed linen and then did the same for himself, like he didn't want to scare you. I swear that boy would do anything for you. He absolutely adores you, you know." She tipped the cup up so I could finish off the milk.

There's more to it than you realise. I smiled and licked

the milk off my lips before replying, "I know. No, I just miss my father, is all. He called and he works away so much. I don't want him to see me like this – he'd treat me like a child and it wouldn't help me recover any faster."

Carol lifted her shoulders in a checked-shirt shrug. "Sounds like my dad. They can't deal with their daughters growing up. Let me know if there's anything else you need."

The phone rang.

She looked at me for a moment.

I held up my useless hands. "Could you hit the speakerphone button, please?"

"Oh! Sure," she replied, doing so.

"Hello?" I said uncertainly.

"I'm after Miss Caitlin Lockyer. This is Detective Neil McGuinness."

Carol's eyes widened and she hurried out, mug in hand. I heard the door close quietly as I directed my voice at the phone. "That's me, Detective."

His tone turned warmer. "I'm happy to hear you're awake. You must have been through a lot. I bet there are a few people who hoped you wouldn't wake up."

"Not here, Detective," I replied softly. "Here in the hospital, everyone's been really helpful."

He coughed. "Good. Look, I've been working on your case ever since you disappeared and I'd like nothing better than to catch the people who hurt you so I can put them in prison for a long time. Can I come visit you in hospital so we can have a little chat about anything you can remember that might help me find them?"

Prison? But they might leave there still alive. . . if there's enough evidence to convict them at all. What if a court finds them not guilty?

"Miss Lockyer?"

I stared at the empty pill cup Carol had left behind in her haste. "Yes."

"Can I come to the hospital tomorrow and. . ."

"I said yes, Detective. See you tomorrow."

This time, I managed to get the button on the second bat with my bandaged hand.

Do I tell the police everything tomorrow and trust them to take care of the men who hurt me, or do I find another way – one that will make sure they can never hurt me again?

Do I trust the police?

I knew the answer to that one, if I had to ask myself such a question. Before all this, perhaps, but now? No. They shot me.

Do I trust Nathan?

I pressed my head into the pillow, closing my eyes.

I heard the man himself enter the room, but I didn't move nor open my eyes. I didn't want to look at him, for fear I'd say something I shouldn't.

That boy would do anything for you.

Would you kill for me, Nathan?

TWENTY TWO

Dark – Mike – Chris – Kiss – No – Beautiful – Bastard

He caught me around the waist before I could move away. My terror rose, not knowing what he was going to do. I couldn't move my arms – they tingled painfully from whatever hold Mike had locked them in.

"You could start with a kiss. Even I did," Mike derided.

Chris pulled me closer, holding me tighter, and I couldn't struggle.

His hands were gentler than Mike's, nervous and uncertain. Aloud, he whispered, again, "I'm not going to hurt you." Begging me to believe him.

One arm a steel band around my waist, with his other hand he gently cupped my face. The heel of his hand under my chin, his fingers curved up around my cheek. "Forgive me," he breathed, his face so close to mine I could feel the heat of his breath on my lips.

Then he kissed me, too. A world of

difference. Careful and hesitant, more like a real kiss. I drew in a breath of surprise and closed my eyes. I almost forgot who he was and where we were. Almost.

I turned my head away. "Don't do that again."

His lips almost touched my ear. "Thank you. A priceless kiss stolen from a beautiful woman."

You smooth, sleazy bastard! I felt my cheeks heat up against my will. For the first time, I was happy it was dark.

He released me and I stumbled back. Two steps and I tripped over the edge of the mattress, which sent me sprawling.

"You did want her lying down," Mike said with a laugh. "What are you waiting for?"

Realising my danger, I raised my voice as I struggled to get up. "Touch me and I'll kick your fucking face in!" I screamed at Chris. Mike. Both of them.

Chris's weight landed on top of me, crushing me into the mattress. I raised my hands to claw his eyes out, but he was ready for me, catching my hands in his as Mike had. He wasn't as cruel – he pinned my hands to the mattress above my head instead. I tried to bend my knees up so I could kick him across the room, but he forced his knees between mine, leaving me more vulnerable than before.

"No..." I whispered again, my voice stolen by fear.

Mike's voice seemed thunderous in comparison. "How are you going to do that with him holding you down? Just lie back and take it, bitch. I've got better waiting for you right here." He grabbed his crotch to demonstrate. "Give her an extra five minutes

for me, Chris." He left, laughing.
  Chris shifted between my legs.
  "No, please," I whimpered.

TWENTY THREE

I couldn't sleep. I heard Nathan settle into his own bed and turn the lights off. I listened to his breathing gradually become even as he drifted off to sleep, but such things eluded me.

I turned on one side and then the other, pressing my face into the pillow or staring at the darkened ceiling. Nothing helped.

Tomorrow I could tell the police everything or nothing. I could be completely honest and describe my living hell in graphic detail, or I could plead my weakened state as an excuse to delay. After all, it would be normal for someone in my situation not to want to discuss the violence and abuse to which I'd fallen victim. Not everyone had my memory, nor would they have spent their captivity repeating all the facts I knew so I wouldn't forget anything.

And Nathan? What about Nathan?

I turned to look at him. He appeared to be having as restless a night as I was, moving around in bed a bit like a fish on a hook. It looks like he's having nightmares, I thought. Hopefully not about me.

I rolled onto my back and stared at the ceiling again, then turned toward the bathroom so I couldn't see Nathan any more.

What about Nathan?

I wondered what he'd do if he heard me tell my memories. If he wasn't having nightmares now, he would once he'd heard the substance of mine. I couldn't do that to him. He didn't deserve to carry the weight in my head. Knowing those bastards had hurt me was enough for him – he leaped to my defence already.

I heard voices and the patter of feet on the floor, so I looked around to see who'd entered the room. A shadow loomed over my bed and I screamed.

Closer, closer, reaching for me. . .

No.

The light over my bed clicked on and I blinked in the suddenly bright light. Nathan squinted back at me.

Not a shadow. Nathan. No need to worry. Shouldn't have screamed. Silly. "What is it, Nathan?"

He smiled at me as I tried to slow my racing heart. I'd been imagining the menace in the shadow as he leaned over me, surely. He'd never hurt me.

"I'm safe in hospital with you. Right?" I tested.

His expression didn't change as he replied, "Yeah." I couldn't tell if his yawn was real or fake.

I stared at him, trying to decide.

"Who gave you your afternoon meds?" he asked, looking worried.

You scared the shit out of me just to ask me stupid

questions? "Judith. . . no, Carol. Carol was on last night. I said I was having trouble sleeping so she found me some milk in the handover room fridge. I was out like a light." I didn't want to tell him that I'd been ignoring him when he came in. Better if he thought I'd been asleep.

"I won't keep you up. You need your rest to heal." His smile was so filled with sympathy I didn't know how to respond. And he looked so sad, somehow. He headed back to bed before I could work out what to say.

It's not like I was going to get much more sleep. Maybe we could both use the company. And he could help me decide what to do tomorrow. Time to find out if he'd really do anything for me, like Carol said.

I swallowed. "Would you please sit by me for a little bit, 'til I calm down properly? I just want to get some of the horrible pictures out of my head. The police come to take my statement tomorrow and I can't stop thinking about all the things I have to say. . ."

I held my breath as he returned to my side. I exhaled slowly, hoping he didn't notice.

"Can you tell me about them? Maybe that'll help them go away faster."

I stared at him. He meant it. He seriously wanted to hear about the horrible things I'd been through. Didn't he realise how graphic my memories were? They'd give him nightmares.

"Nathan, I don't even want to think about them. Talking about my nightmares will only bring them back," I told him gently. This was a horror movie he didn't want to see.

"No it won't." He sounded like he was trying to convince himself he wanted to hear it. "That's what all the psychologists and counsellors say. You wait. They'll tell you it's good to get it out and your heart will feel lighter."

Lightening my heart to burden his? Not likely.

"Nathan," I began, wanting to ask about his nightmares. Did he dream of me or his sister? Both of us?

He looked like he was ready to cry and I could feel tears on my own cheeks. I sucked in a breath as I held out my arms, offering him a hug. The least comfort I could give him.

"I can't, Nathan, not yet. I can't tell you all the horrors that happened – you already have enough to deal with. . ." His arms tightened around me, as if he were desperately seeking some sort of solace. I wish I had some to offer him, but I was the wrong person for that. I could only offer darkness.

TWENTY FOUR

"I'm Detective McGuinness. We need a statement from you, Miss Lockyer." The detective was an older man who looked sympathetic and understanding. He hadn't trusted this to any underling – he wanted to be the one who asked me questions. "I understand this will be upsetting for you, but we need your assistance to catch the people who did this to you."

I nodded, thinking, Don't you dare leave. Somehow during the night I'd decided I needed Nathan. I reached for Nathan's hand, but I couldn't feel a damn thing through the bandages today. I looked down, carefully placing my fingers between Nathan's as I held his hand. I could feel a faint pressure as his fingers curled around mine.

I looked up and found Detective McGuinness' eyes on our linked hands. He cleared his throat and looked at Nathan. "Mr Miller, I'll have to ask you to leave or at least step outside."

NO!

Nathan stood up, but I wasn't letting go of his hand. I could feel the pain in my fingers as he tugged on them, but I gritted my teeth and looked away, determined not to let go.

What do I do? Let him go? Tell this detective everything?

No, no, NO!

"I'm sorry? You won't give a statement yet?" Detective McGuinness said suddenly.

Oh shit. I must have said it aloud and not realised.

I hesitated a second before I looked at the detective. "I'll make a statement now, but I want Nathan to stay."

Detective McGuinness looked at me with pity in his eyes, before he turned his gaze to Nathan and his expression hardened. "Mr Miller is a suspect in this matter and we would prefer that your statement is made privately, so you feel safe and don't hold back information. Your statement will remain confidential."

He wanted to take Nathan away from me before I could defend myself. I didn't trust him. I'd hold back anything I damn well liked. Did he seriously think I was stupid enough to let a man who'd hurt me get anywhere near me? I wasn't telling him a damn thing.

I realised I wasn't ready to give up Nathan.

I glared at the detective and weighed my words carefully. "Officer, I'll never feel safe until I know every one of those bastards can't touch me again. And I'll never feel safe alone with a police officer after one of them shot at me."

He winced at this and glanced down at my legs, before meeting my eyes again. His gaze was steady.

"Nathan. . ." I started to say.

The detective jerked his head, his eyes narrowing as they fixed on Nathan.

I bet he thought Nathan had threatened me with something and he wouldn't back down until he got Nathan out of the room. He'd push us until Nathan left and he had me alone. . . what if he tried to hurt me and Nathan didn't come back? Hadn't I been through enough already?

As I felt tears build, hopelessness set in. My voice squeaked a little as the tears started to flow. "Nathan shouldn't be a suspect in this. He never. . . He didn't. . . He's about the only person who hasn't hurt me."

I reached for a tissue automatically with my free hand.

Nathan, please help me out here, I thought desperately, releasing his hand to reach for a tissue with the other bandaged hand, too.

Relieved, I watched Nathan pull out some tissues for me.

Now show him you're my caregiver when I'm helpless, not the violent threatening bastard he thinks you are, I begged Nathan with my eyes. Please. . .

For the second time in as many days, Nathan helped me to wipe the tears off my face and blow my nose. His expression held only concern.

I glanced at the detective. His eyes were on Nathan and he looked thoughtful.

I made my voice quiet and sad. "I can't use my hands and I can barely stand, let alone walk. I feel so helpless one of these pillows would probably be an effective weapon against me." As the detective looked back at me I tried to smile, but I just didn't feel it. "I know I need to make a statement so you can catch the people who did this to me, no matter how upset talking about it will make me feel. I'll do it, however many tears it takes, but please don't make me do this alone."

Alone. I don't want to be alone. As the tears came to my eyes again, I looked from the detective to Nathan, begging both of them for help.

To my surprise, the first voice I heard was Nathan's. "If you want me to stay, I'll be here for you." He sat down carefully on the bed beside me, taking my hand.

Detective McGuinness just looked at us, not saying anything.

I tried again. "I don't know how long it will take before I'm strong enough to tell this story without someone to support me. I don't even know if I can. I want you to catch them and I want to help you do it. I want to know they can't touch me and that I'll be safe as soon as possible. Please — let me use the little courage I have left before it's gone to tell this story now. I don't know when I'll be brave enough to attempt it again." Slowly, slowly. I forced myself to look down at my lap, hugging my arms to my chest.

An arm snaked around my shoulder and I let out a little gasp of surprise, before I relaxed at the sound of Nathan's voice in my ear. "I promised I won't let them hurt you again. They won't touch you — you'll be safe."

Three times. That's three times today Nathan had come to my rescue, two more than I'd counted on. If he cared about my wellbeing so much, I didn't want to give him up yet.

I heard Detective McGuinness clear his throat and I held my breath. "I think that if you'd like to make your statement with him present, under the circumstances, you can do so. Provided, of course, that Mr Miller doesn't interrupt or interfere in any way."

I breathed a sigh of relief. "Thank you." Then I proceeded to tell him. . . nothing.

TWENTY FIVE

Dark – Mike – Chris – Kiss – Sorry – Bastard

Mike's laughter died away as Chris lay like a dead weight on top of me.

Maybe he's dead, I thought, hoping.

I squirmed, trying to push him off. "Get off me."

"Shh." He held my wrists with one hand and pressed the other over my mouth.

No such luck.

He didn't do anything else, though, for a long moment. My tears trickled into my hair. He hadn't hurt me yet and I was crying already. I sniffled, wishing I could wipe the tears away.

He turned his face toward me at the sound. He shifted again, up and off me, backing away until he hit the door. Closed, of course. He knocked over the torch as he slid down the door to slump to the floor. He lifted his head to look at me, clapping both hands to his mouth as if he were going to be sick. I heard him say, "Oh God, I'm so sorry," in a desperate rush.

I sat up, hugging my knees to my chest. My

tears still flowed freely. I wiped my nose on my sleeve. "Why?" I whispered. I couldn't stop shaking.

"They'll hurt my family if I don't do what I'm told," he said in a dead voice.

"If you don't hurt me?" I asked, a little louder.

"Yes. And I can't do it." He buried his face in his hands again.

"I'll say you're a brutal, callous, raping bastard if anyone asks me," I offered. I meant it, too.

Shakily, he replied, "Thanks."

TWENTY SIX

"I'll go get the laptop now – I'll be an hour, tops. Will you be okay for that long without me?" Nathan asked, looking worried.

I shrugged and summoned a small smile, despite secretly wondering if he thought my sheets would turn sentient and strangle me in his absence. "I'll be fine."

Carol came in. "Time for physio!" she sang out. "Your doctor pulled some strings and persuaded one of our best physiotherapists to take you on, though she barely had space for any more new patients."

Nathan stopped dead. "The laptop can wait."

I ignored him. "Which one?" I asked Carol.

Her smile widened. "Althea. I heard she asked for a very personal favour from the doctor as payment, though. And he turned up this morning looking like he hadn't slept, so we're all wondering just how personal it got last night. . ." Her laughter was wicked.

I didn't believe it. "But he's married. . ." I objected.

She shrugged. "You ask her. Maybe she'll tell you."

"Nathan," I said suddenly. "You go get that laptop. It'll be okay."

He shook his head. "What if she hurts you?"

I tried to smile, but I think all I managed was a sick grimace. "She's a physio. She's supposed to hurt me a little in order to help me get better. It's probably best that you're not here for that. After the session, all I'll want to do is rest, which I can do if I'm telling you what happened so you can write it down."

He bit his lip. "Are you sure?"

I forced myself to nod.

"Then I'll be as quick as I can," he replied, hurrying out of the room.

I felt a twinge of fear, but I brushed it away. Nathan wouldn't have left me unguarded.

"Don't you get sick of having him here constantly?" Carol asked.

I shook my head. "I like him. When he's here, I feel safe. That's a lot for me."

Her eyes filled with tears. "I wish you didn't need it, but it's good he's so devoted to you."

You have no idea.

"You must be Caitlin."

I didn't recognise the musical voice that spoke the words, nor the tall, African woman who entered the room.

I nodded.

Carol smiled. "I'll leave you two for your session." She left quickly.

"You must be Althea," I replied.

She laughed. "I am indeed. My husband said you needed

the very best of care, but because of the trauma you've been through, you wouldn't trust a physio you hadn't met. So he asked me to take care of you and I promised I would."

"Your husband?" I asked, mystified.

"Your doctor," she replied with a smile. "We haven't told many people at work. He wants to keep his personal life separate. Something about how he was engaged to marry another girl and she left him. He said everyone looked at him with such pity he couldn't stand it and he didn't want to jinx us. So, it's a secret few people know. You were there the day he proposed, so I thought you knew."

I drew a blank and it embarrassed me. "I'm really sorry, but I don't remember ever meeting you before."

Her laughter was deep and infectious. I wanted to hear it again. "We were trapped in a lift together once. You fainted in the heat. I'm not surprised you don't remember it. He didn't propose until after he made sure you were okay. His patients always come first, even before me." She nodded fiercely, evidently proud of her husband. "Now. Tell me about your injuries, so I can help you like I promised."

My hands she dismissed until later, when I no longer needed the bandages. My legs were another matter — and the subject of much poking, prodding and manipulation, before she started giving me exercises to help strengthen my muscles.

"How often should I do them?" I asked eagerly.

"At least once a day, if you can," she replied.

I met her eyes. "You know the men who did this are still hunting me, right? I need to recover as fast as I can — I need to be able to defend myself. I have all the time in the world while I'm stuck in bed. How often can I do them, without doing myself further damage?"

She must have seen my determination. "You can do a set or two every hour, but make sure you take breaks in between and stop if it hurts. You don't need to push yourself that hard."

"I do. It'll hurt far more if they get their hands on me again. I won't let that happen."

She smiled sadly. "Good luck with that, honey. You take care and I'll see you for another session in a few days."

As soon as she'd left, I started my exercises again. I couldn't get my strength back fast enough.

TWENTY SEVEN

Nathan placed a pastel pink laptop by my lunch tray.

I looked at him, wondering how he'd come to choose a pink computer. I hadn't thought he was gay, but who knew? Maybe the sleazy manner was an act to hide where his tastes really lay.

He saw me looking from the laptop to him and he started to explain, "It's my sister's old laptop. She doesn't need it any more. You can borrow this as long as you need to, so you can record what you remember."

I nodded, trying to steel myself.

I could have said I lost my nerve, as he took an inordinately long time setting up the laptop, plugging it in, turning it on and waiting for it to boot up. I could have said the sheer trauma and pain had made my memories hazy and I experienced some sort of amnesia. But I didn't.

I can't repeat what I said, because what started as an effort to remember became an exercise in forgetting. I'd start telling Nathan about one memory, then realise that the memory was too painful to focus on or, with increasing frequency, too graphic for me to burden Nathan with. I used vague words and half-finished sentences to describe the very clear nightmares in my head.

Every time I returned to that Word document to add to the record of my memories, I shuddered at the memory of that first session, when I had to describe the PG version of the horrors aloud to Nathan. He typed it all in, his expression holding pity, sadness, desperation and furious resolve, as my memories subjected me to the R-rated version that could never be censored in my head.

What would Nathan do if I told him the uncensored version in all its detail? I wondered every time I remembered his reaction to the little I told him that day.

I lost track of time, but I kept going until the horrible memories wouldn't go away, with my eyes open or closed. I tried to shut them out, but even that failed.

Nathan wrapped his arms around me in an attempt at comfort. Instead it felt like a reminder of help, which, when it came, was too little, too late. His pity only made it worse.

I pushed away from him and lay down on the crisp white sheets, not looking at him because I knew if I apologised for my rudeness, I'd cry again.

When Nathan suggested he leave for a bit, I panicked. The thought of being alone with my memories was terrifying. Especially if his alone time brought him to the realisation that he couldn't handle this any more. I need him to come back.

He must have seen it mirrored in my eyes, our mutual desire to escape from my memories. He was already up and poised for flight. After a slight hesitation, he invited me to the coffee shop downstairs for cake.

I felt wrung out like a dishcloth that had been used on one too many dirty pots. Yet even the thought of caffeine and sugar had me sitting up again, seriously considering his half-hearted offer.

I opened my mouth to accept, but he pulled his shirt over his head. Oh.

Beneath his loose-fitting shirt, Nathan had been hiding more than just his injuries. I wondered how many hours he spent in the gym to maintain those muscles. Looking at his biceps, I could see how he managed to lift me so effortlessly. The dressing was gone from his shoulder, but an angry patch of red remained. What I'd thought to be a mortal injury had only been a bad graze. There'd only been a lot of blood because of the amount of skin scraped off by the bullet as it sped past him. Damage he sustained while trying to help me, I reminded myself. It could have killed him and then I'd have been here, alone and helpless and. . .

I felt a sob rise in my throat and choked it down.

Nathan must have heard me, for he turned toward me, looking concerned as he touched my arm lightly. He extended his other hand toward me, too, the shirt still hanging from his fingers.

Chris, offering me his sweater to cover my nakedness. Kindness in the dark. . .

The memory came without warning and I curled up in horror, trying to fight the dark dream in my head. The day they took my clothes.

I mumbled some reply to Nathan's worried question about my wellbeing, struggling to stay out of the memory. I bit back a scream.

I was so preoccupied I never heard him leave the room. Before I realised it, I was alone with Judith holding the sort of hospital uniform the surgeons wore, a grumpy look on her face. It dawned on me slowly that I wasn't going to wear my backless nightgown in public, something I hadn't thought about. I was relieved, before I'd had a chance to worry.

Judith's grumpy because she didn't like Nathan, I realised as she started speaking, her hissed whisper trying hard not to be heard. "He never leaves. The whole time you were unconscious, he barely left the room. He just kept talking to you. It didn't stop him trying to chat up the nurses, though, sleazy bastard. He sat in the chair by your bed and wouldn't leave, even when I was changing your dressings." She slid my hospital gown down and pulled the surgeon's top over my head.

My voice was muffled by the dark blue cotton. "Really? Why? Did he say?" What did he do to make her dislike him so much?

"He said he'd promised you something and he wasn't letting you out of his sight." She snorted as she helped me to pull on the pants. She evidently didn't believe it.

Wow. He really did keep his promise. I still owed him for a lot. "Then I should thank him, when he gets back." My voice was fainter than I wanted it to be.

"No!" She was vehement. She picked up my hairbrush and set to work on my hair. "Don't trust him. The way he looked at you. . . When I changed your dressings, the way he just *stared* at you, without any emotion at all. He didn't look angry or upset or even interested, like he cared that you'd been hurt. It wasn't normal." She cleared her throat.

"We've all been really hoping you'd recover, with all you've been through. All the staff on the ward, I mean, and in the ED. We don't want your boyfriend making life difficult for you, when you've been through enough." Her expression held dire consequences for Nathan.

I was at a loss for words. Hadn't I already noticed that Nathan's treatment of me was far more clinical than the brand of charm he used on the nurses? Of course his behaviour would seem strange, if they thought he was my boyfriend. "He does care that I've been hurt. It's. . . complicated." I tried to be honest, which also meant incredibly vague.

"If you don't want him here, all you have to do is say and he'll be thrown out of the hospital. He won't be allowed back in." She smacked the brush down hard on the bedside table. She looked and sounded like she'd like to do something similar to Nathan.

I was touched that the hospital staff would be so kind to me, especially as I still flinched when they actually, physically touched me. "He's only here because I want him to be," I told her carefully. "If I didn't want him here, I'm sure he'd go home without you all needing to go that far." I paused, registering her disappointment at not getting to evict Nathan. "But it's wonderful to know that if I needed help, you'd do that for me. Thank you."

We both saw Nathan coming up the corridor and she left the room quickly, not saying another word, though she definitely looked daggers at him.

TWENTY EIGHT

Nathan looked hesitant as he came back in, but he didn't back out. He took me downstairs and made sure I was seated at a table in the coffee shop, before asking what sort of coffee I liked.

Rather than betray my limited knowledge of coffee, I asked him for a cappuccino. I could count on one hand the times I'd asked someone else to make me a coffee. To me, coffee meant whatever instant blend was available, mixed with enough sugar and milk to help me choke the bitter brew down.

He didn't ask me about cake and I wondered if he'd forgotten about it. Or was he one of those domineering men who ordered for you because he felt girls were too helpless to make their own decisions? I was betting on the first option.

I looked around. The cafe was perhaps a third full. I wasn't the only patient there, though I was probably the only patient who wasn't wearing pyjamas. There were a few people in the same scrubs I wore, but their name badges identified them as staff who were supposed to wear them. I couldn't suppress a sigh and looked away.

I'll get there, I told myself. I'll go back to uni and one day I'll get there. All I have to do is recover so I can.

I closed my eyes and listened to the music over the speakers. It was an old song, something cheerful. I tried to remember the words, but the sound of the coffee machine hissing drowned out the music.

I looked over at the counter. It was Nathan's turn.

He ordered and paid for something, then came and sat across from me, empty handed and smiling nervously. "They'll make the coffee and bring them out together."

"So, what kind of cake did you get?" I asked brightly.

He looked rueful. "I don't know."

Puzzled, I opened my mouth to ask a question that began with *how*...

He cut me off. "I didn't know what you wanted, so I got a bit of everything. There wasn't much to choose from." He looked apologetic.

Right on cue, a waitress came with a fully loaded tray and started putting plates down on our table. Some kind of cheesecake, something that looked like an overgrown chocolate brownie, some sort of tart that was covered in strawberries... and two frothy cups of coffee.

"Decaf cappuccino?" she asked, waving the hot drink dangerously close to me.

"Mine," Nathan said quietly, indicating the space on the table in front of him.

Decaf? He didn't want any caffeine? Odd, I thought, avoiding looking at the diabetic coma waiting to happen, spread across the remainder of the table.

I looked down at the coffee the waitress set in front of me, trying to work out how best to drink it. Maybe if I turned it this way, I could get both hands around it. If I was careful, I might be able to do it, but I'd get froth on my face...

Nathan unwrapped a straw and stuck it in my coffee.

I looked at him. He just smiled and picked up a cake fork. "So, which one would you like first?"

I reached for the plate with the strawberries at the same time as he did. I expected a fight, but he held the edge of the plate with one hand and sliced a bite off the cake with the other.

My heart sank. I couldn't handle a cake fork yet.

Nathan hadn't missed my expression. He held the fork out to me, cake first. Like that first bite of egg, I took it.

"Is it good?" he asked, taking the fork to the cake again.

"Yeah," I admitted, my mouth full. I tried to cover it with a bandaged hand.

He popped the next bite in his own mouth. "You're right," he agreed.

He set the fork on the table, the tines resting on the edge of his saucer. Picking up a clean fork, he loaded up another bite. "More?" he asked with a smile.

He waited until my mouth was full before he asked. "So, when you were sitting here with your eyes closed and your mouth open, what were you thinking about?"

He was watching me, I realised. I waited until I'd swallowed before I spoke again. "The music playing on the radio," I told him.

He looked surprised for a moment, then sat, listening.

I did, too. The song had changed – now it was some perky boy band and the song involved frequent use of the word beautiful. My memory stirred faintly. It had been a long time since I'd heard any music. Something called One Direction?

Nathan asked me if I knew the song, a kind smile on his face.

This isn't my style of music and you're not going to stereotype me that easily, I thought furiously. "No," I lied smoothly.

His teeth ticking against the tines, Nathan swallowed another bite of cake. "So, what sort of music do you like?"

Mine, I thought but didn't say. I liked the music that came into my head and felt so great when I got to play it... but it'd been a long time since I've heard any music and it'd be a while before I could play again... but I would! I would!

I tried to gather my drifting thoughts. "I like Powderfinger," I offered.

He smiled. "Me, too. Baby, I've got you on my mind."

I froze at what sounded like a bad pick-up line, staring at him.

His eyes widened as he realised what he'd said. "That's my favourite one of their songs. *Baby I've got you on my mind.* What's your favourite?"

"*Burn your name,*" I said immediately. Because it's the most fun to perform...

He looked confused. "I'm not sure I know that one."

I replied, without thinking, "It was one of the last ones they released. The one that goes..." I sang the first few lines, before I realised that people were starting to stare at me. I clamped my mouth shut.

Oh hell. The pain medication must be messing with my head. I just started singing in a cafe full of people...

Even Nathan stared at me. "You sing really well," he managed to say.

"Thanks," I replied, as politely as I could. "Your turn. What music do you like?"

"Um, my favourite band at the moment is Evanescence." He sounded hesitant.

"They're good, but very dark," I replied, closing my eyes. "I think if I was dying, I would want the last song I heard to be one of theirs. If I were to commit suicide, I would definitely be playing one of their albums."

I opened my eyes to find Nathan staring at me again, more worried than ever. What did I say? I thought a moment. Oh shit. Pain drugs were definitely messing with my head and my inhibitions.

"But I wouldn't say they're my favourite," I finished lamely.

He grabbed my hands and held them on the table, looking into my eyes with a fierce intensity. "Why would you say that?" he blurted out, his eyes wide with horror.

I tried to sound dismissive. "I studied music at school and there was a section on music in soundtracks. We had to assign songs to specific scripts. My group got some action movie where the hero sacrifices himself at the end and we picked an Evanescence song for the death scene." I shrugged. "The teacher didn't like ours much. The group that got the best mark picked *Bohemian Rhapsody*."

He looked confused again. "They picked what?"

It was my turn to stare. "Queen's *Bohemian Rhapsody*. You have to know it – it's a classic." I'm going to have to sing this one too, I thought. At least this one was quieter... I took a deep breath and tried to be as quiet as possible.

It only took a few lines before comprehension dawned on his face, but his eyes were still wide after I stopped singing. He seemed unable to think of a single thing to say. To buy himself time, he lowered his fork toward the cake plate in front of him.

He'd eaten the last bite of cake, without realising it. I watched him try to cut another bite with his fork, but it only scraped the empty plate. He looked down in surprise.

"Do you think we have time for another round before the staff upstairs realise I've kidnapped you and decide to report you missing?" He had a cheerful smile on his face, his eyes already straying to the cafe counter.

Did he realise what he'd said? That he was responsible for my injuries? I felt the fury build. If it's true, I'm going to kill you, but first, I'm going to kick you under the table so hard...

I drew my foot back under my chair, ready to deliver a kick that would help him hit the high notes of any song — even *Bohemian Rhapsody*.

He looked back at me, still smiling as he waited for an answer to his question. It took a moment before it registered in his head what he'd said. His expression slid from smiling back to horrified and he closed his eyes in mortification.

"Oh God, I'm sorry. I didn't mean to..." he babbled.

It was a fucking pick-up line. He'd fallen for me. He'd fallen for me so hard that when he turned on the charm, he managed to forget what I looked like now and what happened to me.

I could feel the laughter bubbling up inside me, as I broke into a grin and carefully placed my feet flat on the floor.

He opened his eyes again and he was absolutely transfixed. He seemed unable to stop staring at me, a battered girl with so many bandages I had to wear surgical scrubs instead of real clothes. Mr Sleazy Roommate, in love with a well-wrapped mummy.

I lost it laughing. It felt so good, after so long. Even my face felt lighter.

I realised that the hospital staff a few tables over were staring at me, too, looking concerned. I managed to get control of myself eventually, but Nathan didn't take his eyes off me.

I looked down at my lap, willing the hospital staff to leave me alone. I'm fine, I'm fine, he just made a funny joke...

I kept my voice as low as I could. I told him I'd had enough cake for now and I wanted to go back to my hospital room.

I heard his voice, talking too fast for me to understand half of it, as we went back upstairs. It sounded like he was just letting off pure nervous energy.

To think he charmed the nurses as easily as breathing.

As he was about to help me back into bed, he paused to take a deep breath and close his eyes before he touched me. His hands were as careful and decorous as ever, not even lingering as I half expected him to. Mr Sleazy Roommate, the perfect gentleman.

I could feel the smile lifting my lips, now light as air.

Nathan was looking at me, a question in his eyes.

What did he ask me? Oh, if I wanted more cake. Yet his eyes were offering far more than cake. Everything. Longing that I'd accept his offer of himself.

I smiled at him. Two could play at this game, and I was holding all the cards.

I could have been answering either question.

"Perhaps, Nathan," I told him, still smiling. "But not before tomorrow."

He opened his mouth, as if he wanted to ask which question I was answering, but he couldn't say the words.

I tried to sound rueful. "I'll be sick if I have any more cake today." My eyes dared him to ask me the other question, the one that wasn't about cake.

He smiled uncertainly. "Me, too," he said nervously.

I'll bet, my queasy roommate.

TWENTY NINE

Dark - Mike - Simon - Knife - Fighting - Police

I woke in the dark, not sure why.

There was no light - just rapid breathing. Not mine, either.

"Help me. Get me out of here," I said, hoping it was Chris.

No response.

I held my breath, waiting.

The rapid breathing didn't change. If anything, it grew faster and louder.

I couldn't see him, only hear his panting.

"Are you going to hurt me?" I demanded. I reached into my pocket for the card, going straight for the knife.

I felt the bump as his scraping steps hit the side of the mattress. He gasped in surprise.

Too close. "ARE YOU GOING TO HURT ME?" I shouted, scrambling up.

Something brushed against my chest, before fingers grasped at my breast.

I slashed forward with my knife and met

resistance.

"What the fuck? She's free and she has a knife?" an unfamiliar voice wailed. "She stabbed me! My son's a police officer, I'll have her arrested for attempted murder..."

Behind him, the door flew open, dim light framing a bulky shadow.

THIRTY

"Cancellation in theatre. . ."

I blinked and focussed on the woman hovering above me. Her name badge told me her name was Claire and she was a CN, if the theatre uniform hadn't told me that already.

"They've moved your skin graft up to this morning," Claire the clinical nurse told me, pressing her lips together. I nodded and she left.

Time to heal some of the scars. This meant I'd be allowed to leave hospital soon, if my skin had healed enough to start using it for grafts on the bits that hadn't. . .

I both heard and smelled breakfast approaching. Hunger wasn't hard to ignore, especially if I could have breakfast vicariously through Nathan. I looked over at him, hoping he'd chosen bacon and eggs.

"I won't have any," he told the lady from catering.

"Why not?" I asked, disappointed.

"I don't want to throw up on the operating theatre

floor," he replied.

But he didn't need surgery – just me. "You mean you're coming in with me?" I blurted out. It still didn't make sense. I knew he'd been a med student, too – and he wouldn't have lasted past first year if he threw up at the sight of blood, like Jason did.

Nathan looked shifty. "They'll put you under. . ."

Unconscious on an operating table, alone. "Fuck." I'd forgotten grafts are done under a general anaesthetic.

Nathan's warm hand on my wrist brought me back to the present. "I'll be there. I'll scrub up and watch over you as you sleep until your eyes open in Recovery."

He sounded like a perverted stalker. I told him so.

He laughed and I joined in, but there was no humour in mine. I knew he heard it. "You're going to be fine. I'll make sure of it."

He didn't know how relieved he made me feel. Nor would he, if I could help it.

THIRTY ONE

Nathan's shouting roused me from my nightmare. I caught the words, "Leave her alone!" and I realised the hands gripping my shoulders weren't his. Then the hands were gone and I fell back against the bed. The impact jolted the breath from my lungs.

I struggled to bring my head out of the dark nightmare and back to the bright hospital room. I took an inventory as I lay down, trying to orient myself.

There's the ceiling light, there's Nathan to my right, shouting at someone. On my left was the wash basin, which had two bunches of flowers in it, still wrapped in florist's paper. I looked further along the bed and saw a worried face I hadn't seen in a long time – a face I never expected to see visiting me in hospital. Jason.

Jason said something, his eyes on me, but I couldn't hear him over Nathan's shouting.

I didn't expect what happened next, though maybe I should have. Nathan took a swing at Jason and his fist connected with Jason's jaw. Jason's response was to ball up his fists and aim a punch at Nathan. His face, his hands. That's my fucking lead guitarist and vocalist. NO!

In my head, the dark nightmare I'd been woken from was happening again in this brightly lit room. I shook myself, gritted my teeth and fought not to scream at the pain as I stood up. This would end, or so help me, I would stick them both in a head lock as long as I could stay conscious.

Step after agonising step, I crossed the room and shoved between them. I was so close to Nathan, his shirt brushed my back, but I faced Jason. Nathan wouldn't hurt me, but for Jason to lose control like this, who knew what he'd do?

Jason's fists stayed up, as if he was going to hurt me, or at least push me out of the way to get to Nathan.

"Don't you dare touch me." I don't think I'd ever been this angry with Jason.

His hands flew up in surrender as he backed away. His fingers looked intact; his face would bruise, but there was probably no harm done. I kept my glare on him for a few more moments.

"I want nothing to do with either of you if you're going to fight like animals!" I shouted at Jason.

He turned pale, suddenly horrified as he saw his future job prospects, all of our future plans, destroyed. Finally, he understood.

"Caitlin, careful. . . you'll tear your stitches," I heard Nathan's voice murmur behind me.

I took a deep breath, relaxing the iron control for just a moment, and looked down. He was too late – one of the wounds on my leg was bleeding, so I'd already ripped the stitches. I started to crumple as the pain came flooding in, with the realisation that Nathan was behind me, trying to support me.

Nathan started this. He had no idea what he almost did.

"Get your hands off me!" I shouted at Nathan over my shoulder.

"No." His voice was a barely audible whisper in my ear.

I'd rather fall flat on my face than let him touch me with the hand that threw the first punch. In my fury, I tried to turn on my heel to face Nathan. I wanted to give him an earful, too. Yet as I started to shift my weight, pain and dizziness overwhelmed me. Strong arms lifted me as Nathan's voice murmured soothingly in my ear.

My eyes tightly closed, I fought to hold onto consciousness, without the use of even my fingernails to claw my way out of the threatening dark.

I needed to reassure Jason, to tell him that everything would be okay. I forced my eyes open to find the room still drained of colour. Stay down. Don't get up 'til the colours come back or you'll pass out.

"Jason." I fought to get the words out. "Something else scared me and I was just shocked to be woken up." I stretched out my hand to him, trying and failing to wiggle my fingers as a silent reminder of what he'd risked. Too late did I realise that else I was showing him.

He stared at my bandaged hand and the fingers I couldn't move, let alone play with. "Oh my God, what did they do to you?" Dreams, career, plans, gone. I could see it in his eyes. He bolted before I could say anything.

I called after him, but he didn't stop, nor return. He didn't let me tell him that I would be okay, that I'd recover and everything would go back to normal.

What if they had taken everything from me, even my music? What if my hands were so badly damaged they wouldn't heal? I could feel my eyes filling with tears and forced myself to think of other things. No need for self-pity. Why was he here, when I knew he threw up at the sight of blood? Why were there flowers in the sink?

I didn't realise the answer until Nathan stood at my side again, holding the larger bunch of flowers as a peace offering in front of him. "Happy birthday," he said apologetically.

Today I was legally old enough to drink and the only alcohol I'd see was some form of disinfectant. I wondered if you could drink the alcohol handwash.

I buried my face in my pillow, laughing hysterically 'til I cried. A normal girl would have just cried, but I was no longer normal, by any stretch of the imagination.

THIRTY TWO

Mike – Simon – Knife – Fighting

"No. She can't have a knife. Chris searched her..." Mike's voice said from the doorway. He moved into the darkness, toward me.

"Stay away from me!" I insisted, waving the tiny blade.

A torch beam blinded my eyes, gleaming on the knife.

"She has a knife!" the smaller man shrieked, pointing.

"I'll kill him," Mike swore, striding over to me.

I brandished the knife, lifting it toward his eyes. "Either of you touch me again and I'll cut your fucking dick off!"

I didn't see the blow that crashed into the side of my face, sending me flying. I hit the concrete blindingly hard and heard the knife skitter away from me.

"I'll do what I fucking well like," Mike answered.

I couldn't see. My face ached and my eyes

blurred with tears. I wondered if my jaw was broken.

I heard the scrape of metal on stone. "There, got it," Mike said. A hand closed around my throat. I could see the knife wavering above my face. "Where did you get this, little bitch?"

"I had it in my pocket," I spat. "I've got a bigger one for killing you in the other pocket. Don't need a big knife to cut off your prick."

Mike threw me back down on the floor. "She's all yours."

"What about this cut? And her other knife? I'm not staying here with that hellcat, getting infected or maybe bleeding to death. I'm not touching her again unless you make sure she can't do it again. And a bodyguard to hold her down, too."

Somewhere under the pain, I felt grim satisfaction that I'd scared the shit out of the idiot I'd stabbed. He deserved it.

"Fine. You come with me and we'll see if there's a first aid kit up at the house." A kick connected with my shin. "You stay here, little bitch. Chris is in deep shit. If she doesn't kill him, I will."

THIRTY THREE

"Today we'll take the dressings off your hands. Your fingers should have almost healed up by now." Judith's expression turned from sweet to sour as she shifted her focus from me to Nathan. "You, out."

Nathan stood up slowly. The question in his eyes was directed at me, not her. Other than that, his face was impassive.

What if my hands were permanently damaged, or twisted? I couldn't face that alone. I lifted my chin. "No," I said quietly. "I want Nathan to stay."

I caught the fleeting smile on his face as he sat down again, but it was gone so quickly I don't know if the nurse saw it. If she did, she probably ignored it.

Nathan stretched an arm across the pillow behind me, as if to exaggerate how little concern he had for what the nurse thought. I wished I was as confident as he was. I leaned back on the pillows so his arm was against my back, hoping I could absorb some of his assurance to blot out my fear. I felt his arm stiffen at the contact and realised his relaxed stance was more brittle than it seemed. Instead of worrying me, somehow I found it reassuring, sinking deeper into the pillows. He responded by curling his right hand lightly around my shoulder, giving it the slightest squeeze.

We're not scared. Just nervous as all hell, I thought. I swallowed and bit the proverbial bullet. "Do it," I told the nurse as I gave a sharp nod.

I held out my hand, trying hard not to flinch as she touched me. I forced myself to hold still until she let go of my freshly freed fingers. I held them up, trying to work out if all of them had healed properly.

Judith's slight smile told me she saw the same straight fingers that I did, but that wasn't the only thing that mattered. "Okay, let's see how well you can move these. Just bend them, one at a time," she said, looking serious once more.

I was afraid it would hurt. I bent my littlest finger slowly, waiting for the shock of pain to tell me I'd pushed even the tiniest part of my damaged body too far. My nail touched my palm and I almost whimpered in relief.

The nurse nodded eagerly as I tried my other fingers — thumb, index finger, middle, ring, before my little finger again. The first two were fine, so I curled my middle finger with more confidence than the others. The protesting muscles cramped and I bit back a cry of pain. I was more careful after that, but I needn't have worried.

Judith made a cautious comment about how well my hands had recovered so far and how I could make do without full use of my hands if I had to.

I looked at her in disbelief. She knew as well as I did that her spiel was silly, a hospital requirement to state risks just in case there was some adverse issue arising from my injuries. I bent all my perfect fingers, leaving only the middle one erect – my reaction to getting a standard statement from her when we both knew better.

She tried not to laugh, but I wasn't similarly restrained. "I'll be fine. You'll see."

She muttered something about arrogant doctors as I continued to laugh and offered her my other hand.

I played the fingers of my right hand out on the sheet, to the rhythm of the cheery little tune in my head. I didn't know where it had come from, but it wasn't going away. *Necessary evil, joy and pain. . .* Idly, I played with words as the silent notes rang in my ears. I wanted my left hand free so I could work a bass line beneath the melody. Something dark to contrast properly . .

"And the other hand?" Judith asked, as if she'd read my mind. I curled my left hand into a fist before splaying my fingers out. I wanted to play.

I stretched both hands again, as if I was going to play the piano for the first time in two months. Some stiffness, but better than nothing. I looked up to find both Judith and Nathan looking at me expectantly. "Physio with finger exercises next. Won't that be fun!" My hands ached to be on a piano keyboard, but I'd have to wait 'til I got home. Then music would be recommended physiotherapy, several times a day. My heart flew in hope. I wanted to play and write and start something new. . .

Judith touched a wet cloth to my hands and I let her wipe them clean, my mind spinning with a song that I was struggling not to sing. She looked amused. "Do you want me to go see if I can get some bubbly from the kitchen?"

It was a standing joke that there was no alcohol in the hospital, when most of the doctors drank like dried-out fish, so I responded like a normal patient who didn't know. "I don't believe there's any alcohol for drinking in a hospital."

Judith glanced at Nathan and winked at me. "There is — for the candlelight dinners in the maternity ward. I'll go get you some and you can toast having your hands back!"

She hurried out before I could say anything. She was talking about the sparkling grape juice, surely — they didn't give out alcohol in the maternity ward. I hoped for better, though. There was wine for the doctors' functions in the kitchen all the time. My first legal drink to celebrate having my hands back. I could have danced, if I could have stood up long enough to do so.

"Congratulations," Nathan said, pulling his arm away from me as he sat up properly.

I looked at him, unable to wipe the smile from my face as I held out my healing hands. My ragged nails could do with a manicure, but I'd have to cut them short to play, anyway. I wondered if I should ask Judith for a nail file when she came back.

To my surprise, Nathan carefully took my hands in his, startling me out of my skittering thoughts. He kissed the back of my right hand, then my left. Even his light touch felt strange on my skin, hypersensitised from being covered for so long.

With an effort, I chose not to pull away. "What was that for?"

He looked surprised. "I'm not sure. It just. . . seemed

like the right thing to do." He let go of me and looked away.

THIRTY FOUR

Sick of looking out of the window at the garden below, I announced my intention of going outside. I wanted to sit in the sun, if just for a few minutes.

Nathan made as many excuses as he could for why I shouldn't.

Eventually, I tuned out as I realised I could go outside without him – now my hands were free, I could push a wheelchair, even if I couldn't walk far yet without it.

The surgeon's dark blue pyjama set I'd been loaned was still tucked into my bedside cabinet, where I'd left it after the trip downstairs to the coffee shop.

I'd never appreciated how easily they slipped on before, with no zips or buttons to complicate matters.

I tried to pull the hospital gown over my head, but it got stuck and I realised I'd have to untie it at the back first. As I dropped it to start on the ties holding it closed, I caught Nathan staring at me wistfully and I realised I'd just given him an eyeful. For the first time in my life, I was glad my boobs weren't all that big — maybe he hadn't seen much. Trusting him to have the courtesy to turn his back or look away, I kept getting changed. My fingers were clumsy as I undid the knots, but I wasn't going to ask him for help.

I glanced at him again and his eyes were still on me, as if he were mesmerised. He was probably hoping I'd flash my boobs again, I thought sulphurously, clamping my mouth shut so I didn't shout at him, no matter how much I felt like it.

Self-consciously, I tried to keep the hospital gown covering as much as possible as I slipped on the dark blue top, followed by the pants.

When I thought I'd be able to keep my temper, I gritted my teeth as I tried to stay civil to Mr Sleazy Roommate. "You could have averted your eyes. It's considered polite."

He told me he'd been waiting for me to ask for help.

I never ask for help. I definitely wasn't asking him. I paused to make up my mind. I was going downstairs into the garden by myself. Fuck you, you sleazy bastard.

The wheelchair was outside my room. It was a little further than I'd walked in my physio sessions so far, but if I held onto the wall, the door frame and possibly the table on wheels, I knew I could reach it.

I stood up carefully and put my hands on the table that still held my lunch tray. I took a step and found I had to lean on the table more than I'd expected. This hurt my hands, so I let go of the table. Right, I guess it'd be the hard way.

I edged my foot forward, gritting my teeth as I lifted my head to focus on my goal. Instead, Nathan's chest blocked my view as his body barred my way. I glared up at him, but he didn't move. I could feel my control wavering. I opened my mouth to tell him to get out of my way and the haze of pain descended, turning the world grey and threatening to take my consciousness with it.

Get out of my fucking way!

I closed my eyes and took a deep breath. I'd walk with my eyes closed if I had to.

Before I could take another step, Nathan lifted me off my feet. When he put me down, it was on the edge of the bed, I knew, from the feel of the cotton sheets on the firm mattress.

You bastard, you're going to make me take those painful steps again, taking me back to where I started. In my fury, I wasn't game to open my mouth. I just sat there, fuming and ignoring him, as I waited for the pain to ebb so I could try again.

He sat on the floor in front of me, ducking his head until his face was about level with my feet as he looked up at me. The perfect level to kick him if he tried to stop me again, I thought. I was going to break his fucking nose with my foot.

"If you don't recover, they win." His words surprised me.

If he'd get out of my way and let me try to walk, I'd have a better chance at recovery than staying in bed all day.

"I'm getting better," I told him, stating the obvious that he apparently hadn't seen.

His tone was melting, barely more than a whisper. "If you let me help you, you'll get better faster. And it won't hurt as much, either."

I shook myself. I'd get better faster if I tried to get back to normal as quickly as I could. "I'm not asking for your help," I snapped. I voiced my suspicions. "You know I won't."

"Who helped you before, Caitlin? Who brought you food, water, medicine? Someone helped you survive." He looked up at me urgently. *Do you remember?* said his eyes.

Of course. Don't you? Are you sure you want me to remember Chris and what he did? What YOU did?

In surprise and anger, I blurted out the first things that came to my head. "Someone who didn't wait for me to ask. Someone kind. Someone. . . I haven't told the police about." *Yet.* I left the last word unsaid, regretting every word I'd voiced.

I waited for him to say something, to ask more questions that I didn't want to answer. I'd said more than I'd intended to already. Lost in thought, I wasn't paying attention when he did speak. Something about how he was going to help me?

Enough waiting. "I want to go outside," I told him.

"And how are you going to get there?" he asked, amused.

Well, first you're going to get out of my fucking way if I have to kick you. . . I bit back that response. "I'm going to get to that wheelchair, take it down in the lift and then outside."

"What if you fall again?"

Not bloody likely. "Then I'll crawl."

"How will you push the wheelchair?" The bastard was making fun of me.

I held out my hands, struggling not to throttle him with them. *Just get out of my way!* I tried to remember what the gardens outside looked like. "I can use my hands a little. It's downhill from the front entrance to the gardens, so that should be easy."

"How will you get back up the hill to the hospital?" he asked.

This was the bit I hadn't thought through. I had hoped to ask him to come and get me in an hour or so, but now I'd be damned before I'd ask him for help.

I mumbled a response, but he was already laughing at me.

I turned away from him, eying the wheelchair again as I steeled myself for another attempt. Fighting with him sapped my energy and I'd need it if I was going outside.

As if he'd read my mind, he lifted me up again, this time taking me over to the wheelchair. As always, his hands were deft, gentle and courteous. Anything else would be unprofessional, I realised. Shit, when he watched me change earlier, he was probably checking to see how I was healing up. Always, he'd tried to help me. If I hadn't seen him flirt with the nurses, would I have thought him any less gallant? Especially with me always in that horrible, skimpy hospital gown. I felt bad that I hadn't trusted him to help me get dressed. Belatedly, I voiced the words I should have said much earlier. "Thank you."

Experimentally, I bent my fingers around the wheels. I can do this, I told myself with relief. Now don't be a coward and look at him.

Nathan stood in the doorway, looking lost and worried.

"Are you coming?" I asked him, trying to cross my fingers for the first time.

"Sure," he replied.

My heart leaped and I realised how relieved I was.

He started pushing me down to the lift, telling me about the gardens.

When the sunlight kissed my skin, warmer than anything I could remember in weeks, I laughed for joy.

I'll never let them win. I didn't want to lose this.

THIRTY FIVE

Mike — Pills — Dark — Fighting — Chris — Clothes

"If you don't do it, I'll shoot you here and now," a voice drawled, across the room or maybe outside of it. "Get her undressed and you know what to do next, don't you?"

"All right, all right!" Chris's voice sounded scared and much closer.

The creep of fingers on my skin, beneath my clothes.

I rolled away from him, scrambling to my feet. I tried to ignore the dizziness, back with a vengeance. "What the fuck do you think you're doing? I'll break your bloody hand if you touch me without my permission again!"

I could see him only as a stationary shadow, perhaps two metres from me. Between me and the door. Chris's voice was barely audible, but I recognised it all the same. Maybe it was the way it shook, like he was terrified of me. "I have to."

"Like hell you do!" The dizziness didn't

fade and my head started to ache unbearably. So did my jaw. I lifted a hand to my face, trying to rub the pain away.

"Your head still hurts?" Concern coloured his tone.

"Yes," I admitted. "What's it to you?"

"I have some more pain relief." I heard the rustle and crackle as he pulled the pills out and pressed them from the packet. "And water..." He leaned over to retrieve the bottle. He held out both to me, his arms stretched like a zombie in the dark.

I hesitated. Not because I thought he resembled a zombie. I suspected trickery of a different kind.

My biggest worry was that he'd grab me once I was close enough, overpowering me easily as his strength overcame mine. I decided it didn't matter – if he wanted to grab me, I had nowhere to run. The pills and water were worth the risk. Chris hadn't hurt me yet.

Carefully, I reached out and took both from him. He made no move to approach closer, though I kept my eyes on him as I swallowed the pills and gulped a little more water.

"You stay there," I warned him as I backed away with the water. He didn't attempt to stop me.

I should have wondered why.

Instead, I sat on the edge of the mattress, sipping in silence while he stood between me and the door, a silent sentinel. A standoff. Who would break first? Not me. I had nothing left to lose.

Boredom set in and I found myself drifting. My eyes started to close and I swayed. Muzzily, I decided to stretch out on the mattress, just for a moment, to deal with the drowsiness while the pain ebbed away. He hadn't hurt me. Wouldn't hurt me. Maybe I could trust...

"Finally."

A hand groped its way up my leg. I kicked out feebly and it let go. I barely had a moment to breathe my relief when cold fingers crept beneath the waistband of my jeans. The scratch of the zip before he started tugging on them, denim sliding down my skin and exposing it to the freezing air.

"Let go of me, you bastard!" I screamed out, struggling. Fear turned me colder still. Couldn't trust anyone. Not even the one who helped me.

The hands only tightened their grip, stripping my jeans from me, no matter how hard I fought. My body was too sluggish and slow to respond. Did he even notice my poor attempt to struggle?

"I'm not hurting you. Just let me," he begged.

I couldn't believe my ears. "You want me to let you rape me? To make it easier for you?" I tried desperately to twist away from him, but his grip was unbreakable. "I said let me go, loser!"

"Can't. If I don't do what I'm told, someone else will get hurt. And they'll hurt you, too." The sound of him licking his lips. Nervous. Good. "We have to get these clothes off you... then I have to... have to... I've got a gun."

I froze. I wasn't ready to die yet. I didn't know him, nor what he was capable of doing.

Hands slid beneath my shirt once more, pulling the fabric up. I swatted at him with hands so heavy I could barely lift them. Helpless. I couldn't stop him.

"No, please... please... don't... you don't

have to do this," I whimpered.

"I do." He sounded like he was in pain. I wished he'd go curl up and die of it. A pause as he yanked my t-shirt over my head. "I won't hurt you. Relax and it'll be over soon."

I smothered a sob and sent my mind somewhere else. Anywhere not here.

THIRTY SIX

"Are you ready to give press interviews yet?"

I stared at Nathan. If it was a joke, it sure as hell wasn't funny.

He looked apologetic. "There's a press crew around, waiting for you. I heard them talking."

Fuck. Nosy people asking me questions I didn't want to answer. Telling the world what I didn't want to tell anyone, even Nathan. "I don't want to, oh hell, not yet."

The sun slid behind a cloud, making my mind up. The light seemed so dim by comparison. Then the cloud was gone.

Nathan wanted to go back inside. I could see that, but I wanted just a little more sun. After all, we were pretty well hidden and I said as much to Nathan.

Reluctantly, he agreed to stay outside with me, so he could help me back inside when it became necessary.

It felt like no time at all before Nathan's voice told me with regret, "Time to go, angel." He pointed. "Look, they're taking photos of us."

With his help, I switched my seat on the bricks beside the pool in a patch of sunlight for the wheelchair. I had to hold on, as he whipped it around and started up the hill at a faster speed than I expected.

I heard voices shouting behind us and curled up in the wheelchair, praying that Nathan was wrong and they weren't following us. The voices grew louder. "No," I whispered, closing my eyes.

I heard the pounding of Nathan's feet on the path paving, feeling the breath of breeze increase as we gained speed. I didn't feel the warmth of the sun any more — I felt a chill to the depth of my bones.

When Nathan lifted me into bed, I could feel his chest heaving through his sweat-soaked shirt. I watched and waited as he poured himself some water, drank it and tried to slow his breathing.

"Why would any reporter want to interview me?" I asked carefully, when it looked like he had the breath to talk.

When he started throwing around phrases like "back from the dead" and "Harry Potter" I thought he was joking. If I was in a story, it was most certainly horror — a far cry from children's stories where the main character survived through magic, miracles or some form of paranormal occurrence. Vampires, wizards, mermaids. . . no, just me.

But maybe, just maybe. . . there was a story to tell. No less fictional than any other, really, but who'd want the truth?

The rustling of paper brought me back to the present. Nathan proffered a newspaper, plastered with my name and my picture. I scanned the first few lines and realised it was the print version of the news I'd heard in the Emergency Department when I arrived.

One day I'll tell this story, I promised myself. I'd sell it to the highest bidder and to hell with the horror. It wouldn't be my problem any more.

I looked at Nathan, considering. Every story needs a hero. Even mine.

THIRTY SEVEN

"You've made a remarkable recovery. You take care – I don't want to see you back here unless you're on prac again," Dr Aidan said with a smile.

"Me, too," I admitted as I watched him sign my discharge papers. He'd already arranged more meds through the hospital pharmacy – one of the staff was sending them up now.

I could go home!

"Would you like me to drive you home?" Nathan asked, the moment the doctor left.

I hesitated for an instant before I nodded. I'd trusted him so far – a short car trip was hardly a risk.

A nurse whisked me downstairs, Nathan and a guard following behind. The nameless guard did his best not to make eye contact with me, even as I gave him a beaming smile. Nathan wasn't the only man I owed gratitude for keeping me safe in hospital.

Nathan wanted me to sit in one of the seats inside the

foyer while he brought the car around, but I wouldn't do it. The outside bench looked far too inviting. I'd been cooped up inside for too long and the perfect day begged to be enjoyed. He exchanged a glance with the guard before he headed off into the car park.

As he passed the doctors' car park, I smothered a laugh at the sight of Dr Aidan's red Mini. It looked silly between the huge four-wheel-drives and flashy sports cars, but he refused to drive anything else. Idly, I wondered what it was like to drive. Now I was eighteen, Dad would permit me to buy my own car instead of borrowing his and I'd barely considered what I wanted.

The guard sauntered into view, headed for the car park. He wouldn't have left unless Nathan was back, so I looked around for him.

Déjà vu. A red Mercedes pulled up in front of me.

The first time, I should have run. Now I could barely walk, but I knew what I had to do. I had to get back inside. I wouldn't let them take me back. I'd die first.

When I saw Nathan get out of the car, I almost cried.

I won't get into their car again. I won't, I swore.

"Not you. You can't take me back there to them!" I insisted.

He stared at the car as if he didn't remember. Slowly, he told me that the car belonged to him.

My fear spiralled out of control. "No – I trusted you!" Had I trusted the wrong man?

Nathan backed away from me, his hands up in some sort of surrender. I glanced over my shoulder and saw two hospital security guards watching us intently. I'd never been so relieved.

Nathan asked me to sit down again – on the bench, not in his scary car – and I did. He started to explain how he owned a red Mercedes.

When his voice faded into silence, I kept my voice steady, reminding him of what he already knew, as I fixed my eyes on his shiny mag wheels. "They had a car just like this one. They pulled me into it and drove me. . . there. . . and. . ."

Nathan wouldn't be so stupid as to kidnap me again in broad daylight, under the eyes of security guards who had a clear view of both his car and the number plate. He'd take me home or the police would hunt him down. I was being suspicious and silly. He'd sworn to protect me. Of course he wouldn't hurt me. I laughed at my own silliness.

"But you. . ." I began, not sure how to finish. I shook my head. "Swear you don't work for them."

"No," Nathan said.

My mind whirled. No he wouldn't swear to it, or no he didn't work for them?

Hoping I hadn't missed anything important, I tried to pay attention as he continued, "One of them decided to try and kill me on that beach where I found you."

No one tried to kill him on the beach. They tried to kill me. The police officer tried to shoot him on the road. Didn't he remember or was he trying to cover up the truth?

"Would you still like a lift home?" Nathan held out his hand.

Again, I hesitated. I glanced back at the staring security guards and made a decision. I'd get into his car, but not willingly. He'd have to carry me in, which meant the security guards would be suspicious. Just in case.

Nathan believed in my weakness and lifted me into his horrible car without a qualm. Still I worried. At least I was in the passenger seat and not child-locked into the back with Saucer Eyes.

I watched Nathan key my address into his GPS, not saying a word. I knew I hadn't told him where I lived, but he was too flustered to notice his slip. When his eyes strayed to me again, I carefully looked out the window instead.

I wondered what waited for me at home. If he was so familiar with my address, did that mean his colleagues had searched it thoroughly? Had they planted some form of surveillance in there, to keep watch on my house? Why had he bought me new clothes from a supermarket instead of sending someone to my place for mine? Or did he truly not want me to know who he worked for? My head was a mess and Nathan wasn't helping. Tears of frustration sprang to my eyes. I didn't understand him at all.

Nathan wiped the first tear away and I looked up at him in surprise. His fingers closed over mine, but I didn't drop my gaze to look. "Caitlin, it's over. They can't touch you any more." I'd never seen him look so intense. "Or are you upset that I was checking you out?"

Of all the ridiculous things to say to break the serious mood. . . I burst out laughing. Nathan, checking out my damaged body? He wouldn't hurt me. He wouldn't even touch me. I was going to be fine.

"Please, can you take me home now?" I asked aloud.

"Sure, angel," he murmured, starting the engine.

It seemed like no time before he said, "You're home."

I looked out the window and realised he was right. I was

home and it hadn't changed at all – the opposite to me. I thanked Nathan as he helped me from the car and into the house.

I told him where we kept the spare key and watched as he dug it out.

I stepped inside, following Nathan's gaze to see where the surveillance cameras were. Ah, on the burglar alarm sensors. That meant the bathrooms, toilet and bedrooms had no cameras – just the living areas.

He turned his eyes to the floor. Before I could ask why, he said abruptly, "You can use my sister's laptop for as long as you need to."

I nodded, thinking of how much I'd have to add to the vague descriptions of my memories. More than Nathan should ever see. Yet I didn't want to say goodbye to him yet. He'd been so kind in driving me home, despite my unfounded fears and my dislike for his car.

"Did you want to have dinner here, or do you have something planned at home?" I offered uncertainly. I had no idea what to offer him for dinner. I didn't even know if we had food in the house, with Dad gone for so long.

I'd have to ask him to order and pay for pizza. I laughed at my own stupidity.

As if he'd read my mind and didn't like the pizza box he saw there, Nathan said, "You should probably have a rest, maybe even a couple of hours' sleep, and I'd stop you from doing that if I stayed. I'll leave you to it. . . Here's my phone number. If you need me at any time, feel free to call."

He took a moment to pull a receipt out of his wallet, looking around for a pen. I grabbed one from the hall table and held it out. He smiled his thanks as he scribbled his number on the receipt. I read the numbers over his shoulder – the landline looked like a South Perth one, not far from here, I guessed.

"How about I see myself out?" Nathan's words startled me.

Hastily, I smiled and agreed. Maybe he was the one on surveillance. I hoped he was the one watching me through the cameras. Better than a stranger.

He walked slowly out, offering to return tomorrow.

I grasped at the straw. I didn't want to be alone. "Thank you, yes. That'd be wonderful." I wished I had the temerity to demand he stay with me now, but he seemed jumpy, somehow. Maybe he wanted to go home and check on his sister. Surely she had surveillance in her house, too.

I forced myself to close the door behind Nathan, before I hurried to the lounge room window to watch him drive off, my hand pressed against the net curtains and glass as if I could bring him back if I reached out far enough.

Nathan, please don't go.

Yet he did, pulling smoothly out of my driveway and driving away. It felt like he'd taken my heart with him. Lost, somehow.

How strange.

THIRTY EIGHT

Mike – Hide – Dark – Fighting – Chris – Clothes

He took my clothes. All of them. Cold and clinical as if it were surgery. He bundled them up and took them to the door while I shivered. I heard his voice as a low hum in the distance.

"You got all of them? Fuck, have fun with her. Mind if I wank while I watch?" Mike's voice said.

My heart froze as I felt cold fingers on my skin again. The mattress moved as his weight crushed it, close to crushing me. And worse.

"No," I whimpered. "Please..."

Never had unzipping sounded so loud. To me, it was louder than the scream I tried and failed to summon from my own lungs. His panting drowned out even my breathing – I didn't want to breathe if it meant the pain that would come next.

"Please," I whispered.

Laughter from further away. "Come on, fuck her. She's begging for it. Just shove it in. I'll do it if you won't. She looks real uptight..."

"NO!" His shout echoed through the room, telling me it was bigger than I thought. He swallowed noisily as he pulled his hands away from me. "I can't."

"You sure about that?" the big bastard asked, an edge to his tone.

"I... can't... not with you watching," Chris said finally. He stood up and moved toward the other bastard.

I struggled to sit up, moving into a clumsy crouch.

"Performance issue, huh? Why am I not surprised?" The rustle of fabric. "I'll take her clothes, then. Anything else you need? A dildo, maybe, if you can't get it up?"

Where to go? The door was out, with two of them there. My next best option was to try and hide in the darkest corner I could find. I moved into the darkness.

Chris sounded upset. Good. Two-faced prick. "No. Just... no audience."

The bastard snorted. "Wish it was my turn. Ah, she'll keep." The door slammed shut. Shuffling footsteps on concrete, fading away.

One down. One to go.

"Oh shit. Angel?"

He'd discovered I wasn't where he'd left me. I stayed silent and tried to move deeper into the dark — away from him. My back touched the concrete wall, cold and rough against my bare skin. I edged along it, trying not to make a sound. I backed into a corner, almost screaming as soft, sticky cobwebs clung to my skin. What if the spiders were still home? I bit down on my lips to keep the scream inside. A deadly spider bite was preferable to what he had in store.

"C'mon, angel. It's dark and it's cold, you have no clothes and you'll freeze. I'm not going to hurt you," he pleaded. He clicked on a torch and started sweeping it around the room.

Knowing he'd find me soon enough, I spat, "No, you just took my clothes and you want to rape me. Like that won't hurt. Fuck you!" The words came out thickly, like I was drunk.

His voice was anxious. "Look, I'm just doing what I'm told."

"So you're going to rape me because you were told to. Big bloody hero." My voice was flat. I edged around the wall, hoping to find another way out. A corner gave way to an alcove and I backed into deeper darkness, where I couldn't see him - only the light from his torch beam. I grazed my foot on a brick, searing pain spreading as it scraped away skin. I didn't make a sound.

"No. I swear - I won't touch you again. They want me to, but I can't do it. C'mon, I know you're not feeling well."

His torch beam played across the edge of my alcove, then approached along the floor. The light touched my toes and moved away quickly.

"Here." The torch clinked to the floor, casting weird shadows as it shone up his body. He started to pull his sweater over his head. I caught a glimpse of the ripple of muscle beneath.

Now or never. I reached down and grabbed the brick, sprinting toward him. With his head covered, he wouldn't see me coming. I brought the brick down on his torch, smashing the glass and the globe inside. Light died.

I brought the brick up to hit him with it next.

"What the hell?" He flailed around and sent

me sprawling before I could clock him with the brick.

I scrambled to my feet, stumbling for the door. My fingers touched wood and I felt around for the handle.

There wasn't one.

I shoved at the door, kicking at the lock, but nothing happened. I remembered this door opened into the room - kicking wouldn't help. I sank to the floor, dizzy.

His voice was alarmingly close. "Here." Something soft touched my face. Not fingers. Fabric.

In the dim light, I could barely make him out as a dark shadow looming over me. I was too tired. He was going to win. My only hope now was that he'd knock me out and I wouldn't feel him hurt me.

"Just fucking get it over with," I panted. I was close to passing out.

"Here. Take my jumper. You must be freezing."

"I give up. You win." I slid down the wall. The concrete under my head was cold but I was drifting out of consciousness anyway. I barely felt it.

"No, angel. I can't win. I've lost too much already. Don't you ever give up. Keep fighting. Don't let them win."

His hands touched me again. I couldn't move to resist them any more.

Darkness descended.

THIRTY NINE

I sank onto a stool by the phone and pulled out the phone book. I had a lot of cards to cancel and new ones to request. An hour later, sick of spelling out my name and telling everyone my birth date, I left the kitchen and headed for the pathetic collection of belongings I'd brought home with me from hospital.

I pulled the laptop bag onto my shoulder and carried it to my bedroom, looking for the camera on the hall sensor. Once I'd spotted it, I felt a little safer. At least someone was watching out for me, somewhere. I hoped they were close by – close enough to come if I needed them.

Unzipping the bag, I lifted the pink 'puter out and started to connect the power cables. I didn't flick the switch on the wifi modem. I didn't want to check my emails, Facebook and all the rest. Answering all the panicked questions would take me ages and I just wanted to focus on the worst things first.

Jo had told me about the Facebook tribute page, RIP

Caitlin, that some idiot had set up. Almost, but not yet, asshole, I thought. I wasn't dead yet. I had too much to do. A little justice was in order.

I watched the machine power up, tears springing to my eyes as I saw a photo of Alanna and Nathan on the desktop. They looked like they were on a boat at Rottnest — and they both looked so happy. I'd never seen him smile like that. Perhaps a part of him really had died with her. She'd been so vibrant.

But not stupid. She'd told me to watch out for him. Had she seen danger when it came for her?

I shook the thought from my head. I knew now what they'd done to her, more clearly than anyone else could, for I bore the same injuries. I'd lived to tell the tale it was time to tell.

The file was saved directly on the desktop, neatly called *Nightmares of Caitlin Lockyer*. Like the title of a horror novel, I thought. I'd never liked horror stories, but I opened this one.

I skimmed through what I'd already told Nathan in the vaguest terms. The most brutal of rapes reduced to thirty words? No, twenty-nine. I could reduce the whole thing to just four, if I really thought about it: It hurt. Never again.

But brevity wasn't called for now. Brutal detail, so I could find them. Hunt them down. Somehow make them pay for what they'd done to me. Like Alanna, I probably should have died. But I didn't. I was on borrowed time. Borrowed for vengeance, for I had no life left as long as they had theirs. I'd never be free until they were all dead.

I carefully stretched my fingers and started to type.

Chris.

The car.

The stolen kiss.

How he took my clothes.

The horror of the first rape. And another. . .

The cruelty of cuts, breaks, bruises and other brutality.

The horror of help not given, however desperately begged for.

Bloody breakfast cereal that I'd never eat again, no matter how hungry.

And the beach. . . darkness, freedom, stars, blood and gunshots. . . almost losing everything.

As I reached the bit where my fingers were broken, I stopped, the tears too much. Now I wanted a hug from Nathan, a promise of cake and comfort. I toyed with calling him, but I didn't. After all, I didn't need him – I just felt a little lost and lonely. Hardly an emergency.

I read through the harrowing account of how Pete. . . and couldn't do it any more.

As the sky turned mauve, I sat back, looking at the horrible text with some satisfaction. I'd done enough for one day. I hit save.

My stomach rumbled to remind me that I had other concerns than catching criminals. I closed the lid of the laptop and rose, heading for the kitchen.

I opened the fridge first, out of sheer force of habit. The smell that assaulted me was like nothing on Earth I'd ever smelled before. I grabbed the orange juice and slammed it shut quickly. The juice bottle was the only item that hadn't been furry.

I set the bottle on the sink and found a glass. Barbara had kept our house immaculately clean, as always. Having a cleaning lady like her was a luxury I hoped would continue for a long time.

I uncapped the juice bottle and started to pour.

Nothing came out.

I set the bottle on the bench, checking to see if the seal was still on it. It wasn't. I tipped the bottle over the glass again.

A little liquid started trickling into the glass, followed by an enormous blob of goo that splashed over the glass and the draining board in a spectacular orange inkblot.

What does this remind you of?

I could almost hear the hospital psychologist's coaxing voice.

I inclined my head, looking closely.

It reminds me that I've been away for a long time and I need to go food shopping. It reminds me not to drink the orange juice.

I capped the bottle and dropped it into the bin.

As if the clink of the bottle hitting the bin-bottom were some kind of cue, I heard knocking.

FORTY

The knocking continued as I made my way to the front door.

Jagadamba from across the road stood on my doorstep, her dark eyes worried. "Caitlin! We were all so worried about you and the newspapers kept saying you would not return alive. . ."

I smiled. "You know me, Jaga. I'm too tough to kill."

"What happened to you?" she asked.

I sighed. "More than any girl should have to put up with." She smelled of spices – the sort that set my hungry stomach off again.

"Oh, don't you worry. You'll be back into life in no time. I know you!" she said fiercely. She dropped her voice. "Would you like some biryani? I made extra when I saw you arrive home, because I thought you'd have nothing in the house and no time to cook." She held up a covered dish and the spicy smell intensified.

I think I drooled a little. I covered my mouth with my

hand. "That would be amazing. . . thanks, Jaga." I took the warm dish from her hands, cradling it in my arms like a baby.

"If there's anything you need, you just call us," she said. "I'll send my husband over if you get any more men visiting who shouldn't be here."

I smiled tiredly. "It's okay. The men before were putting in a new security system." I hoped it was true. Surveillance cameras were a sort of security system, after all.

We both said goodbye and she crossed the road to return home.

I carried my dinner into the kitchen and set it on the bench. Lifting the lid, I inhaled the spicy smell of the still-warm curry. I was ready to eat it all on the spot. Forcing myself to wait, I stuck some rice and water in the rice cooker and turned it on.

While I waited for the rice to cook, I stretched out on the lounge room floor and started doing the exercises Althea had given me. I did two sets of everything, then started on the third before the timer beeped. I clambered to my feet, feeling the burn of exhaustion in my thighs as I stood. I took a deep breath and forced myself to walk normally, despite the pain. I could ignore it. I'd ignored worse pain before and no amount of limping would make those bastards pity me if they turned up here. Or her.

If I wanted to kill her and all the rest of them, I needed my strength.

I served up the biryani and rice, spooning a much larger serving than I normally would. I'd need the energy to do more exercises after dinner. I ate the lot, though I felt bloated afterwards as I washed the dishes.

I stuck the rice in the dish Jaga had given me and opened the fridge without thinking. The smell hit me again, just as bad as before. I took a moment to see if I could remove the source. . . but my fridge looked like something out of a horror movie. Something had gone mouldy in the crisper and the mould had spread from shelf to shelf while I'd been away. It looked like I'd been dissecting calico cats and kept the body parts in my fridge.

I shut the door again, without leaving the dish in there. I popped it in the freezer instead, which bore no fur – just a thin crust of frost.

I headed back to the lounge room, dropping to the floor to repeat my physio exercises until I ran out of strength. I couldn't recover fast enough.

After an hour, a sheen of sweat made my clothes stick to my skin. My legs were protesting in pain even as I lay on the floor. I decided to try taking a shower.

I managed to stagger to the bathroom, only to collapse in a heap on the bathmat. There was no way I could stand long enough for a shower. Hauling myself up on the side of the bath, I filled the tub instead and crawled laboriously in.

I wanted to sink beneath the bubbles and sleep, but I had my own bed for that – a bed I was definitely looking forward to, after weeks of cold concrete followed by a slightly softer hospital bed.

I drained the tub and crept over to the cupboard for a towel to dry myself with. I was so exhausted I knew as soon as I reached my bed I'd fall in and sleep – I wouldn't want to come back to hang my towel up. I hesitated for a moment, before remembering that Nathan would be monitoring the surveillance cameras. He'd seen me naked only this morning. Taking a deep breath, I tried to walk nonchalantly down the hall to my bedroom.

I closed my bedroom door and pulled on a nightie, before palming the light switch and falling into bed. The soft mattress cuddled me as the quilt enveloped me in what I can only describe as heaven. Home.

FORTY ONE

Forgiveness – Superman – Chris – Clothes

I jerked awake.

Beneath me was the mattress, not concrete. Back where I started. "What'd you do to me?" I demanded, my voice hoarse. I could barely move my legs.

His voice came from over by the door. I could just make out a shadow crouched by the wall. "I gave you my jumper. I moved you to the mattress so you'd be more comfortable. I wrapped you in a blanket so you'd be warm. And I took the other blanket for myself, because it's freezing in here and you're wearing my jumper." He sounded... pleading. Like he wanted my forgiveness or something. He wasn't going to get it.

I could feel the fleece on my skin and the scratchy blanket wrapped around my legs, restricting my movement. "And how many times did you rape me while I was unconscious?" I spat angrily.

"None." His quiet response shocked me,

especially as it sounded like he was telling the truth. "And I'm not going to. Save your strength. You don't need to fight me. I'm trying to help you."

"Helping me is getting me out of here. Not stealing my clothes," I pointed out.

"No and I'm sorry. I gave you mine, though. If you don't want it, I'll trade you my blanket for my Superman jumper back."

I forced myself to laugh. "Superman? You think you're Superman? I wouldn't ask you for help even if you were Superman! Hell, that's what I need. A real superhero, to beat the crap out of all these bastards, including you, and get me the hell out of here. I'll keep your damn sweater."

"There are no superheroes, here or anywhere. All you have is me."

You're a pretty poor excuse for my last hope. Yet I'll work with what I have to try to get out.

He continued, "Rest while you can. While I'm here, the others won't touch you."

I hesitated, but I had to ask. "Why not?"

He sounded like it pained him to say it. "Because they think it's my turn to hurt you."

FORTY TWO

I woke myself with my own scream.

Tom had hit me. He'd broken my fingers. And then he'd. . .

I bit back another scream, trying to slow my breathing and my heart rate. I was on a comfortable bed, not there. I groped for the bedside table, hoping I had a bedside lamp. I couldn't remember any more – it had been so long since I'd slept in my own bed.

My fingers felt the tingle of the touch lamp as the globe lit up. . . and died.

Swearing, I slid out of bed and tried to find the light switch.

I barely managed to get to the door on my shaky legs, swatting at the switch until it turned on and I could sink to the floor.

I hugged my knees to my chest, feeling very alone.

I wanted Nathan. I wanted to feel his arms around me. I wanted to hear him tell me that I was safe.

I thought about calling him, but my clock told me it was almost midnight. Who would watch the surveillance cameras if he was here, soothing me to sleep like a big baby?

I forced myself to stand and walk over to the desk, my muscles screaming in protest until I sank into the desk chair. I powered up Alanna's laptop and promptly typed in everything I could remember of my nightmare about Tom, sparing no detail. I got to the worst part and stopped.

No one needed to know how it felt when they raped me. It's no one's damn business. All they needed to know was that it happened. And all of them did it.

Quickly, I typed in the four bastards' names. I started to fill in sketchy details of what I remembered about each of them. It was nearing two in the morning by the time I'd finished, but I didn't dare stop until it was done.

Feeling a bit better, I lay down again, deciding to leave the light on. I felt a little afraid of the dark.

I fell asleep and woke screaming. Tom had raped me again in my sleep and I couldn't. . . couldn't. . .

I stumbled out of bed and down the hall. Nothing calmed me like music. Nothing.

With shaking hands, I lifted the lid on the piano.

It was time for more exercise. The best kind.

I touched my fingers lightly to the keys, praying it wouldn't hurt too much. I needed to hear music – mine, no one else's.

I tried. I really tried. But my fingers were stiff and my playing was stiffer still. As the sun rose, I played scales. Up and down my piano, limbering my fingers up until they worked again. Yet with every scale, a tune kept creeping into my head. I wanted to hear it on guitar, but I picked it out in piano notes, just letting the sound colour the air around me. Even after hours of scales, my music was still stiff and jerky, but that seemed to suit this piece. A necessary evil, perhaps. Part of the discord in my head.

I shook my discordant head and resumed my scales.

A tattoo on the door matched the rhythm perfectly, but I knew it meant the person knocking wanted my attention. I staggered to my feet and looked at the stained glass decorating my front door, glowing in the early morning sunlight.

A new day had dawned – yet I hadn't slept.

FORTY THREE

I dragged my feet to the door and managed to unlock it. All that playing made it easier to twist the locks, though it still hurt to stand. I had to lean on the door to rest.

I shifted my weight from the wooden door to the screen one, swinging it out to see my visitor better.

Stronger hands than mine moved the door as I did, dragging me along with it and partway down the steps. I tried to hang on, but my fingers weren't strong enough.

Fortunately, Nathan's arms were. The only reason I didn't fall was because he caught me.

"What happened?" I heard him say.

I mumbled something about how I couldn't sleep with the nightmares. How the nightmares wouldn't go away.

He lifted me in his arms and told me he was taking me to bed. I wanted to laugh, thinking that such a seduction seemed too sudden, but I contented myself with a smile as I snuggled closer to his chest. I wanted him to comfort me. To stay.

I felt the bed beneath me and he tried to pull away.

No. Not alone again. Please stay.

I reached for him.

As sleep washed over me like a warm wave, I heard him say he would.

I smiled as I drifted off.

In the dark, the bastard took my clothes and I was helpless to stop him. I tried to fight him, but my hands met nothing but air and a pillow. A sweet, soft pillow.

I'm home. Safe.

Where was Nathan?

"I'm here, angel, like I promised. It's okay. . ." He took my hand in his.

I could barely believe that he'd stayed. I wanted to kiss him, I was so happy to see him. So silly.

He rested his head on the pillow beside me, facing me. "Bad dream?" he asked.

I nodded and he pulled me into a comforting hug.

Somehow this seemed more intimate than before. I lay in bed in his arms, safe and secure, and slept.

FORTY FOUR

First – Tied – Fingers – Broken – Cut – Rings – Tom

"Right, where's the little bitch?" A new voice startled me. Someone's silhouette stood in the open doorway.

Groggy from sleep, I rolled out of the blankets. As I'd slept, Chris had taken his sweater back. Beneath the blanket, I wore a t-shirt. Chilly, I tried to think fast.

"I heard no one's had you yet and I get to be first."

I didn't know the man, nor his voice. Scared of what the new man meant, I flew at the shape, biting, kicking, punching and scratching.

Déjà vu. Half my face ignited and I flew partway across the room to land heavily on the floor, the result of another blow I hadn't seen. A warm trickle on my cheek told me he'd cut me. With what? Rings?

I tasted blood and a sudden pain in my chest told me at least one of my ribs was broken. I struggled to get up, but the pain of each breath I took slowed me down. His body crushed mine against the concrete before I could get to my feet.

I reached behind me, nails out, in the hope of doing some damage. I raked them down what felt like his arm before he pinned both of my arms behind my back. He roped my wrists together and tied them tightly. There'd be no freeing myself this time. The Swiss Card had stayed in the pocket of my jeans, stolen by Chris and Mike, along with the rest of my clothes.

"I think you drew blood that time, little bitch," he said angrily.

"Fuck you," I replied. I tucked my fingers into fists, so only the middle ones stuck up. "Up yours, you prick."

He snorted.

I screamed as he methodically broke both upright fingers. His rings dug into my flesh.

In a haze of pain, I didn't resist as he got up off me and turned me onto my back.

It was too dark for me to see his face, so I spat, "Who the fuck do you think you are?"

He took out a knife, holding it up so it caught the little light and glinted. It was bigger than the one I'd held, that Mike took from me. The only knife I'd seen bigger than this was my chef's knife at home. Or the ones in the necropsy labs at university. Maybe.

I smothered a sob. I had to keep fighting. Show no fear.

"You can call me Chris," he said, carelessly slicing the sides and shoulders of my borrowed t-shirt so it fell away from me. The blade was sharp, nicking my skin in several places, but he didn't seem to notice in the dark. Or maybe he did and he'd meant to hurt me.

Now I wore nothing but fear and a few spots of blood. Oh God, please... no.

He stood back and looked at me for a few seconds, unzipping his jeans. He took a step closer.

One more, you prick. One more step... and he took it.

I kicked out at him with both feet together, but he moved and grabbed my legs, forcing them back down to the floor, spread wide apart.

"If you think you're going to..." I began angrily.

"Fuck you, little bitch." He grunted, lowering himself to the floor between my legs.

That was the fucking beginning. I won't let him live to see the end.

FORTY FIVE

After a lot of persuasion, Nathan managed to talk me into going shopping with him. I'd intended to use Dad's credit card details to do my grocery shopping online and make them deliver it all for me, but he reminded me that I had no cash, no phone, no wallet and no idea what the newspapers had invented about me overnight. Some things don't get delivered.

He swore he'd help me with everything, so I reluctantly agreed. It felt strange going out in public, after so long in captivity, in the dark and in hospital. At least I didn't have to do it alone.

So I'd feel like a right invalid, he got me a wheelchair. Despite all my piano practise, my fingers still felt clumsy as I pushed the damn thing. I resolved to play for an extra hour when I got home. The new song – the one that wouldn't leave my head. I focussed so completely on the song that I almost crashed my wheelchair into someone's shopping trolley. She glared at me as I mumbled an apology, but her expression quickly changed to shock and she hurried away.

She wasn't the only one to wear that expression. I felt like everyone was staring at me — had they all seen my photo in the paper?

Every shop we went to, it seemed they had. Everyone looked at me for a second longer than they normally would, giving me pained, sympathetic smiles as they nodded to me as if they knew me.

"Do you need anything?" I asked Nathan, wondering. He didn't seem to be the type of bloke who'd volunteer to go shopping for no reason.

"Something to sleep in," he said quickly. He made a big show of buying himself boxer shorts and t-shirts in Myer, asking my opinion of an expensive satin pair and some cheap cotton ones.

I looked at them both and wondered how he'd look in the deep blue satin, six-pack and all, but I tried to control my face. "Weren't you going to buy pyjamas?" I asked innocently.

To hide his panic, he picked the first pair he saw — a pink pair parked haphazardly on the rack marked: *50% off already reduced items.*

I couldn't help it. I laughed so loud I couldn't stop.

"Can I help you?" the shop assistant asked as she hurried over.

"He needs some new pyjamas. Probably not in pink," I said, pointing.

Nathan's cheeks flushed to match the pyjamas as he put them back.

"We don't have much left after Father's Day, but the

best ones are over here. . ." she said, leading the way over to a rack that looked a bit more his style. "What do you normally wear? Long sleeve, short, buttons, long pants, shorts. . ."

I heard Nathan mumble something about how he normally just slept in his shorts or nothing at all. I'd seen him mostly in his shorts and a t-shirt in hospital, so I already knew he'd dressed up for me. I hadn't realised he'd dressed for me.

It was the shop assistant's turn to blush as she managed to say, "I'll just be over at the counter if you need any help. Just let me know, okay?" She beat a hasty retreat.

Nathan quickly picked something with long pants and long sleeves, before pushing me up to the counter with his proposed purchases.

I'd never seen a shop assistant process a payment so fast – and say so little while doing it, too.

"Time for food shopping?" Nathan asked, breaking into my thoughts.

I agreed, so we headed for Woolworths. As we wove through the crowded shopping centre, dodging trolleys and kamikaze pram-pushers, a thought struck me. He'd wrapped himself in the sheets when he'd shared my bed in hospital. Maybe the conservative sleepwear was part of his bid to be allowed to sleep with me.

I led the way to the frozen food section, where the pre-prepared food was kept. The less time I spent cooking, the more time I'd have for exercises and recovery. The display of strawberry punnets broke my resolve, though – it had been so long since I'd had fresh ones. I stuck some in the trolley, on top of everything else, and kept my eyes on them as Nathan pushed our soon-to-be purchases toward the till.

"Anything else you need?" I murmured, looking at the newspaper rack by the register.

"Coffee," he replied.

"I have some already, look." I pointed at the big jar of instant coffee hidden beneath a frozen pizza.

"No – I don't drink that stuff. I'll get my own," he said vaguely, hurrying off to do so. I wondered what sort of coffee he'd come back with. If he was really so fussy, he must've wanted that expensive stuff that had to be brewed or needed specialist equipment to make.

To my complete shock, he returned with a jar of decaffeinated instant coffee. "What?" he asked, catching sight of my expression. He tossed the jar into the trolley.

"Nothing," I replied, wincing as the jar landed on one of my precious punnets. "Not on the strawberries!"

He apologised and moved it, but it was too late – the damage was done. He'd squashed part of one punnet. Annoyed, I led the way to the register. I wanted to go home.

He reached for the newspaper before I could, laying it carefully on the conveyor belt at the checkout. Actually, he'd grabbed two, but he seemed happy to pay for them, so I didn't argue.

As we waited for the girl at the checkout to finish scanning our purchases, I caught Nathan glancing from the newspapers to me, a bemused smile on his face.

It wasn't a bad photo of me – though it was a terrible one of him. You couldn't even see his face. I scanned the article, which didn't tell me anything I didn't know. Apparently, I'd been found near death, on a beach early one morning by a mystery man. A reward was offered for an exclusive interview with the man, I read, as I turned to page seven for the rest of the article, but Nathan hadn't seen it yet. I wondered if he'd take them up on it, or if there were some confidentiality conditions inherent in his job that said he couldn't give press interviews. More importantly, looking at the offered reward, I wondered what they'd offer for an interview with me. Perhaps I should check my email and Facebook messages.

Nathan's expression turned dreamy and I wondered what he was thinking about. From the way he looked at the paper, I suspected it was me. I smothered a smile and decided to cause a little trouble.

I had to call his name a couple of times to get his attention before I asked, "Will you stay with me tonight?"

"Sure," he replied promptly.

Thinking of the pyjamas, I waited until we were in the car park with no one in earshot before I said what I was thinking.

"I want you to sleep with me."

His eyes positively shone for a second, before he realised I couldn't be serious about sex with him. But for that second, he'd hoped. . .

Feeling perhaps a tiny bit penitent, I explained that I wanted him to stay with me like he had in hospital – or like this morning.

Instantly, he agreed.

As he lifted me into the car, I felt for a moment that he lingered to savour the feel of me in his arms.

The thought that coalesced in my mind was that if I did choose to get naked with Nathan, he'd never hurt me. For he knew I'd kill him if he did.

Maybe one day. . . but not yet.

"Should we pick up a pizza on the way home?"

It took me a moment to understand what he'd said, but once I had, I agreed.

He handed me his phone, as my brand-new one was still in the box, and told me to order whatever I wanted for both of us.

I had to search for the number, but I found it and ordered for us. While Nathan focussed on driving, I flipped idly through his phone. He had a text message he hadn't read. I accidentally hit the touch screen in the wrong place and it sent me to his list of messages. The unread one was about his latest phone bill being ready to pay. I moved my fingers to send the phone back to its home screen when the first line of another message caught my eye.

"Maintain cover. Build trust." The number had no name associated with it.

I glanced at Nathan, but he was busy swearing at some Landcruiser that'd just cut him off.

I opened the message so I could read the rest – there was a whole conversation preceding it. I scrolled down to the first message in the chain.

It'd been sent from Nathan's phone – presumably, by him. It dated back to 3rd July, the day before I was kidnapped. "Made contact. Will attempt to obtain information."

The reply. "Stay with contact. Establish trust. Cooperate. Use any means necessary. And condoms."

Nathan's next message was dated 4th July. The complete lack of punctuation emphasised the urgency of the text.

"Drugged saw kidnapping trapped in car girl taken must break cover need backup now."

The last and most recent message was the one I'd seen initially. I read the message in full, dread sinking in my stomach. "Maintain cover. Build trust. Do anything they ask until further notice. Will contact."

I poked blindly at the touch screen, trying to exit out of Nathan's messages as if I'd never read them. When I saw the home screen again, my nerveless hands dropped the phone in my lap.

Someone had ordered him not to help me – to let me be taken. I needed to get into ASIO and find out who. There was no way in hell that was legal or procedure.

I closed my eyes and added one more bastard to my list. A nameless bastard, for the moment, but not for long, I vowed.

FORTY SIX

In the morning, Nathan headed off home, promising to return that night and take me out to dinner.

I'd fallen asleep far too early last night, so I had an extra hour of piano practise to put in before starting any other exercises. I'd finally managed to limber up my fingers enough to work a bass line beneath the melody that wouldn't leave me alone. One more run through and I'd write it down. . .

A heavy knocking jarred with my timing. I stopped playing and stood, making my way to the front door.

As I approached, I heard a gruff voice say, "Sit. Caesar, sit."

I smiled and threw the door open, unlocking the screen door before I could even see him clearly. "Good morning, Bruce. What can I do for you?"

Bruce looked hard at me, as if he couldn't decide which weighty matter to bring up first. "It's good to see you home, Caitlin. Wendy and I didn't believe anyone could hate you enough to do something like this. The bastards should be castrated and hung. They should bring back the death penalty for people like them. . ."

I fought to keep the smile on my face as I nodded my agreement. The bastards should be castrated, then their corpses hung up like dead meat. . .

"So I've come to give you Caesar and Cleo," he announced proudly, waving at the two dogs sitting at the bottom of my front steps.

The two enormous Rottweilers wagged their stumpy tails. I'd taken these two to training a couple of times for Bruce, so I was on their short list of favourite people.

"But I don't have any dog food, Bruce. And you know Dad doesn't like dogs. . ." I began.

"While you're home alone, you can keep them in your yard – I'll come over and feed them every day. They'll help protect you." His fierce grin was hard to resist. "You won't have to worry about a thing. If you have any intruders. . . Caesar and Cleo will take care of them for you. You know how much they love you."

Holding carefully to the rail, I proceeded down the steps to the two dogs. I held out my hand for each of them to sniff before I patted them both gently. The dogs did love me, but I wasn't sure I could control them if they attacked someone. They didn't know Nathan.

"Bruce," I said carefully. "It's such a lovely, kind offer, but one of my friends is coming to stay with me at night, to keep me company. Caesar and Cleo don't know him. What would I do if they attacked my friend?"

He scratched his head. "Ah. Should I just leave you the block-splitter, then?"

I noticed the heavy axe he held by his leg and smiled. "You know I can't lift that. You keep it. If I need help, I know where to come."

He seemed agitated, but he knew better than to push me. Bruce had known me since I was six. "All right," he said finally. "You know if you need any help, or anything at all – just ring me or come over. If you get anyone so much as look at you wrong, you run straight to my place and set the dogs on them. I'll leave the gate unlocked."

I thanked both him and his two dogs, then watched as all three crossed the road back to his house.

I breathed a sigh of relief as I locked the door behind me. Even without Nathan, there was always someone watching out for me. Even my neighbour's scary guard dogs.

FORTY SEVEN

Tied – Dark – Chris – Water – Pills

I awakened and it was still dark. I tried to rub my eyes, to see if they were really open, but my hands just didn't move. I ached deep inside from what the bastard had done to me.

I tried to stand up, but my feet were forced too close together, my thigh muscles unable to move. I twisted around, trying to see where I was, but there was nothing visible in the darkness. Someone's breathing was the only sound.

"Awake?" It came in a barely audible whisper.

"Where's Chris?" I demanded. Which Chris, I should have said. The bastard who could barely touch me or the one who broke my fingers and...

Slightly louder this time. "Right here."

His hand lightly touched my shoulder.

My throat was dry as I whimpered, "I need water." No need to defy him.

"I know." The cool rim of a cup pressed to my lips. "I'll help you where I can. Here –

something for the pain." Pills, then the cup back. I didn't question it, I just took them. I realised I was a drug addict and I didn't even know what the drug was.

My tears chilled my cheeks. I couldn't wipe them away. They flowed down my face, unchecked, a tribute to my own weakness. They fell faster - Chris witnessed this, me losing everything I'd ever had.

I began to sob uncontrollably. What did it matter - Chris was no one! "Untie me and take me home!" I begged him. "I can't stay here - let me go!"

Almost totally unhinged, I strained at the ropes that held me, willing there to be a weakness to let me free. All that broke was my skin, blood oozing out of the burning cuts. Warm and strange, the added pain brought on a fresh flood of tears.

"You have to let me go, now," I told him urgently.

"No, not now. Be patient." He hesitated a moment before he continued, "You'll get out of here. If you keep believing it, they can't win."

I felt so tired and drowsy, my eyes began to close again. "Bullshit," I mumbled.

"You'll be fine," he soothed.

No I won't, I thought as consciousness faded.

FORTY EIGHT

Nathan was late. I'd put on lipstick then chewed it off as I waited. I'd replaced it with the all-day colour stuff that stained my lips. I'd played piano until even I'd gotten sick of the sound, so I stretched out on the floor and turned on the TV. Some reality show about people who could dance. . . or sing. . . or something. I let the music wash over me as I started another set of physiotherapy exercises. I could feel my legs getting stronger day by day.

I even felt sweaty from the exercise – it sure was a warm day for September. Almost October now – where had the year gone?

I heard the sound of a car in the driveway.

Nathan! Finally.

I jumped to my feet, clicking off the TV. I hurried to the door so I could see him. I'd taken particular care to look good tonight – he'd promised to take me out for dinner. Not really a date, but I'd dressed for it anyway. A pretty red satin shirt over dress pants. I felt giddy.

Maybe that's why I made such a stupid mistake.

I flung the door open and stood on the doorstep, wondering why his engine sounded so loud today. I was halfway down the steps when I realised the car wasn't his.

I saw a white convertible – a woman's car, definitely. It still had a crystal hanging from the rear vision mirror, catching the sunlight and throwing rainbows across the dash. Yet it wasn't a woman who climbed out. It was a big, bulky bloke, wearing a heavy coat and cap, so I couldn't see his face at all.

It was her. She'd given her car to one of the bastards and he was here to take me back!

My hesitation lasted barely a moment, before I realised that I couldn't go back inside. The only way to survive was to run and hope he didn't catch me. So run I did, bolting through the garden and onto the footpath.

I thought of Bruce's guard dogs, but didn't dare cross the road when my pursuer had a car at his disposal. He'd run me down before I could make it to the gate.

There were some Moreton Bay fig trees in the park up the road that I might be able to climb. If I could reach them without him seeing me, I could hide up there until he gave up. He couldn't get a car into the park without drawing a hell of a lot of attention – and none of my neighbours would stand for that.

I wasn't prepared for the pounding footsteps of him following me on foot.

I tried to speed up, but my muscles screamed. This was the first time I'd tried to run since I got out of hospital and I wasn't really ready for it.

I wasn't ready to die yet, either. Faster!

Over my panicked panting, I heard his breathless voice. "No, stop. Come back. You can't outrun me."

Oh God, it sounded familiar. It had to be one of them — and I had nothing to kill him with.

I put on another spurt of speed. I couldn't keep it up much longer, but I knew what would happen if he caught me.

It was almost as if he'd read my mind. "Come back. Please let me. . ."

No. I'd rather die than let you hurt me again!

A hand landed heavily on my shoulder. If I'd had enough breath, I'd have screamed. Instead, I tried to shake him off.

I hit Margaret's garden edging and lost my footing, tumbling onto her lawn. I rolled as I hit, determined to at least face the man who was trying to kill me. I wanted to spit in his face, as it was the only projectile I had to hand. Maybe I could blind him with phlegm. . .

He pulled the cap off. I almost cried.

"Angel, are you okay?" Nathan asked.

"How could you scare me like that? Why did you. . ." My throat hurt too much to speak. I could barely breathe.

"What do you think of my new car?"

"You're. . . a fucking. . . dickhead! You're late because you got a new car?"

"Yes." He looked uncomfortable. "I know you didn't like the old one, so I figured it was time for something new."

His eyes kept darting every which way except my face. I followed his gaze and saw Margaret, standing with her son's hockey stick. I'd seen her chase an escaped pitbull at the park with that hockey stick. She'd stunned the dog senseless with one swipe – it'd still been unconscious when the guys from the pound showed up. She was a mean shot.

For a moment, I wondered if I should let her hit Nathan a couple of times for scaring me. I smiled grimly at the thought, before I drove it from my head. I couldn't let her hit him – I'd need his help to get home. And we had a date tonight.

"The car's fine. Please, help me up and back to my house," I said shortly.

He slid an arm under my legs, but even that hurt.

"Just help me walk," I told him, trying to steel myself against the pain I knew it would cost me. Better walking in pain than screaming while he carried me. What would my neighbours think?

He protested a bit, but I stayed firm, so he helped me stand. When my legs threatened to collapse beneath me, his supportive arm was the only thing keeping my upright.

I smiled at the neighbours we passed, who all seemed to be doing gardening or sports on their front lawns in the last of the evening sunlight.

I managed okay until we reached the bottom of the steps to my front door. I leaned heavily against the rail, not sure how I was going to make it up those last few steps. Maybe if I rested for a few minutes and Nathan held the door open, I could stagger in and collapse on the couch. Maybe. . . No. I couldn't stop now. Had to climb those steps and then I could rest.

He swept me up and carried me across the threshold.

"Rest," I heard him say, as he carefully laid me on the couch.

With my legs screaming at me, it was hard to do anything else. I couldn't remember hurting this much – not even when the bastards had me. I vaguely remembered something about how the memory of pain fades, but I still wasn't prepared for it.

I focussed on my breathing. If I could stay conscious, then maybe I could take some pain medication to help it go away.

Bruce from over the road came to check that I was okay. I smiled and thanked him, heartened by how helpful my neighbours were. He'd brought the block-splitter, too, I saw. I made sure to tell him that Nathan was my friend before he headed back home.

Nathan asked me if anything had happened while I'd been home alone and I reassured him that it hadn't. I almost told him about the new song that was taking shape, but I couldn't summon the energy to walk to the piano to play it for him. Another time, maybe.

I started to ask about our date, but Nathan was kind enough to postpone it to another night.

I relaxed on the couch, finally giving in to the pain, hoping it would fade if I lay still long enough.

As if to make up for frightening me, Nathan was more caring than usual. He murmured my name as he stroked my hair, before moving my body into the recovery position I remembered from my first aid courses.

How sweet. He thought I was unconscious. He evidently didn't know how incapacitating severe pain could be. It didn't affect my hearing, though, as he keyed in a call on his phone.

As he spoke to the stranger on the other end of the

phone line, I realised he was talking to the person watching the surveillance cameras – he had backup. At first, I was relieved, then mortified, as I thought of the times I'd walked around the house without clothes on. I never wanted to meet this surveillance person. If I did, I might have to shoot him.

Once he'd ended the call, Nathan leaned over me and stroked my neck. Before I could ask him why, he removed his hand. I heard him turn the TV on. It sounded like he was watching a cooking show. I let the commentary form a dull buzz in my brain, sitting somewhere behind the pain, until someone mentioned a dessert with strawberries.

My stomach reminded me it was dinner time, but I'd have given anything for the dessert on the cooking show. I swear I could almost smell it, I wanted strawberries so badly. I knew I had some in the fridge, but I wasn't sure I could walk that far without hurting myself.

I looked at Nathan, who was intent on the TV programme. I called his name hesitantly, not sure how much to ask him for. Maybe if he could carry me to the kitchen and pull up a chair, I could sit down while I washed and hulled the strawberries. . .

He didn't say a word. He just held out the bowl. He'd even sliced them. I could have kissed him. I nearly did.

He looked embarrassed, as if he could read my mind. "Eat something so you can take pain medication." He nodded at the pills beside a glass of water on the table.

I couldn't thank him enough. I wanted to kiss him more than ever, but I banished the thought. I savoured my strawberries instead.

FORTY NINE

"You've really recovered remarkably well," Althea told me. "I wish some of my other patients were as diligent with their exercises as you!" She lowered her voice. "Just don't overdo, it, okay?"

I nodded and smiled, not bothering to tell her that, by her standards, I probably overdid it every day. I figured it was better to work hard on my recovery than to baby myself and die as a result. If I was meant to die on that beach, it was only a matter of time before they returned for me. And I intended to be ready. I had death to deliver and pain in bulk quantity.

Nathan sat in the waiting room, impatiently tapping at the touchscreen on his phone. He looked like he was ordering hits on violent criminals, but I knew he wore that expression when he played games. He pocketed his phone before I reached him, though, so I couldn't check to see if I was right.

I paid for the session, booked my next appointment and

walked out of the physiotherapy clinic. Nathan matched my steps, offering a welcome arm to help me walk to the car. Tired and hurting, I accepted his assistance and leaned against him as we made slow progress through the car park.

"How was the session?" he asked. "Are you recovering well?"

"Yes. She was quite impressed at my progress," I admitted, not meeting his eyes. I didn't want him to know just how well I'd healed. If he thought I didn't need his help, he might not stay with me. I could walk, but I wasn't sure I could defend myself well enough to take them all out if the bastards turned up together.

Almost automatically, Nathan lifted me into the car and fastened my seat belt for me. I said nothing except to thank him for his kindness.

The drive back seemed very short, as I was lost in thought. I wondered how much longer Nathan would stay if they didn't come after me soon. I dreaded an attack, yet if the delay meant losing Nathan, an attack couldn't come soon enough.

The moment I saw my house, I knew my wish had been granted. Someone had been there and they hadn't hidden their visit, either. The front door gaped open like a fresh wound.

Nathan dithered for a minute or two. I wondered why he didn't call his colleagues. Maybe they'd given up waiting for something bad to happen to me. . . was he the only one left? He confirmed my suspicions by suggesting we call the police instead of his team.

While he made the call, I fished through his glove box, desperately hoping for a weapon. A screwdriver, a can of pepper spray. . . I hit the jackpot with a pocket knife. Feverishly, while Nathan was still distracted, I folded out the blade, resolving to stab anyone in the groin who got too close. Castration sounded like a really good idea.

I dropped the knife when Nathan came close – I didn't want him to try and take it off me.

His reassuring litany lasted until the police arrived, in a proper patrol car and all. I let Nathan carry me inside once they'd given the all clear – my intruders had already left. I wasn't prepared for the mess they'd left behind, though.

I curled up in an armchair, afraid to touch anything that might be evidence. It took me a moment for my shocked brain to realise that it didn't matter what I touched – my fingerprints and DNA would be everywhere, anyway. Nathan's, too.

I saw the empty knife block in the kitchen and immediately thought of her. A knife would have been my first choice of weapon, too.

If she'd come and gone without staying to hurt me more, she must have left something behind – either a message or something that would hurt me in her absence. The most personal place for her to do that would be my bedroom, so that's where I bent my steps.

Cruel and unusual were her style, so I was mystified by the mess in my bedroom. It looked like she'd gone through my wardrobe, trying on and discarding items as if she was choosing the perfect outfit for a special occasion. Killing me, I guessed.

A flash of blue caught my eye – the dress I'd worn to my high school graduation, hanging askew on the hanger. It was the most expensive dress I'd ever owned – it cost more than my ballgown. I'd hoped one day to wear it again, but she'd shattered that dream with a slash of my scissors. I almost cried.

From underwear I'd never worn to dresses I'd hoped to wear again – all had fallen victim to her blade. Much like me, except the clothes hadn't fought back.

Nathan murmured soothing words while the police officers took notes. I paid little attention to any of them. More than ever, I wanted this to be over. My fingers tightened around the filleting knife I'd found on my bed, as I crushed lacy lingerie in my other fist.

I intended to gut her like a fish. But first, I'd seduce my sleazy roommate and see if the suggestion of sex could persuade him to stay long enough to assist with the slaughter. With his help, I might survive.

As if he'd read my thoughts, Nathan offered, "I won't let them hurt you. I'll even take you shopping to buy more clothes to replace these."

I left the shredded lace on the bed. Lingerie shopping with Nathan sounded like fun – and perfectly in line with my plan. I headed off to wash any intact clothes that remained, while Nathan dealt with the mess. Over my shoulder, I saw him staring at the shredded g-string I'd balled up on the bed. I smothered a smile and kept going.

FIFTY

Her – Tied – Mike – Tom – Cut

"What the hell? I said not her face – we need her to stay pretty." An angry woman's voice broke through the darkness.

"She attacked me with a knife," Mike muttered.

I'll do it again. Cut me free and I'll claw something off with my bare hands...

"What's your excuse, Tom?" She sounded bored.

"She tried to take her nails to my face. She almost scratched my eye. I didn't hit her hard. She just landed on her face, is all." He sounded even more bored than her.

Not Chris. Tom. Tom's the prick who first raped me, who broke my fingers, who's also going to die... I listed it all out in my head. If only I could see his face, so I could memorise his features.

"You've got the rest of her to do what you want with. Just leave her face, is all. It'd be nice if you didn't kill her yet, too." She paused, taking a deep breath. "Who wants her next?"

My blood ran cold. Please, not more pain.

"I do," both men said together.

I held my breath, hoping they'd decide to fight to the death over me or something equally stupid. Something that kept me safe from both of them, or one, at worst.

"I haven't had her yet," Mike said. "I'd like to wake her up and give her a big surprise."

So would I. I'd like to give you a bullet in the brain.

"I don't like sloppy seconds," Tom said with disgust. "If I don't have her first, I'm not interested."

I wanted to curl into a ball and hide at the memory of what he did to me first. Don't let him touch me again.

"Sloppy seconds! Hell yeah!" Mike laughed. "You can go first, if you get her wet for me, mate."

No, please...

"Fine by me."

No. Not fine at all. Fucking horrible. I froze and tried not to let them know I was awake enough to hear them.

A hiss of breath. "Then it's all arranged to your satisfaction. You both remember what I said and have your fun. Mike, can you make sure the others know? Any more damage to her face and I'll do some damage. They'll believe you."

"Yes, ma'am," Mike said.

I wanted to laugh out loud. Hysterical laughter, but laughter nonetheless. Mike the big bastard had a woman boss who he called 'ma'am' and obeyed? Too funny.

I hadn't been paying attention. Cold air

chilled my bare skin, for the blankets had been ripped away. A cold blade slipped between my legs, freezing me further. The rope dropped from my legs, cut.

"I know you're awake. You're too stiff to be asleep. Spread your legs for me like a good girl and you might even enjoy it." His voice was quiet and emotionless. "And no, don't think you'll get your hands on my knife. Try anything like you did yesterday and I'll cut you instead."

He shoved my legs apart and I found my voice, desperate to say something that might delay the pain or stop it altogether. I heard the squeal of a zip, then the crackle of plastic.

"Why bother? Chris's had me every night. He's more a man than you'll ever be. You're the sloppy seconds, not me," I spat.

He grunted and I felt his weight on the mattress. "Shut up or I'll break your jaw."

"But she won't let you do that. The bitch you work for," I taunted.

"The bitch I work for won't care if I cut you a wider cunt, though. So shut the fuck up or I'll do it," he threatened.

I gritted my teeth as he grunted.

Please, let it be over soon. Or I'll go away in my head and not come back.

FIFTY ONE

I needed cheese. If I didn't get cheese, the zombie mice would be hungry and they'd cry. But all I could find at shop after shop was cheddar and camembert. They'd only eat Persian feta and I could hear them crying already as I took longer and longer. . .

Mice don't eat cheese.

I startled myself awake, trying not to laugh at the sheer stupidity of my dream. There was no such thing as zombie mice and they definitely didn't eat cheese.

As I stifled my laughter, I realised Nathan was thrashing around beside me, his breathing fast and panicked. "No. . . no. . ." he murmured, the breathy whisper hard to understand.

Nathan had nightmares. I should wake him from this one, as he'd done so many times for me.

"Nathan, it's just a bad dream, like mine. Please. Don't let them. . ."

He threw his arms around me, tightening them into an

inescapable hug.

"It's okay, angel. A bad dream. You're safe — safe at home." He choked back a sob. "You're okay."

Oh God. His nightmares were about me.

I made an excuse about needing to write my dreams down and his hold loosened enough for me to leave the bed.

He offered to help.

"No — you don't need to hear this." Not if it gave him nightmares worse than mine. "Go back to sleep, Nathan. I won't be long," I lied.

I turned the laptop on, feeling his eyes on me the whole time. He didn't go back to sleep for a while and he was restless soon after. Feeling like a sick stalker as I watched him sleep, I waited to see if he'd have another nightmare.

"No. . . not her. . . no. . ."

I felt tears streak my cheeks at the agony in his voice.

"Not Caitlin."

I stumbled back to my bed, moving as close to Nathan as I could.

"You're okay. Just a dream. . ." he murmured, stroking my hair as he pulled me closer to him. I could feel him shaking.

I gave him nightmares. I should never have told him. "I'm sorry."

"I'm here now and I'm helping you. No one's going to hurt you again, I swear. Definitely not her." He sounded so fierce, as if he was trying to fight off his own nightmares as well as mine. What could I say to that?

"Thanks, Nathan," I murmured, wishing I could offer more. Yet a small part of me whispered, Serves you right, you bastard, taking so long to help me. I tried to silence it, but the niggling thought remained.

FIFTY TWO

I saved the lingerie shopping for last. Nathan made appreciative noises when I showed him some of the clothes, but it was the sexier stuff I wanted him to see.

I deliberately took him to the lingerie shop with notoriously bad service. The teenagers at the counter only served their friends and ignored everyone else. In the past, it had annoyed me beyond belief, but today their inattention was perfect.

After several unsuccessful attempts to get their attention, Nathan agreed to help me fasten things. No matter how much he averted his eyes, I knew the mirrors would make sure he saw everything.

The longing in his eyes as he stared at the red satin padded one made me smother a smile as I set it on the pile of items I wanted. He swallowed as if his mouth was dry for the black lace. I added that to the pile, too.

He didn't seem to like the patterned ones as much and one didn't fit very well, either. A little bit too much padding, perhaps. He shuddered at the black and red one I thought quite pretty, but I set it aside. He seemed to grow more and more agitated as I switched to some plain satin ones and I opened my mouth to ask why

Of course, that's when the stupid shop assistant decided to try to be helpful. "Can I help you with anything?" she simpered, shoving the curtain open without caring whether I was naked or decent.

I quickly slipped a sweet little chemise over my head.

"Oh, thank God!" Nathan exclaimed. I could see his hands shaking, but his eyes were on her and not me.

I glanced at the bulge in the front of his pants and tried to distract the shop assistant before she noticed, too. I handed her the pile of items Nathan had expressed his appreciation over and asked her to get me matching knickers for the lot. Nathan adjusted himself while her eyes were on me.

"You look beautiful in that one," he murmured, as soon as she was out of earshot.

I tried not to cheer — no matter how much I wanted to — as I asked him to assist me back into my own clothes.

Once dressed, I snatched up the chemise that Nathan had admired. I intended to wear it tonight — and see how long he could resist.

FIFTY THREE

Her - Tied - Alanna - Chris - Personal

"My husband is weak. He wants you, but he hasn't given in to temptation yet."

I blinked at the torch she shone into my eyes. I didn't uncurl from my foetal ball.

I saw her lift her shoulders in a shrug. "He will. You look too much like me. He'll never dominate me, for he's too weak. Perhaps I should watch when he takes you." The torch played over my body. "So dirty, though." She shuddered.

"So give me a shower and a change of clothes," I said hoarsely.

"You won't live long enough to need one," she said softly. "It's only a matter of time. He killed the last one. The ASIO boy's twin. She fought too hard."

Realisation hit - I knew who she meant. Found dead on a beach, bloodied and broken. The bloke who found her had talked to the news and he'd looked green.

"Alanna," I blurted out. "He killed Alanna."

She shrugged again. "Was that her name? I didn't care to find out. Like her, you won't last long."

"I just have to last long enough to kill you," I rasped.

"You won't get a chance. The one you call Chris - he'll kill you first. To save his family, he thinks." She laughed. "He can't save his family." She walked to the door. "It's not personal. He could have picked anyone. It didn't matter to me. It'll all be over soon."

The hell it isn't personal. It is to me. This is my body they're hurting. It may not be personal to you yet, but I'll sure as hell make it personal when I kill you, bitch.

FIFTY FOUR

"How many?" A pause. "I'll take care of it. Let them in."

My hand hovered over the just-pressed flush button when I heard Nathan's low voice in the hallway. I froze, stunned, as the water swirled around the bowl.

Nathan burst in on me, kicking the door shut behind him. I felt his whole body tense as he crushed me against the wall. His hand silenced the shocked scream that wanted to escape from my mouth. I swallowed it down. Fear had no place in my head when it was swiftly replaced with fury.

You bastard. Tell me you didn't just. . .

He was breathing heavily, desperation in his expression.

I gazed steadily back into his panicked eyes, trying to decide what my next action should be.

Nathan carefully took his hand away from my mouth, his look apologetic.

Oh no you don't. . . The hell you're handing me over to them!

I forced myself to relax in his grip, dropping my head

and closing my eyes, from fierce to pitiful in a moment. I took a calculated risk, distracting him in the most underhanded way possible. "Nathan, please don't hurt me," I begged him as desperately as I could manage.

He was still for a moment, trying to shut out the memory I knew my words would inspire. His weight against me lessened and he made an effort to control his rapid breathing.

"I'm not going to hurt you." His tone was calm and low, so reassuring he disarmed me completely.

You've said that before, I thought uneasily. You've never hurt me. But they. . .

The gentle kiss as his lips met mine shocked me.

Nathan would never hurt me. Just like he wasn't hurting me now. . .

The memory came unbidden – forced kisses in the dark. One rough and unpleasant; one gentle and insistent. My lips parted and I responded. . .

"Chris." I forced my eyes open as I spoke the name, not wanting to be in the dark with memories I didn't trust. Remember?

You bastard. How dare you. Never without my permission. . . I glared at him, trying to decide what to say first, as I shoved his shoulders away with both hands.

He moved back, so only his hands touched me, still pinning me to the wall. "I'm sorry. . ." he started to say.

I should have done this a long time ago.

I was too close to kick him and in bare feet I'd only hurt my toes, but I could and did drive my knee up to where I could still cause considerable pain.

He gasped as my knee connected, leaning over to move

his most sensitive parts away from me, while putting more weight on pinning me to the wall. His forehead nearly rested on my shoulder.

"You prick. You did that before *and* you hoped I wouldn't remember." I tried to scare him into letting him go, but still he held me firmly. I pushed against him and tried to twist away, to no avail.

His voice was wheezy and breathless, but still audible. "I need you to stay in here. The house is being watched and I need you to hide in here, where no one will guess you are." His weight on my shoulders intensified and my knees folded. He was ready for it, pushing me into the tight space between the toilet and the wall, as I sank to the floor.

Hurt me and I'll kill you. I glared up at him.

But instead of approaching me, he turned to go. He's serious, I realised.

I found my voice. "You can't leave me here alone – give me something to defend myself with, or stay here with me!" It was painful for me to admit, but that was the reason I hadn't kneed him where it hurt before now.

He knelt down on the floor in front of me. I must have hurt him, I realised. He had tears in his eyes. Good.

His voice was low and painful. "I can't. They've seen me come in here – and if I stay, this is the first place they'll check, because they know I'll be here. Then they'll find you, too."

Shit. Shouldn't have hurt him. Not yet. I still needed him. Hell, if he got me through this alive, maybe I could even forgive him.

I looked up at him. You really want my forgiveness? Fine. "Make sure you kill them all."

He winked and nodded. Through the rapidly narrowing gap as he shut the door, I could see him adjusting himself, wincing.

Maybe I'll apologise for that, I thought. When it's all over.

Maybe.

FIFTY FIVE

I watched the light from the frosted toilet window fade from orange to pink to darkness.

Jammed between tiled wall and toilet bowl in the dark, I heard sounds that might have been gunshots, but they were muffled – sounding far away. My heart raced with fear and a sort of thrill that I'd felt before, but I'd forgotten.

I realised that I wanted Nathan to be there with me – I didn't want to cringe in a corner like a frightened rabbit. All someone had to do was open the door and I was a sitting duck – they couldn't miss me. Nathan should have given me a weapon, not left me here alone, near helpless, confident I was so well hidden that they'd never find me. Fucking bastards. Leaving me in no state to fight. Hell, I wanted to fight, but I feared I hadn't recovered enough to be any use. I'd distract Nathan from them if he had to focus on my fragility.

He still should have left me a fucking weapon – one I didn't need much strength for. A small automatic pistol, perhaps. . . or was he just afraid I'd hold it to his head if he tried to kiss me again?

I remembered the burn of his lips on mine. The unexpected, urgent kiss. When he knew what they'd done to me. . . The dark memory hovered in the back of my mind, the one that had yawned open like a chasm when I'd closed my eyes earlier, but I pushed it away. I didn't want to give in to it. It'd come back in my nightmares soon enough.

I pushed that thought away, too. Burning fury is better for a fight than fear for the future.

Never hurt me again, I thought fiercely.

If Nathan gave me a gun, I probably wouldn't shoot him. I felt like kicking him instead – far more satisfying. I flexed my foot, wondering at one of the few parts of my body without scars. My feet and my face. My face I knew why; my feet. . . perhaps none of them had a foot fetish. They were definitely fucked up in their preferences otherwise – maybe feet were just too tame.

I heard a faint sound and looked up. The door started to open – the handle turned and the door moved inward. I scanned the room, looking for anything I could use as a weapon. The toilet brush or the bottle of toilet cleaner? Laughter threatened to erupt, but I held it in. She didn't seem to see me until the door was fully open, but by then she blocked the doorway. She was armed.

"Hello." She was short, like me, with dark hair, dark eyes and a petite build. Very like me, but older. A face I hadn't forgotten. "Come on, get up. I'm taking you away from here."

She was dressed in a dark vest and shirt with dark pants, far more practical than the new nightdress I wore. I should have been wearing something like that. I just stared at her for a moment. I needed to get up and get close to her, or I'd never stand a chance. I might even have to kill her. Oh God, how? I'd never killed anyone before.

At least I had a tiny bit of time to find my courage and decide to do it, desperately hoping Nathan would come back in time to save me. Despite the impressive weapon, I knew she wasn't going to shoot me yet. If she was, she'd have had me at hello.

"I can't get up by myself. I need help," I blurted out.

"Where's Al Himar when I need him? He liked being your nursemaid more than he liked fucking you." She snorted.

Realisation dawned. "You mean Nathan? You're calling Nathan Al Himar?" I forced myself to laugh. "The man you call an ass shot your husband stone dead. For me. And he'll happily do the same to you."

"Bullshit." Her eyes flickered, as if she didn't know what to believe. She shook her head "He'll do what I tell him, as always. I might have him eat me out again, on the leather back seat of his lovely car, while your corpse is cooling in the boot."

Again? Nathan slept with this bitch? How?

She saw my confusion and smiled. "He may be a donkey, but his performance was quite impressive. Of course, you wouldn't know — he never tried to please you like he did me. He was trying to seduce me for information, so I really got him at his best."

No. Nathan wouldn't sleep with her for information. He wouldn't. . . surely! She's full of shit, trying to shake me. He swore he'd protect me. He promised he wouldn't let her. . .

"Come on." She leaned closer to me and held out a hand, the one without the gun. Not a little weapon like the one on the beach – something newer and bigger; the type you see on American action movies that spit out bullets far faster. She waved the gun toward the door and the hallway outside, telling me to go that way.

I'm going to die. She's going to shoot me with that overpowered weapon while I have. . . shit. Damned if I'd go out cringing in a corner, though.

I took her arm and stood up. We stood eye to eye for a second, though I was unsteady.

She smiled. "The boys have missed you. And your pet donkey, the ASIO ass-boy you think will save you? He'll kill you for me, to protect his family, even without orders from his boss. Who is quite an obedient bitch himself, as I recall. He's pulling the rest of his team out as I speak, so there won't be anyone to help you. Just the inconstant donkey. Maybe I'll let him fuck me one last time before I kill him, too."

Doubt hit for the second time, harder than before. If his boss was implicated in this, too, I didn't know what Nathan would do. What if she was right – and he'd choose her and his sister over me? Maybe he'd wanted the bitch all along.

The bitch who'd hit me and pushed me into the car. The bitch who'd slashed my clothes and was back to do the same to me. I couldn't count on any help from Nathan or anyone else.

Fuck you, Nathan, if you want her. I'd rather die than go back. What did I have to lose? If I'm going to hell, I'll take you with me, bitch. You're going to pay for what you did to me.

I lifted my arm, and the toilet brush with it, to her face. She recoiled from the brown bristles, coated and dripping with blue toilet cleaner. Her mouth opened wide with horror. I smiled and shoved the foul thing down her throat. As she choked, I grabbed for the gun and I didn't let go.

She could have squeezed the trigger in surprise.

But she didn't.

Both of her hands were clamped around the handle of the toilet brush, trying to drag it out so she could breathe. I knew the cleaner would already be burning her insides. The bitch deserved it.

I yanked the gun from her hands, shoving her against the wall tiles. I'm not sure she even saw it coming. I squeezed off one round into her face and I didn't stop until I'd run out. I had no bullets left and the bitch was missing a face.

The shots echoed in my head, so loud I couldn't hear anything else. Her blood was everywhere – coating the tiled walls and the floor. The acrid smoke burned my throat and made it hard to breathe. I felt her body go limp and fall.

Good.

I pulled the blood-spattered satin chemise off, trying to wipe some of her blood off my face as I did so, and dropped it on the floor. Carefully, I edged her shirt and vest over what was left of her head and put them on. The vest seemed to be some kind of armour, its pockets loaded with extra ammunition. This'd be handy.

I took her pants and put them on. Strapped to her ankle was a big, wicked-looking knife. I hesitated, before taking that, too. She wouldn't need it. Her shoes looked too big for me, so I left them. I dressed her in my ruined nightie, then pushed her over so she lay face-down on the floor. Maybe they'd think she was me and buy me some time. I picked up her gun, wiping some of the blood off it with the skirt of the nightie.

Then I tried to heave open the door, but her feet were jammed up against it. I managed to push it open wide enough to squeeze out into the hallway, but the weight of her legs shut the door as soon as I was through.

Oh well, it'd take them longer to find her and realise it's not me, I thought.

I looked around for somewhere to hide, ideally where I could make use of the gun. The laundry and bathroom were the nearest rooms, but they had no obvious hiding places. I wished I had the flexibility and strength to brace myself in the corner of a ceiling, like people did in movies, as I looked up at the high ceilings. Maybe if I could climb onto the dryer. I'd be out of sight and I'd have a clear shot at anyone trying to get me down. I just had to get up there.

For the first time, I blessed Jo's addiction to the shooting range. I'd handled a fair few pistols and I wasn't a bad shot. I hoped I wasn't too out of practise.

I stuck the gun and the knife up on the dryer, so I wouldn't have any accidents with either of them. Then I took a deep breath and started to haul myself up.

By the time I'd climbed from the top of the washing machine to the top of the dryer, I figured everything hurt and I might have injured some muscles I didn't know I had. I hope I get to rest up here a while before I need to climb down, I thought as I shoved a clip of bullets from my vest pocket into the gun. I fully intended to shoot first and say *fuck you* later.

FIFTY SIX

Tied - Help - Pills - Chris

Perhaps I was so exhausted I fell asleep. Perhaps one of them knocked me unconscious. I went away to places in my head that were as far from the cold concrete as I could, so I don't remember. All I remember is every one of them making a point of telling me his name was Chris, with not a single voice matching the one they called Chris.

When I woke up, it was to something cold and wet touching my cheek, which now felt horribly bruised. The rest of my body felt worse - violated in every way. I'd force him to kill me before I let him rape me again.

"What in hell are you doing this time?" I said tersely.

"Shh," came Chris's whispered reply. "They won't let me near you unless I... they want me to... so keep it down, please, so they don't hear us. I'm here to help you."

"Find me a good pair of rusty garden shears... and untie me." I snapped back. "Help

me and I'll let you keep all your bits intact.
I'm going to fucking castrate the rest of them,
so they'll never..."

"I can't untie you. They'd know I helped
you. I brought you some food and drink... and
something for the pain. Did they hurt you when
they tied you up?"

Of course they fucking hurt me, stupid. My
face hurt too much to eat or even talk. I
didn't want to think about the rest of me. I
didn't say anything else. He gave me some
pills, holding the water to my lips as I drank.
A nice pair of garden shears and they'd know I
was there... and they wouldn't be doing it
again, either.

"Did they hurt you?" asked the pathetic
Chris's voice again.

That's an understatement, I thought, as I
nodded in the dark.

Keep fighting. Don't let them win.

And he was gone.

FIFTY SEVEN

Nathan went past the door. Another man paused to point a gun into the laundry, before he kept going. Silently, he followed Nathan.

I slid down from the dryer to the floor, as quietly as I could. I clicked the safety off my gun, knowing what I had to do. Nathan had already reached the toilet, with the mystery man still a few steps behind him.

I grabbed the guy's shoulder, sticking the gun into his neck. I hissed at him to drop his weapon. He leaned down to place it on the hall rug and I kicked it, sending it spinning across the laundry floor. He even stuck his hands in the air. I couldn't see over his shoulder or his raised hands – I was too short. "Tell him he's been followed," I hissed.

"You missed one," the man squeaked out. He jerked his head a little behind him.

I couldn't see Nathan. Was he angry at me for killing her?

"You killed her," Nathan accused.

Oh shit.

I couldn't deny it. "Yes." It came out as a whisper – my voice had failed. The man I held at gunpoint nodded for Nathan's benefit.

I'd killed her. I'd been so scared of them taking me back that I'd killed to stop her. What else had he expected me to do?

So lost in thought – when I should have been thinking about the present. Nathan hit the other man like a truck, barrelling us both into the wall, with me cushioning the big man's fall. Desperately, I tried to shoot him so he wouldn't touch me again.

Get off me!

The gun jammed. The stupid bitch probably hadn't even loaded the bullets into the clip properly. I wanted to kill her all over again.

The big one kept me pinned to the wall as Nathan did his utmost to get me free of him. Large hands grabbed my frail fingers, trying to pry the gun out of them. Out of spite, I threw it down on the floor, hoping to dislodge the clip so I could reload it properly. Then I could shoot him.

Nathan somehow got the big bloke's attention and his weight on me lessened enough for me to slide away from him to the floor. I dived for my weapon but it skittered out of my reach. I didn't have even a moment to breathe before a crushing weight knocked the breath out of me. The big bastard covered my body with his and I didn't even have the air to scream.

I'll kill you. . . I'll fucking kill you. . . Nathan, get him off me. . .

The touch of cold restraints around my wrists froze me

entirely. The scars had barely healed from the last set. . .

I'll die first! And I'll fucking take you with me. . .

I tried desperately to throw him off, to escape from his grasp, but I heard metal snap closed and almost cried.

Nathan. . . please help me. . .

Nothing. Not a sound from Nathan. In my ear, the big bastard's quiet words sounded perfectly calm. He told me there was nothing I could do, that he was taking me with him and he was going to knock me out.

I had only one reply. The same as the first time. "FUCK YOU!"

His grip on me loosened and I used the little freedom I had to look for Nathan.

Nathan. Please help me. Nathan. . .

I saw his face, but he stood back, panicking as if he was scared to step forward and help me. Why did he hesitate? What did I miss? What did the big bastard threaten me with that had Nathan so scared to help me?

If I'd thought his eyes were desperate before, they were nothing to what his expression held now. Insanity, desperation, anguish, despair, horror, grief: I could take my pick, they were all there. Yet he still stumbled toward me.

I felt the cold prick at my neck. Oh, fuck. What was he injecting me with? As if Nathan's single step was his cue, I felt the liquid forced beneath my skin. No. . .

I closed my eyes.

FIFTY EIGHT

Darkness swirled, but Nathan's voice pierced it as if sound were light.

"You're not taking her anywhere."

I tried to move, but everything felt too heavy. It was like being unconscious in hospital again. Why give me pain drugs when last time they used chloroform? And why such a tiny dose, when a heavier one could knock me out for hours?

I felt arms lift me, desperately wishing I could fight to free myself. I must have made some movement, because I heard Nathan's voice apologise for hurting me. So close a whisper. . . the arms holding me were his. In relief, I relaxed.

"Navid!" The way he said it, the strange word sounded like he was calling a name.

The deep voice responding confirmed it. "She killed the girl we were trying to protect. . ."

He was a guard. One of Nathan's colleagues. And he

thought I was her! Relief cycled to triumph as I realised switching clothes with her had worked – only I'd fooled the wrong person. I wanted to laugh, but my body didn't respond.

"Caitlin killed the bitch. . ." Nathan said the words so calmly, as if he knew I'd do it all along. I hadn't known if I'd manage to survive, let alone kill someone. Even if she did deserve it.

I killed the bitch. The relief and joy of it knew no bounds. She'd never hurt me again.

"That was Laura." I heard the venom in Nathan's tone. The bitch's name was Laura and Nathan didn't like her at all. But she'd always be the bitch to me.

"It's over. Nick, Pete, Tom. . . they're all dead. Make this all go away before she wakes up. . ." Blissfully, I listened as I floated in the dark. In Nathan's arms. And in safety.

I drifted as both voices murmured. I heard the unfamiliar deep voice realise Nathan was right. "It's over."

Nathan's reply washed over me, until he raised his voice a little to stress the words. "Please. I can't stand to lose her again. . ."

I wanted to smile. What more evidence did I need to know that Nathan cared deeply for me? He'd killed for me. He'd admitted it to one of the blokes he worked with.

I felt the gentle bump of Nathan's footsteps as he carried me away.

FIFTY NINE

Brick – Fingers – Broken – Nose – Pete

What was in those pills? They left me so drowsy I couldn't stay awake.

Groggily, I tried to work out what had woken me.

"I like the colour. Like you're gift-wrapped, just for me." I heard the sound of sawing and felt the rope constrict around my legs. The sawing stopped and his voice sounded closer. "Pity your tits aren't bigger, though."

I pulled my knees up, my muscles screaming as the rope constricted, and kicked out with both feet together. I heard a satisfying grunt and a thump.

"Fuck! You broke my nose, you bitch." The blade bit into my calf instead of the rope and I screamed. "That's better."

"Try that again and I'll break the rest of your face, too," I panted, praying he wouldn't cut me again.

"The other blokes said you like it rough. Fine by me, but I'm not into pain. Mine, that is. So we'll do things differently."

He grabbed my feet and dragged me off the mattress, onto the cold concrete. He shoved a foot under my back and kicked me over, mashing my face into the concrete. I tried to kick him, but it was harder lying on my tummy.

"Better," he said. He seized my hair and pulled my head back. "Scream for me again."

My scalp screamed in pain, yet I swallowed mine. "Go fuck yourself."

By my hip I could feel the rough edge of a brick. I tried to move my hands to the side so I could grab it. Maybe if I rubbed the rope around my wrists against it, I could free myself...

"You want the brick?"

Fuck. He saw what I saw doing. I felt the brick move as he lifted it out of my reach.

"Okay." He smashed it down on my hand, shattering my fingers.

I screamed until I ran out of breath.

"Well, that's foreplay out the way. Time for the best part."

I heard the scream of his zip and the crackle of plastic.

With my legs still tied together and me lying face-down on the concrete, I wondered what the hell he intended to do. I hoped he'd decide to wank instead of running the risk of getting closer to me again. My fingers hurt too much to cross them.

"It's better this way." He shoved me down as he stretched himself out on top of me. He gave my backside a stinging slap. "Such a sweet little arse. I bet it's tight, too. Oh, fuck yeah. You like it rough, right?"

I screamed again.

SIXTY

Cool air chilled my bare legs.

A hand touched my chest between my breasts. I curled up to protect myself, bringing my knees up so I could kick the bastard so hard he sang soprano.

Nathan, if you sold me out to them, I will hunt you down and kill you in the most painful way I can devise.

I relaxed a little when I heard Nathan's voice. I listened to the litany of reassurance that didn't tell me why he'd taken my pants.

"You're covered in blood, angel."

Laura's blood, I wanted to say. As soon as I could move properly again, I'd wash it off with disinfectant and then maybe I'd feel clean again for the first time since she touched me.

"Just me, angel. I'm not going to hurt you."

So he didn't sell me out. I breathed again.

His hands touched my chest again and I heard the purr of the vest zip. I was too tired to resist as his hands examined me carefully, like a doctor would. His voice shook and squeaked a little, but the words kept coming. He intended to take my clothes off to wash the blood from my body. I wanted to nod my acquiescence, but my head felt too heavy.

Cold air touched my chest as he peeled the shirt from my skin, the blood making it stick to me. After Nathan's horror earlier, I didn't want to see his expression now. He'd never see my body as anything but damaged – he could only see the scars and what they once were. I could control my eyelids again, but I felt no desire to lift them. Not even when the hiss of warm spray hit my skin, from my shins to my face.

Maybe the medication had made me more pliant, too, I mused, letting my body flop like a doll as Nathan enveloped me in towels. Lifting, carrying and laying me down – encased in flannel, as I felt a towel smoothed over my body like a hospital sheet.

The shower spray hissed again. Nathan's turn?

I tested my body, trying to work out if I could control it yet or not. I moved my toes under the towel, trying not to wince as I flexed my aching thighs. Do not climb on dryers. I arched my back a little, shrugging my shoulders simply because I could. I played air with my fingers. *Necessary evil, the evil and the good. . .* I felt the smile lift my lips. After all, wasn't killing people supposed to be evil? Yet I felt so good now she was gone, as if the world was a better place. Necessary evil, indeed.

Distantly, I heard the shower stop and Nathan's footsteps approached. The slap of wet feet on tiles ceased as water splattered beside me, some of it soaking through my towel. Nathan swore and stepped away.

Curious, I carefully opened my eyes. I watched Nathan struggle out of his soaked clothes until I could see the pale skin of his bare backside. Not a bad backside, either. He wrapped my pink towel around his waist, his arm muscles bulging a little with the death grip he held the towel together with. Was he afraid his bits would fall off if the towel did?

He turned around and my smothered laugh died in my throat. The fearful, worried look at me said more than words. No. He didn't want the sight of so much skin to scare me.

It's not the sight. It's the feeling of it in close proximity to mine, I wanted to explain. But to do that, I'd have to tell him everything and why. Burden him with graphic descriptions of rape. I closed my eyes. No, Nathan, I can't do that to you.

The shock of his skin on mine almost broke my resolve. I sucked in a breath to scream.

His soothing voice cut me short. That and the slide of satin over my skin, as he clothed me once more.

Soothed, dressed and dry, I sank into Nathan's arms, secure and safe. Because the bitch was dead.

Nathan set me down on a soft mattress. Mine.

Cool cotton covered me, slowly starting to warm me. Quilt.

I heard a voice say they were all dead. I started to relax, relieved, before I realised the voice wasn't Nathan's. The voice called me beautiful, then said something about stealing souls. Cold fingers touched my face.

No. NO. Nathan? Nathan, you promised. . .

His arms were around me and the quilt, cocooning me tightly. "I'm here," I heard his voice murmur. "I'm here." A pause. "No one's going to hurt you, ever again. They're all dead."

It's over. Oh thank God, it's over.

I could feel my mind floating. Nathan's voice said something else, but I couldn't focus on it. I drifted off to sleep. Safe.

SIXTY ONE

It was dark when I woke up. Nathan was beside me – I'd just woken him up.

In my dream it had happened again. She'd come and tried to take me back; I'd shot her and her blood had splashed. . .

I tried to take stock of what was real, here, now.

I was wearing little more than my underwear – shortie satin pjs. Nothing else. Not someone else's clothes.

My hands were clean. There was no blood on them.

It couldn't have been just a dream.

But Nathan didn't have a gun – I didn't have a gun.

I couldn't have murdered anyone.

Oh, but I did. I killed the bitch who hurt me, whose husband. . .

"Hey, are you all right?" Nathan's sleepy voice in my ear. "You were lying there on the toilet floor when I got there. You passed out. You've been out of it for hours."

That couldn't be right. I remembered. . . Memory mixed

with dream. Did I shoot her or was it an accident? It's not murder when it's self defence. No accident. . .

"I dreamed that. . . they were trying to take me back and I killed someone. You had a gun and they all had guns. . ." I tried to make it sound like any of it made sense, but failed.

"Just a bad dream. It's all over now." His lips on mine.

I gasped in surprise.

I felt him freeze. He hadn't planned this. His breathing was ragged, but I kept mine as even as I could, holding still.

It's your move, Nathan.

Very carefully, he slid his fingers along my pillow, between my cheek and the cotton cover. He kissed my lips as if he was kissing his sister's cheek, a kiss so chaste it was hard to believe I was sharing a bed with a man who'd seen me naked. Then he pulled away from me slightly, his breathing fast and nervous.

Why so slow and hesitant? What happened to Mr Sleazy Roommate in the toilet tonight? Unless he hadn't planned that, either. . .

A faint idea coalesced in my head and I did what my body had wanted to do in the toilet earlier this evening, before I pushed him away so I didn't. I wrapped my arms around him and kissed him properly.

He was too shocked to kiss me back for a second or two – he even forgot to breathe.

When he did respond, his every movement was careful and tender, as if he were savouring each moment.

I could do this. I could let him touch me. I could respond. I even wanted to. After the pain, confusion and killing tonight, I wanted this. I wanted whatever pleasure this man could give me. If only to feel wanted again.

He had no shirt on. My hands smoothed his skin. He kissed me as urgently as I kissed him.

"Let me help take your mind off it."

He was so gentle.

Was he this gentle with her?

Ugh, could he really have slept with her?

I don't care how gentle you are now, you bastard. You touched me without my permission and then nearly got me killed. The hell you're touching me now – and definitely not if you slept with her. How could you fuck that bitch? Knowing what she did?

"NO!" I hissed through gritted teeth and shoved him away.

SIXTY TWO

Four — Mike — Tom — Simon — Pete — Her

I lost track of the days, the difference between day and night and any sense of time. Some minutes stretched for hours when I just wanted it to be over, but it felt like I'd only just gone to sleep when someone else would hurt me and wake me up to start all over again.

I was always tired. Maybe the pain or the horror of it made me so sleepy. Sometimes I was even too tired to fight, too tired to spit the insults at them that I was thinking. Maybe they hurt me less because they didn't get much of a reaction to whatever they did to me. Maybe they hurt me more to get a reaction.

There were four of them who hurt me, all different.

One of them was there more often, a big bully who'd crush me under his weight. He was rough and strong and he probably left bruises wherever he touched me. He'd hit me or hurt me some other way with his big, meaty hands, until I'd at least whimper, before he'd start grunting his way to a climax. He was the one the others called Mike. The bastard who'd drugged me in the car.

Another one liked to break my fingers, or twist the ones he'd already broken. He liked to pinch and slap, too. He was a small, skinny bloke with a nasal, whiny voice. Torture with him couldn't have lasted more than five minutes. I heard Mike say to him once, "C'mon Pete, your five minutes are almost done!" and, thankfully, Pete had been done, too.

One of them always brought one of the others along to "hold me still." He took forever and his hands were everywhere. It was like being groped by two squids. He'd make comments to himself or the guy holding me for him. I know I fell asleep more than once and I doubt he noticed. If Mike was holding me, he'd hit me 'til I woke up and he'd laugh that he and the other guys had exhausted me before it was Simon's turn. The cold fish was called Simon.

Simon's preferred accomplice he called Tom. Tom didn't say much, he just did what he came for and left. I asked him once why he bothered with me at all. He told me to shut up or he'd break my jaw. Don't remember if he came back after that.

Then there was Her. The woman who wanted me to speak to her friend. The woman who drove the red Mercedes. She hit me and pushed me in and she knew what they'd do to me. I'll kill her if I can.

I want them all dead. I want to know they can never hurt me or anyone else again. It'd be satisfying if I can make sure they feel the same pain as what they'd forced on me before they die, but I'll settle for them dead. Maybe.

SIXTY THREE

I didn't regret it properly 'til Nathan had hurried out of my room and I heard the water running in the bathroom. I slipped out of bed and opened my bedroom door silently. I wanted to apologise. I was so messed up after getting into not one but two fights tonight that I'd started a third with Nathan. I didn't want him to leave me alone – not tonight.

Outside the door I came face to face with a man I didn't know. Oh, but I did. Even as his eyes slid away from my face, I realised this was the man who'd tried to crush the life out of me before he stabbed me with a syringe. The man who knew Nathan.

"Are you here to guard me?" I whispered.

He nodded.

I looked into his eyes, keeping my voice low so Nathan wouldn't hear me. "I'm sorry I held a gun to your head. I thought you were going to kill him."

He smiled, nodded and told me it was okay. Haltingly, he said, "I'm sorry for. . . stuff, too."

I heard Nathan splashing in the bathroom and hurried through the house to the toilet. When I opened the door, I half expected to see the blood-spattered walls in my memory, but the gore was gone. The tiles sparkled like they hadn't for months and I know I hadn't cleaned them.

I shut the door again as quietly as I could and headed into the laundry to retrieve my knife. I scrabbled around on top of the dryer until I found it, wedged between the dryer and the wall. I tucked the sheathed blade into the waistband of my pyjamas, pulling my top down to hide it. It was cold against my skin, much like my resolve.

I tiptoed quickly back to my room, listening for the running water in the bathroom. It sounded like Nathan was still there.

The guard hadn't moved. He gave me a nod as I approached.

"Nathan's guarding me, too, right?" I asked.

He nodded.

I hesitated, but I had to ask. "Is he any good? Can I trust him?"

He paused, looking thoughtful. "Well, he's kept you alive this long."

Through blind, dumb luck and help from everyone, including me.

He looked like he was thinking the same thing. He opened his mouth to speak.

"Why did he take so long to come back for me?" I couldn't stop my voice from shaking.

He swallowed. "He disobeyed orders and killed suspects he was supposed to capture. My orders were to get him to the surveillance van. I didn't know he'd missed one."

"Orders? You mean Nathan's not in charge?" I asked quickly.

"No, the unit manager up at the State Office. . ." he began.

That was the man I needed to meet. The man who was ordering him around. The one who told him to let me get hurt. If all of Nathan's fuck-ups weren't his fault – well, most of them, at least – someone else needed to pay. And the price would be high. I'd make sure of that.

I gritted my teeth so hard they grated together. "Tell him I need to talk to him. Without Nathan." I took a deep breath. "I'll tell him everything I know."

He looked at me in consternation.

I heard Nathan turn the water off and his footsteps cross from tiled bathroom floor to hallway carpet. "Thank you," I whispered as I hurried back to bed.

I slipped the knife beneath my pillow while he exchanged words with the guard outside, their voices too low for me to hear. I lay down and focussed on my breathing, allowing my body to relax again. Whether I trusted Nathan or not, at least I wouldn't be unarmed any more. I intended to take this knife everywhere. Especially if I lost Nathan's help.

As he crept into bed beside me once more, I relaxed in relief. I needed him still and the only way I could think to bind him more closely to me involved sex. I only hoped I could do it.

SIXTY FOUR

The plan was so stupid it was hard to believe it'd been mine. Of course, it wasn't until I was in the middle of the crowded nightclub that I realised what a terrible idea it was. I couldn't seduce Nathan in this crush – he couldn't hear a word I said. I needed privacy. And a truckload more courage than I could ever possess.

It took him ten minutes of waiting before he could buy me a drink from the bar – hardly enough liquid courage to bolster my bravery.

So when Nathan asked me if I wanted to go home, I was so happy, I kissed him.

I'd finished two of my stubbies by the time Nathan pulled into an unfamiliar driveway. My head was swimmy with the alcohol. Nathan swirled it round further by lifting me from the car and spinning me around. The empty bottle in my hand slipped from my fumbling fingers and thumped to the grass. A glowing heat spread through my chest, fuelled by the alcohol and more besides. I returned

Nathan's fierce kiss, holding his head in my hands.

I wanted this. Fuck, I wanted this. He'd never hurt me. NEVER.

Something bumped against my leg. I looked down and saw Nathan had hooked his fingers round the handle of the bag from the liquor store. It was coming in with us. If my courage needed any more fodder, he had it. Dutch courage. I giggled. Not my vodka mixers. Russian courage, more like.

Nathan smiled at me, setting me gently on my feet so he could unlock the door. We both lurched through the front door, laughing as our bodies were squeezed together in a doorway that wasn't meant for two at a time.

He dropped the keys as he kicked the door shut, then knelt to retrieve them. I stuck my toes on top of his keys, out of some fuzzy concept of mischief. His hands on my leg, sliding up and lifting, threw me off balance, so I almost fell on top of him. Instead of righting me, he tried to rise to his feet, with me balanced precariously over one shoulder.

He shifted my weight so he had me in more of a fireman's hold over his shoulder — better balanced but hardly dignified. His firm hand on my bare backside steadied me, but it shocked us both. Somehow my skirt had ridden up and my underwear was in clear view.

"You got a red g-string to match the red bra?" he gasped.

Actually, I'd been pretty pissed to discover the idiot of a shop girl had given me a g-string instead of knickers, but it'd been the perfect choice for tonight. Nathan's lips on me drove all thought of anyone else right out of my head.

"Kiss-arse," I murmured, my skin tingling as he did it again. I watched the keys get further away, forgotten on the tiles.

Nathan inverted me and I felt furry fabric beneath my bottom. I looked around fuzzily at the lounge room I didn't recognise. I was sitting on his sofa and he stood near me, holding out a bottle. "Would you like another drink?" He took a deep draught of his own, downing most of the contents before he wiped his mouth and dropped the bottle on a side table.

I watched his throat move as he swallowed. I wanted another drink, but I wanted him first. I struggled to my feet and stuck my arms around his neck, trying to kiss him again.

He lifted his head out of my reach. "You're drunk, angel. I don't want to take advantage of you."

"Not drunk, well, not quite," I managed to say with a giggle. "Very tipsy. I think I want to go to bed."

"Sure, angel. Let me help you." He supported me as we walked together through his lounge room and into the passage to the bedrooms. It wasn't wide enough for both of us together, so he moved behind me, tugging my waist-high skirt down to cover me as he did so.

Annoyed, I yanked my stretchy dress up and up – over my bra and my head, so I stood in my underwear, with my dress dangling from my hand. I turned to face Nathan, whose eyes were huge as they stared down at the red bra between us. "Oh God," he murmured.

I looked at him in consternation. Was he disgusted by what he saw? Would no one ever look at me like I was attractive again? Last night, he'd said. . .

"God, you're beautiful, Caitlin. You have no idea how hard it's been, resisting you." The look in his eyes was one of longing.

Is this what it's like, to be truly loved by someone? I wondered. This isn't just lust. I've seen plenty of that — more than I ever care to.

And me? I want Nathan.

We kissed, long and lingering, until he lifted me in his arms and we began again. I felt the jolt of his footsteps as he carried me through a doorway, from the darkness in the passage to clumsily clicked-on light.

The bed Nathan tenderly placed me on looked black, but as I looked around me I realised that it was a printed quilt cover, the black only a background illuminated by the millions of stars in the Milky Way.

Take me to the stars, Nathan.

Before he could straighten up, I pulled him down to the bed with me. He wasn't clumsy — instead, he was careful to land beside me. He leaned over to kiss me again, one hand lightly stroking my neck.

I moved by instinct, for I knew if I thought about this I'd back down and I didn't want to. I had to know. I rolled, pushing him with me, so instead of lying side by side in the stars, I sat astride him. Stars beneath my knees and his bulging pants between my thighs. I caught his surprised eyes and reached back to unclip my bra, sliding it off to throw it to the floor.

"Angel. . ." he said in wonder. With agonising slowness, he sat up so his breath was a warm breeze across my skin. "You know I'll never hurt you, right?"

I touched trembling hands to the back of his head and gave the slightest push. "I know," I breathed as his lips touched my breast.

I needed to feel his skin against mine, not fabric. I pulled at his shirt and together we hoisted it over his head. His bare chest was as hard with muscle as mine was soft, but it was clear in his kisses that this didn't bother him in the slightest. I undid his belt and slid that off, too. All that was between us were his pants and my g-string.

Nathan sat up straight, his eyes level with mine. "I don't want to take advantage of you," he whispered.

"Last night you said any time, all I needed to do was ask. I'm asking now, Nathan." I could feel the drunken buzz fading, leaving me cold and naked in its wake. Somewhere inside, I felt terror that he was going to reject me. The longer he took, the greater was my desire to curl up in a little ball and give up. "Please?" It came out as a whisper.

With his lingering kiss came relief. "For you, angel, anything. I'll even keep my pants on. Tonight's for you. I can wait."

My brain was still fuzzy and I couldn't work out what he meant. I didn't resist as he lifted me to lay my head on a pillow. His hands stroked the tiny strip of satin I still wore. "Are you sure?"

I laid my hands on his, pushing his fingers into a hook between the stringy satin and the bony skin at my hips. Together we pulled them over my knees, down past my toes. I threw them on the floor. "Yes," I breathed. I'd never been so scared.

SIXTY FIVE

Tied – Chris – Cornflakes – Coke – Superman – Death

"Here, I brought you something to eat," Chris's voice hissed quietly. "Can you sit up?"

Groggily, I struggled and groaned a little, to no avail. Plastic clattered on the concrete floor before his hands slid behind my back, supporting me as I tried to sit.

A flash of pain. I gritted my teeth. I wouldn't let on how much it hurt.

Even in the dark, he noticed something wasn't right, but he didn't mention it. He draped a blanket over my shoulders as he moved to sit partly behind me, so that his body supported my back.

My instincts threatened to shrink away from even this benign body contact, but exhaustion got the better of me. My body sagged against him, with just a blanket between us. All the while, I told myself, He won't hurt you. You don't need to fight right now – just rest. Begging for it to be true.

The clack of cutlery on plastic as some kind of cereal rustled. I registered that part of my pain was hunger and accepted a spoonful of whatever he offered.

Stale, dry cornflakes. Like biting into the plastic packaging. I wanted to spit them out, but my mouth was too dry and I was too hungry. Tears dripped silently as I struggled to chew.

He voiced an apology. "I looked, but that's all there is. There's no milk and they've run out of juice. All I found was Coke - here." The click and hiss of a can being opened, followed by the sound of many bubbles that meant it was warm.

He pressed the can to my lips. Coke warmer than the temperature in the room ran down my chin and onto my legs, which the blanket didn't cover. Bubbles burned into the cuts and bruises.

It was too much. I started to sob and once I started, I couldn't stop.

His arms crept around me in a cautious hug. He was careful to enclose the blanket in his embrace. Unlike the others, he didn't touch my skin at all.

"It'll be okay," he whispered, sounding uncertain.

"No it won't," I said between sobs.

"You have to keep fighting. You can't let them win," he insisted.

The tears flowed faster. "I can't any more. Please. Kill me now. Do it quickly, so they can't hurt me again. I'm begging you. Don't let them... don't let them..."

"You have to hang on. I'll find a way to get you out of here. Both of us."

"Your family..." I started to say, not sure how to finish.

"I'll go to prison to protect them. But I can't kill you. I'll find some other way to protect them. I'll save you."

Him and his Superman complex. He couldn't save me. He couldn't even save himself or his family.

I almost laughed. "If you get me out of here alive, I swear I'll tell everyone from the police right up to the judge that you were a saint and my fellow captive - including how you saved my life."

"What happened to telling them how horrible I am?" He sounded rueful. "Tell them whatever you like, as long as you hang in there, angel. I won't let them hurt you."

A bit bloody late. What about how much I hurt already? Can you take that away, too?

"You need your strength. Please, eat some more?" He sounded apologetic as his arms loosened.

I heard him scrape another spoonful and opened my mouth dutifully.

Eat. Drink. Let him help you rest and take some of the pain away. Let him help you keep your strength long enough to live and get out of here.

If I stopped eating, would this be over sooner? No more pain?

I pushed the traitorous thought away, forcing myself to crunch through the cornflakes and swallow.

"When I get out of here, I'm never going to eat cornflakes again, stale or otherwise," I vowed vehemently, the anger more at my own thoughts than the decrepit cereal.

The only way I'll leave here is if I'm dead. I have nothing left to lose.

"Hold onto that thought." His voice sounded

like it came through gritted teeth. "Here, this will help with the pain." More pills, washed down with warm Coke. I never thought to ask what was in them. I didn't care enough to ask. For a dark moment, I wanted more - enough to stop the pain forever.

But I wouldn't ask. A drugged death was too uncertain. If I had to die, I wanted to take at least one of them with me. For that, I needed my strength. So I needed to eat cardboard cornflakes and drink the Coke to sustain me until I could make them pay, at least in part, for my pain.

More cornflakes until the pills brought more oblivion.

SIXTY SIX

This was no fumble in a dark corner, at some school friend's party with a clumsy boy I barely knew. Nor was this a brutal assault that would leave me bruised and broken. Nathan handled me lovingly, like delicate china.

He held his weight off me, his body hovering above me as his lips kissed mine, then a line of soft kisses down my breasts, firmer as his mouth dipped lower. His gentle hands stroked my thighs, pushing them further apart. I found I was holding my breath in anticipation, but I cried out in shock at the unexpected rasp of his tongue over sensitive skin.

"Caitlin, I don't want to hurt you, or push you too far again. Angel, tell me if you want me to stop." His breath was warm on my skin as he spoke, so I barely heard the words. I couldn't decide if I was trembling with excitement or fear. His eyes looked at mine across the length of my body, worried.

I forced myself to smile and slowly shook my head.

"Don't stop. Please, Nathan, don't stop." For if you do and my courage fails, I'll curl up and never let you or anyone else touch me again.

He didn't stop again. Instead, he was wonderful.

The first time was sudden and explosive. So lost in the sensation, I barely heard my own voice scream his name. I was too caught up in the vibration of his chuckling response.

The second I thought I was more prepared for, a slow burn to a less powerful peak. I found I was lifting my hips to meet him as the warmth washed over me. His hands were firm beneath my backside, supporting me. "Let me improve on that, angel," he murmured and began again. The strokes were slower this time, a long, languorous selection of licking, sucking and stroking all blended together until I sobbed his name again. It struck me that I was sober and there was something else I wanted to do, for I felt so sensitive now I wasn't sure I could take much more. His gentle fingers stroked me again, driving me mad.

"Stop," I begged him. "I want you to kiss me."

Nathan moved quickly from between my legs and off the bed. The hiss of released gas left me looking around in shock. Nathan gulped down half of one of my little vodka drinks and smiled. I wondered how he'd brought them to the bedroom. The bottle clunked to the bedside table as he crept across the bed back to me. His kisses tasted of lemon.

"Thank you," I said when he paused for breath.

"You're welcome, angel. Any time. . ." he murmured, leaning in for another kiss.

I kissed him and pushed him, all in one smooth motion as we rolled together. I was on top once more. I didn't have the courage to do this any other way. I wasn't sure I had the courage now. I gritted my teeth as I felt the heat of him between my legs. I was terrified.

My heart rate still hadn't slowed and my very blood was buzzing from his touch. The least I could do was reciprocate.

I kept kissing him as I unzipped his fly and undid the button. My hands under his bum, I dragged the dress pants down over his hips as he sat up in surprise. Something in my eyes stopped his protest before he gave it voice. "Condoms?" I murmured between kisses.

I couldn't look down. I felt cold at the thought of sex. Of letting him. . . letting him. . .

My courage ebbing as fast as it came, I resolved to give him a blow job. Both the least and the most I could do. I swallowed, hoping I'd be able to follow through with it.

Oh God, I should have had more alcohol to drink. Maybe I wouldn't have been so scared.

I could hear Nathan fumbling around with the bedside table. I heard the drawer slide open and glanced over as he reached for the box on top. There were plenty beneath it, all different.

I looked at the box he handed me. Strawberry-flavoured, it said. You didn't expect this, but you sure as hell hoped, I thought grimly. I grimaced. Pity they taste more like bubblegum than strawberry. Better than bare latex and damned if I'm swallowing for you, Nathan.

He stuck out of the front of his checked boxer shorts like an empty flagpole. I pulled his shorts down, too, so he was bare to his thighs. I didn't want a mouthful of cotton. I stuck on his hot-pink condom one-handed, kissing his mouth the whole time. Angels need two hands and instructions for this, Nathan. I gently massaged him with my hand. Not small, but not enormous, either. I could handle this. I moved quickly, before I could waver in my resolve. I had a warm, bubblegum-flavoured mouthful before he regained the power of speech. What he did say came out sounding like, "Muh." I sucked harder and felt him thrust in response. I almost choked.

A reverent hand stroked my hair. "You don't have to do this, angel."

I'm not a fucking angel. Or maybe I am. An angel of death, more like.

I felt a tear slide down my cheek.

"No. NO!" Nathan's sudden shout scared me. He pushed me away. His face looked afraid and he visibly shrank away from me in more ways than one.

What did I do?

More tears welled up. "I thought you were enjoying it."

He wiped my tears away. "You weren't. Everything I've ever done for you. . . I'd do it again in a heartbeat. All you have to do is ask. And you still wouldn't owe me anything, angel. Least of all this."

He gestured at his rapidly retreating arousal.

"I can do this," I insisted.

He saw my scars. He saw the damage and didn't want me any more.

"I'm sorry, angel, but I can't." He stood up, turning his back as he pulled the condom off. As if he didn't even want to look at me any more.

I was too tired to deal with this now. If he didn't want the best blow job of his life from the girl he loved, then I wanted to curl into a tiny, unwanted ball and sleep.

"I'm tired, Nathan," I confessed.

He was all attention, without a hint of disappointment or disgust. "I'll find you one of my shirts to sleep in. I'll go wash up while you change."

He threw the shirt to me and hurried out of the room. The used condom fluttered to the floor in his wake, limp and unloved. The opposite of me as I stretched out, skin now wrapped in shirt and sheet. Sensationally sated, yet saddened.

SIXTY SEVEN

"Would you like me to sleep on the couch or in here with you? I can sleep on the floor, if you prefer," Nathan offered.

My body was still buzzing as I reached out for him. "Here's fine. Hold me, Nathan. I feel safer that way."

He spooned up to me and I sighed as I relaxed into sleep.

"No. . . no. . . please wake up. No. . . you can't be dead. Caitlin. . . please. . . wake up. . ." I woke to Nathan's panicked voice as his hands patted me.

I'm not dead. I think I'm not dead. No, I'm breathing. Definitely not dead.

I stayed still, trying to keep my breathing even as I gathered my straying thoughts. My dream hadn't been bad.

"Angel, I'm sorry. . . I'm sorry. . . Oh God. . ."

I swallowed and said, "Nathan? It's just a dream, right?"

"Caitlin? Caitlin? Please. . ." I could feel his face through my shirt as he listened to my chest. My shirt felt damp from. . . tears? Could he really be crying?

"It's okay," I murmured, cuddling closer to him.

"Angel?" He lifted his head to kiss me lightly. "It's okay. You're safe. You're safe. . ." His arms tightened around me.

"I'm safe," I repeated, hoping it was true. If he hugged me much tighter, he might break my ribs.

"Safe. . ." he murmured. "I'll keep you safe, angel." His grip relaxed a little.

I waited for his breathing to become even before I dared to fall asleep again. His nightmares were getting worse — and becoming more dangerous, too.

SIXTY EIGHT

Tied – Mike – Her – Knife – Cutting – Blood

I screamed as hot pain sliced across my thigh.

"Hold still. You, hold her still," she said.

A warm body landed on my midsection, crushing me to the cold concrete. Denim-clad legs pinned mine down, apart.

Another slice and another scream.

"I can gag her, too, if it bothers you, ma'am," Mike said.

"No need. There's no one to hear her," she said carelessly. I heard the knife point scrape my skin, the pain a constant burn now. "Shine that torch here. I want the letters clear."

I tried to scream, but there was no voice left. A hoarse whimper was all the sound that came out.

"What the fuck are you doing?" I rasped.

She ignored me, intent on mutilating my body. She lifted the knife, so it glinted in the torchlight. "There. A little present for the ASIO boy." She looked down at my legs. "No. I need to do the other one, too. They must match."

She stabbed the blade into my other leg.

I cried out, but no one took any notice.

You promised. You promised you wouldn't let them hurt me.

I struggled, not caring any more. Chris couldn't keep his promise and I couldn't keep fighting. I'd make them kill me instead.

"Oh shit! The knife dug too deep because you couldn't hold her still. Now she's bleeding everywhere. I must have caught a vein... we're out of time. She won't survive the night, bleeding like that. Send Chris in here. Make sure he knows where you've left the keys, so he can dump the body. Follow him and call the police as soon as you can. We need him caught with it."

When did I become a sexless thing you could call 'it?'

"Yes, ma'am. What do you want me to do with her?" Mike asked.

"Knock her out so I can finish. I only need to cut one more letter."

Something heavy collided with my face and darkness seeped into my head.

SIXTY NINE

When the sun had risen, I woke alone to the sounds of Nathan speaking angrily with another girl. I pulled on one of Nathan's sweaters and approached closer to investigate, just in time to hear her call him a paedophile and me a child.

His sister. The one who was my age. She had to be. But her words didn't make sense. If he was a paedophile and I was a child, he wouldn't have turned me down last night.

She repeatedly warned him away from me as he protested, refused and defended me.

Inwardly, I cheered.

"Can't you put the coffee away when you're done with it?" she muttered.

He mumbled something about leaving it out for her.

"I don't drink decaf. You're the only person I know who drinks coffee without caffeine in the mornings. Where's the point in drinking coffee that doesn't do anything?" I heard the clunk of glass on wood, before a cupboard door slammed.

I wondered about Nathan and his distaste for caffeine. The only people I knew who preferred decaffeinated coffee had it in the evening, so they didn't have trouble sleeping. But Nathan. . . oh! Nightmares and insomnia. . . of course!

I waited for his reply, but the silence stretched until she broke it, her words leaving me cold.

"Not a girl who's been abducted. After she's been raped and God knows what else, the last thing she wants is a man anywhere near her. Least of all you."

I needed to see Nathan's face, to see if her words had any effect on him. Quietly, I stepped into the doorway. Neither of them saw me for a moment.

A thinner, angrier version of Alanna whirled around and started swiping at the bench with a pot-scourer. I wondered if their laminate bench top would lose its surface beneath her frenzied scrubbing. She stood with her back to me, while I could see Nathan's profile as he watched her. He seemed to have trouble forming a response, but he didn't look happy. He rocked a little in his seat, like he was trying to exorcise a memory.

She shouldn't have used the r-word. It'd set off his guilt. Turning my attention to Nathan, I summoned a smile as I called his name.

His smile and, "Good morning," left me feeling like I was his perfect dawn and not the pariah I'd felt like last night. Before the nightmares started. Rescue me, his eyes pleaded.

Thinking quickly, I asked for his help in the shower, hoping he wouldn't freeze up like he had last night. I needed to know if any of her warnings had sunk in to his traumatised consciousness. And if last night was simply a result of him drinking too much, never to be repeated.

He agreed and I left, but I'd barely made it two steps from the door before I realised he hadn't followed me. Carefully, I rested against the wall as I waited.

I let my eyes roam around the ceilings, looking for the surveillance cameras that had to be here. His sister would surely have as much protection as I did. Yet I saw none.

Maybe they'd used better technology for this house because she was more valuable. Or maybe there was no surveillance. . . I sat puzzling out what that meant as they shouted insults at each other for a bit longer.

Nathan finally left, angry and upset, but he stopped as soon as he saw me.

I stretched a hand out for his and let him help me to my feet. He held me tighter than usual as we walked together to the bathroom, as if he was afraid to lose me.

Don't worry, Nathan – I already know your alter-ego is Mr Sleazy Roommate. And last night you showed me you won't take advantage of me. A compunction I don't share.

Once the bathroom door shut behind us and the shower water muffled our conversation, I resolved to find out whether he still wanted me after last night. His sister didn't need to know.

I slid my hands up his shirt, caressing the firm muscles I knew were hidden beneath the fabric. He stiffened at my touch, but he didn't pull away. I tried to pull his shirt off and he lifted his arms to assist me.

So far, so good.

I pulled off my own sweater. My heart sank as he closed his eyes before he could see anything. Did my scars really make me that hideous? Was last night just a drunken mistake?

Cautiously, I pressed my naked body against his. He still had his shorts on, but they weren't much of a hindrance. I could feel his eager response to my proximity.

"Would you like me to help you in the shower?" His breathless voice surprised me, as did his open eyes, fixed on my face. The guilt wasn't gone, but it was fading.

I smiled as I accepted his offer.

His hands on my body were as tender as last night, lifting me into the warm water as he stepped into the shower with me in his arms.

I looked down. His soaked shorts clung to his body, hiding nothing.

"I'll keep it in my pants," he swore.

I laughed, cupping his cheek as I kissed him. "How are we going to do this?" I murmured.

His arms were full of me and I couldn't wash myself with the two of us so close.

He looked puzzled, like he hadn't planned this, either. "I don't know," he said finally. "We don't have a chair I can stick in the shower for you here. Maybe. . . if I set you down on your feet. . . do you think you can hold onto me for support while I help you wash? If you like. I'll be a perfect gentleman, I swear."

Somehow, we ended up standing like dance partners in the shower, swaying a little under the warm rain. The promised perfect gentleman reached for the soap and proceeded to demonstrate his prowess, like a dishwasher with a delicate china plate. No passion – just professional boredom.

I endured it, holding still as he caressed my body with the bar until I was clean. If I couldn't see his strained shorts, I'd have thought my bare skin had no effect on him.

He clinked the soap back into its dish and placed his arms around me again, careful not to let my breasts touch him. "Now, let's get you wet and you'll be all clean," he murmured, turning with me so more of the spray rained down on me.

I chose my words carefully. "What if I'd prefer to be wet and dirty with you, Nathan?"

He stared at me, shocked. "What. . . what do you mean?"

Fuck, Nathan. I know you heard and understood the words. Should I have just said, "Finger me, Nathan," instead?

With equal care, I grasped his hand, pulling it down. "You. . . remember what you did last night? I want to know I didn't dream it." I swallowed, already regretting my impulse. "Please."

His expression softened. "You were a dream last night. I never thought you'd trust me enough to let me touch you like this, let alone pleasure you like last night," he murmured, one finger lightly stroking. I shivered in relief. "Are you sure you want this?"

"Oh yes." I threw my arms around his neck, kissing him deeply as his caresses deepened, too.

"Don't. . . stop," I panted, before returning for another kiss. This kiss didn't cease until I collapsed against him, spent.

He may have been an absolute dream, but Nathan was no nightmare, that was for sure.

SEVENTY

Nathan's hands lingered dreamily on me as he helped me dress, as if the scars didn't deter him in the slightest in the light of day. I wondered what had turned him off so completely last night, if it hadn't been my body.

The sound of crockery scraping in a metal sink reminded me of his angry sister. Perhaps I was asking the wrong person – she knew him better than I did.

Nathan offered to help me to the kitchen and make me breakfast, but I shook my head. I'd never get her to be honest about him within his hearing. "You should go hang the towels up and get into some dry clothes," I suggested, glancing down at the prominent torch he carried for me in his soaked shorts.

He flushed and grabbed the damp towels, mumbling as he strode away.

I waited until I heard the toilet door close before I hurried to speak to Chris. I didn't know how long it'd take him to jerk off.

"How long has he been having nightmares?" I asked softly as I entered the kitchen.

"Since she went missing," she responded, equally softly.

"Has he slept with any girl since?"

"He's fooled around with a few, but none of them ever stayed 'til morning," she replied.

I felt a blush colouring my cheeks. "Maybe it's because we didn't."

She lifted her eyebrows at me.

"Your brother's good with his hands and his tongue. Do you really want the details?" I took in her panicked expression. "Fifty bucks says he's making use of his hands to relieve the pressure right now. Give him some credit."

I heard the slam of a door. That was quick.

She turned away from me, staring out the window. I followed her gaze to where Nathan was pegging the towels on the outside clothesline.

I shrugged and started searching the kitchen, trying to work out what to have for breakfast. For a moment, I regretted not taking Nathan up on his offer of a full cooked breakfast. I had a craving for bacon. . .

"He's not even making you breakfast?" she asked, as if she'd read my mind.

"No, I talked him out of it," I replied in Nathan's defence.

She stared at me in shock, as if she hadn't expected me to reply. "How did you manage that? It's difficult to talk him out of anything."

I warmed to the girl. She did know him and she was going to tell me what I needed to know, even if Nathan was listening. Maybe an insult would make him move out of earshot. "Difficult? He's as stubborn as a mule!"

She evidently thought the same thing, laughing loudly as she agreed with me.

Nathan's scrutiny didn't lessen.

"I'm Caitlin. Nathan seemed too. . . *preoccupied* to introduce me before." I almost said rude, but she seemed to understand anyway.

We shook hands as she introduced herself as his sister, Chris, exactly as I'd surmised.

The girl he'd been trying to protect as he'd let me get hurt. Was it worth it, Nathan?

"Shit, are you all right?"

She'd seen the pain in my expression. I think she took it for real pain instead of bitterness and heartache.

"No, but I will be one day," I replied carefully. I edged away from her, toward one of the kitchen chairs. My legs were cramping a little from the unaccustomed exercise — both last night and in the shower.

She helped me sit down, her voice low in my ear. "He didn't hurt you, did he?"

"No," I whispered back.

"I'll make you a coffee. You just sit and rest. It still hurts you to walk, doesn't it?" she said loudly.

"Not as much as it did at first, but it still does, a bit," I agreed. I dropped my voice lower. "Especially when I've done. . . more than I'm used to." I felt my cheeks redden. She'd made no secret of the fact that she'd heard us last night, when she'd been shouting at Nathan earlier. I hoped we'd been quieter in the shower.

"Does he even know?" she asked, turning to look at Nathan.

"Don't tell him. I'm recovering faster than he realises. Let him play Prince Charming for a bit," I whispered.

"Prince Sleazy, more like," she whispered back, before raising her voice to a more normal volume. I tried to choke back my laughter. "Look, I don't know what you've been through, what they've done to you or anything. Just don't assume he's some kind of Prince Charming because he rescued you. He's nowhere near perfect – he'll probably just end up hurting you, breaking your heart. He's good at that."

I wasn't even sure I had a heart left to break. I didn't dare confess that to his sister, though. "Do you think badly of me for staying last night?" I asked instead.

Her expression told me she did, but she evidently noticed my knowing look and denied it.

"No, it's him!" she insisted. "What you want to do is your business, and you're not the first."

Nathan had killed for other girls? Or let other girls get hurt?

She saw my expression and hurried to explain. "Not the first girl he's ever brought home, I mean. He'd come in late, not alone, and she'd be gone by morning. I've never seen – or heard – the same girl twice, except when they called to try to get in contact with him again."

Well, if he was as good in bed as he was in the shower, it came as no surprise that his conquests would want more. I did. . .

"Have there been many since Alanna disappeared? Or since he found me?" I asked softly.

"It's been a long time since he brought anyone home – more than two months – but I'd have thought he'd know better than to seduce you, or play on what he did for you –

after all you've been through, you don't need him to hurt you as well!" She addressed the last part of her comments out the window at Nathan, who hid behind a towel.

She thought Nathan had seduced me? Hopefully, he thought so, too.

I covered my smile with my coffee cup, drinking deeply.

"Alanna warned me about him, but she knew he wouldn't be able to resist me."

Chris set her cup down in shock. "You knew her? How old are you?"

I lifted my gaze to meet hers. "I'm the same age as you. He told me about you, so I knew. . ." Her shock made me shorten my sentence. He hadn't told her anything. Was he trying to protect her? "I knew who you were when you visited him in hospital. I'm sorry I wasn't awake enough to introduce myself then. The pain drugs kept me pretty out of it."

"He drops girls if they start getting too close. Just don't let him hurt you," she said.

Don't get too attached, in other words. She might be my age, but she knew nothing about bastards who hurt girls.

I smiled. "Nathan? He wouldn't dare hurt me. He'd do anything to help me get well again." I took a mouthful of coffee that went down the wrong way. Coughing, I tried to find my voice again. "He said he never wanted to see me hurt." I coughed again, harder.

Through the window, I saw Nathan start toward the house. I heard the sound of a screen door opening and slamming.

"Are the dreams about her? Is he taking anything for them?" I asked urgently.

"They used to be, but he got better after a while. Maybe it was the Temaze sleeping pills his doctor gave him," she replied in a hurried whisper. "Now they're about you. And he doesn't have any pills left. He won't go to the doctor for more, either. It's like he's afraid to admit how many he's taken. I don't know what to do to help him. He should stay away from you and anything to do with Alanna, but he won't listen to my advice. He won't even talk to me."

Nor me.

My eyes filled with tears of pity for Nathan. He was doing his utmost for me and his sister, but he needed to heal more than I did. And I was in no fit state to help him — I was my own mess. And his sleeping pills. . . he had none left because he'd given them all to me. To save me from pain. So self-absorbed, I hadn't noticed that he was hurting worse than me.

Nathan's arms around me were a warm and welcome addition. I hugged him back, wishing I could take away his pain.

"What did you say to her?" Nathan demanded.

I looked up, but he wasn't talking to me.

"I don't know," Chris said. She gave me a meaningful look, like she wished we could continue the conversation.

I wanted the opposite — time to reflect on what I'd learned about Nathan and his family, before asking her any more. After all, Nathan had told her very little about me for some reason — and I didn't want to burst her bubble that she lived in a perfect world where people didn't get hurt, kidnappings resulted in happy endings and rape was something that happened to other people.

I wished I had the same kind of bubble, but my soap

had turned to scum in the hard water I'd been handed and there was no changing it back. Time to clean up the mess and make the best of it. Of course Nathan would stand by me, no matter what, until they were all dead and I was safe. Or would Chris be right, and he'd hurt me before he left me?

I told them both that I wanted to go home.

"Are you sure?" Nathan and Chris asked at the same time.

I nodded.

I'll be right. I have to be.

SEVENTY ONE

Beach - Stars - Sand - Shots - Surf - Chris - Nathan - Numb

I was floating. No pain - nothing holding me down, any more. Something cold touched my face and I opened my eyes slowly. I recoiled from the dark shape hovering over me.

"It's okay. I'm just washing your face," said a voice I barely recognised.

I shivered in what felt like a cold wind. It couldn't be. I looked around fearfully. I looked up, and saw the contrast of pinprick stars on the darker black of the open sky. "Where are we?"

"We're at a beach, out of there, away from them." His voice sounded different, that was why I didn't recognise it immediately. More abrupt, more certain. More authoritative. "There's something I have to do here."

"You got me out. Thank you, Chris!" I felt a surge of joy well up, bringing tears to my eyes, barely able to believe it was possible.

He was silent, and I looked at him to see

the reason for it. I was shocked to see he held my hands in his - I couldn't feel his touch, and they didn't look like my hands - they were twisted and swollen, dark with blood to well past my wrists. As he held my hands, he said, "Can you trust me?"

"Okay." I was surprised that he'd bothered to ask, after all that had happened.

He suddenly turned to face the dunes, looking worried. "Wait here. I'll be back." He got up and jogged off into the dunes, leaving me alone. "...First aid kit..." were the only words I could discern as he took off.

I tried to move, but my body wouldn't respond. There was no feeling left in my legs, and my hands were numb from the wrists down. I tried to call out, to tell him to wait, not to leave me alone like this, but even my voice wasn't strong enough. Just as I started to panic, I heard footsteps approaching me across the sand.

I struggled to sit up, realising too late as I managed it that I was wrapped in a blanket, which slipped off my shoulders, exposing most of my top half to the freezing wind. I clumsily attempted to pull it back up again with my numb, mangled fingers, but failed miserably.

Somehow, I collapsed on the sand again, my head spinning. So cold already, I barely felt him rip the blanket away from me and toss it aside.

I should have fought, but it was like moving through cold water and I was so tired, so tired! "Sadistic prick," I mumbled.

I couldn't even feel the pain any more. I heard a voice, but I didn't care enough to focus on what it meant. I closed my eyes, drifting into sleep.

A sharp pain woke me and I cried out, opening my eyes as I struggled to sit up, convinced I'd been stabbed.

He pushed me back down, his voice an unintelligible sound that I couldn't focus on, but I fought him now, desperate to see if I'd dreamed it.

Then he was gone.

A gun in my hands. I couldn't feel it, had to touch it to my face to be sure I had it.

"End it," I murmured.

A gasp. No.

Tugging, snapping, took it from me. The gun was gone.

Shots.

"Wake up, angel."

Nathan, saying, "It's over."

"Chris..." I mumbled.

"It's all right, he's dead," Nathan replied.

SEVENTY TWO

Nathan dropped me off at home and I made vague excuses to get rid of him. I had a meeting with his boss and I didn't want him involved in it. I hadn't told him I knew his secret and I didn't want to yet. Not before I knew the whole story.

His colleague Navid drove me. He didn't say a word to me for the whole trip. I wondered if that was protocol or personal.

He escorted me to the reception desk, where he handed me a visitor badge. "You need to sign in here and then I'll take you to see Mr Mott." I lifted the pen to sign the visitor book. "Don't trust him."

I looked up. "What did you say?"

He pressed his lips together. "Sign in?" he prompted.

I finished signing in and clipped on my badge as I followed him into the small office area. ASIO didn't have a very big presence in Perth — presumably the rest of their operations were in Canberra.

The office belonged to Paul Mott — it said so on the

door. Navid knocked cautiously on the glass and was told to come in.

He cracked the door open and ushered me inside, closing it behind me.

"So you're the girl my team has been babysitting," Mott said with a wide smile, holding out his hand to shake mine.

I inclined my head and didn't offer him my fingers. He looked like the type who'd crush them in what bastards like him called, "a firm handshake," but was more like an attempt to break the other man's fingers first. As Navid had advised, I didn't trust a man whose smile didn't reach his eyes.

He recovered quickly. "Have a seat," he said, waving at the one in front of his desk. The client's chair, of course. He ensconced himself in his throne behind the desk. I didn't tell him I had the same sort of desk chair in my music room.

"Now, what was it you wanted to discuss with me?" He arranged his face in another insincere smile.

"Why are your team babysitting me?" I asked bluntly.

"I'd have thought that was obvious," he drawled. "You've been the victim of violence and my team are doing their best to ensure it doesn't happen again."

"I don't buy it," I responded. "ASIO doesn't care about a bunch of rapists and perverts kidnapping a girl. And most ASIO operatives don't carry weapons. Even the police wouldn't assign me a guard when someone broke into my house. Your team was there and didn't prevent the break-in, either."

His face gradually developed two pink spots on his cheeks, reddening as I continued.

"ASIO wouldn't hire Nathan Miller. He has too personal a stake in this. And he's trying to get information out of me, but he's so clumsy at it I find it hard to believe he's ever done this before." I wet my lips. "So. Why are your team babysitting me?"

He hesitated. "Protecting you until Nathan gets your valuable information, as you put it."

"Do you think he'll get it?"

His eyes darted away before returning to me. "Do you?" he countered.

I laughed. A politician's answer from the prick. "Perhaps," I replied. I leaned forward. "What will you do if you don't get it?"

"We can't keep babysitting you forever. Sooner or later I'll reassign resources to where the need is greater."

I decided to try being nice. "It might help if you told me exactly what you need. I mean, I can remember a lot of things. The people who were there the day I was kidnapped. What happened on the beach before and after the police arrived. You, telling Nathan not to let the police know things when I was in hospital." I watched him carefully and was rewarded with a shocked glance before he regained his composure. My suspicion grew – Mott was the bastard who'd sent the message to Nathan's phone.

"Standard practice in counter-terrorism," he blustered. "I wouldn't expect a young girl like yourself to know anything about national security. . ."

"No?" I interrupted. "Then why am I their target?"

"I have no idea," he replied smoothly, as if he expected the question. From the blankness of his expression, I guessed that this was an outright lie. "You tell me. Tell me everything you remember, from the number plate of their car to the size of each dick they shoved up your arse. Tell me that and maybe we can catch them. Or I'll assign your babysitters to more important duties and leave you to be raped to death by the terrorists you know are hunting you."

I swallowed, trying to wrap my head around his offensive, hate-filled threat. I had to – or lose my chance to find out what happened.

"Does that include Nathan Miller? Is he operating completely under your orders?"

He didn't meet my eyes for a moment, so I knew the words he uttered next weren't entirely true. "Yes. Everything Nathan does is in response to a direct order." He laughed and flashed his insincere smile. "Why, did you think he loved you? He's our best interrogator, because he'll sleep with the ugliest hag to earn her trust. I heard his informant was hardly a hag – a really hot dominatrix. I bet he had fun. You must have been a real disappointment after her," he sneered. "I didn't expect he'd sink low enough to seduce a child, but he rose to the occasion like no one else. Call of duty." He shrugged.

Oh God – he'd slept with Laura, too. Who didn't she sleep with? Breathe. Even if this was the man who'd tried to get me killed, I couldn't kill Nathan's boss. Not yet, anyway.

"What will you do if I give you my memories? Everything written down, in as much detail as even you could want?" I asked evenly.

His smile set my teeth on edge. "Why, then you'd be doing your country a great service."

I laughed. "The country thanks me. No, I said what will you do?"

"I'll help you disappear into witness protection, so you'll never need ASIO babysitters again."

I stared at him. "You mean leave my life, my family. . . everything? What kind of life is that?"

"One you get to live," he replied smoothly. "You're young enough to transfer to another university in another city without damaging your career. It's not as if you have a lot of family here – relocation won't be hard for you. And, of course, you'll change your name."

"What about my musical career? My band?" I blurted out, horrified.

His eyebrows rose. "I'm sure you can find some musicians in another city who'd be happy to play with you." He shrugged.

I jumped to my feet. "Music isn't a hobby, like photography or writing stories – we're a band. We've written songs together and we perform them. We have gigs lined up here in Perth. I can't just leave that. If you want me to kiss my whole life goodbye, and make me start over in a new city, you're going to do the same for the rest of my band. Hell, I'd want a signed recording contract before I'd agree to that."

He laughed unpleasantly. "Do you have such a contract now?"

"No," I admitted. "But I never will if we have to start over. It took years to get enough exposure here for paid gigs. In a new city. . . who knows how long it'd take? No. I won't go into witness protection. I'll take my chances with my life here. Nathan won't let anything happen to me."

"Miller will work on whatever case he's ordered to. He's not your personal bodyguard." He stared at me like a snake

– not blinking at all. "I have it on good authority that some of your attackers remain free. Are you willing to take your chances with them?"

I swallowed. I wanted a heavily armed chance with Nathan for back-up. Alone and without him. . . I might not stand a chance at all. "Nathan swore he wouldn't let them hurt me. I believe him."

He laughed, taking his time before he sobered and said, "Very sweet. And you believed him? So all your injuries – the ones he failed to prevent – don't hurt at all?"

You fucking bastard. You ordered him to stand by and do nothing while they raped me.

Tears burned my eyes, but I didn't dare shed them in front of this prick. I tried to keep my voice steady. "If I go into witness protection, it'll only be with my band and a recording contract. I'm not asking for an advance – royalties only. I'll even pay for the recording studio for the first album."

He shook his head. "You can't hide in witness protection and be a pop star. It doesn't work like that."

I pressed my lips together. "Do you honestly think my band is the next One Direction? I'll write you a list of indie recoding labels we'll consider, based on their distribution and touring capability. I just want to make a living while I'm at uni. If you prefer, we can discuss ex gratia payments for people who have been significantly inconvenienced by government. I heard people who have been wrongfully imprisoned can get millions in compensation. . ." I watched him grow pale. Apparently young girls like myself normally didn't do their fucking homework either. "I'll change my name, move to a new city and study there. But only with my band and a contract with an independent music label."

"Not enough," he replied. "What about your memories? If you want all that, I want a full account of everything you remember in relation to the terror suspects and your captivity. In writing."

"Then I want our arrangement in writing, too, with details of the recording contract as part of the agreement," I countered.

"We can discuss that at a later date, when you provide said information," he said smoothly, rising to his feet.

"Thursday," I replied, remaining seated. It was time to seriously look at those media offers – if ever I needed a bargaining chip, it was now. I didn't trust him.

He looked surprised for a moment, but his hesitation didn't last long. Maybe I should have asked for more. "Thursday," he repeated.

I couldn't get out of there fast enough.

Navid waited beside the reception desk. "Sign out, turn in your visitor badge and I'll take you home," he said.

We'd been driving for perhaps two minutes when he asked, "Did you get what you came for?"

"Some of it," I answered. I hesitated. "Is he that rude to everyone?"

Navid glanced at me and laughed. "He's not polite, that's for sure."

I wet my lips. I couldn't take Mott down by myself and he wouldn't physically attack me so I could kill him in self-defence. Nor would Nathan do it for me. I needed Navid's help to get Mott charged for his crimes. "He. . . knew things I've never told anyone. Things that happened while they held me captive. The only person who could have told him is dead. I. . . something's not right."

Navid frowned as he looked out of the windscreen at the traffic. "I know he's rude, but to say he's consorting with terrorists is quite an accusation for someone as high up in ASIO as he is."

"I know," I replied in a small voice. "That's why I'm telling you and not making a formal accusation. You told me not to trust him. I don't. He's dodgy and someone needs to find out how he knows these things. . ."

"I'll keep an eye out, Miss Lockyer," he said. "But it's not your problem any more. You should focus on recovering and getting on with your own life. Catching terrorists is our job."

Mutely, I nodded, while crossing my fingers. I'd planted the seed and I only hoped it would take root and flower. If I had my botany right, this was going to be a big, stinking Rafflesia — a corpse flower.

SEVENTY THREE

"Hello?" I answered cautiously, holding the phone receiver to my ear.

"Miss Lockyer? This is Detective McGuinness. I'm sorry I didn't get back to you sooner about the break-in at your house – I managed to pick up a cold somewhere. . . and just as I thought I was fine, my wife caught it, too, and she was in bed for a solid week. She couldn't do anything – I even had to take the kids to school, cook dinner, do all the cleaning. . . I don't know how nurses do it – I've been on chicken soup and tissues duty for a week. It's a relief to be back at work."

"I hope everyone's okay now," I replied politely, wondering what he wanted.

"Back at work and all," he said. "But I didn't call to talk about me. I wanted to know if anything else had happened since the break-in. Did you notice anything missing, or anything in the house that shouldn't be? Had any further intruders?"

I hesitated. Nathan hadn't said anything about keeping Laura's attack secret, but if he hadn't told the police how he and I'd killed four people between us that night, I couldn't just blurt it out. "No, no intruders after last week," I answered truthfully. I didn't have to mention that they'd come back two days running last week. . .

"You keep a look out, and call me if you see anything suspicious," he insisted. "It'd be a hell of a relief if there was anything else you could tell me about what you remember from your captivity. Stuff we could use to track them down, so you wouldn't have to worry about an attack."

"I've been writing down a little of what I remember," I replied cautiously. "I could give you a copy on CD when I see you next."

"That'd be a great help," he said. "I'll have to get back to you on when I can meet with you again. I seem to be snowed under in the office. You'd think I'd been on holidays instead of home sick. . ."

We both said polite goodbyes and ended the call.

I headed back to my room to finish off the Nightmares file so I could give copies to everyone who seemed to want my memories.

One version for the police and Mott, which didn't include a single mention of Chris. From the police to the judge, just like I promised. One complete version for Nathan, omitting nothing.

I paused for a moment. There was one thing I wanted to keep from Nathan, if I could. He felt guilty enough now, with his vague knowledge of what they'd done. He didn't need to know explicit details. I took out every mention of rape and replaced it with other words for the same thing.

Torture. They hurt me. Pain. . . but never admitted to him that they raped me. I imagined the look on his face if he read it. . . and removed the lot. He knew. He didn't need to be reminded. I hoped he never read it.

I set a copy of Nathan's version to print, too, just in case something went wrong with the data copy. A hard copy backup – I wasn't taking any chances. Just as the first page hummed off the printer, I heard Jo's car pull up, perfectly on time.

I headed for the front door to let her in, then led the way back to my room. My work was only half done.

"So, what are you doing?" Jo asked, seating herself on my bed.

I squinted at the screen. "I've been writing down the details of everything they did to me so I can give it to ASIO and the police. Now, I'm checking my emails to see how much I can sell the story for."

"You're selling your story? To who?" she squealed.

I grimaced. "I haven't decided yet. This one's offering the most money, but. . . they want to interview Nathan as well as me. I'm not sure if that's a good idea."

She clapped her hands like an excited child. "Are you serious? It's a brilliant idea. Hell, I'd pay to see his face when you tell people on live television how much of a pervert he is! I still don't understand how you can stand to have him around after all he did to you. You know there's a condition called Stockholm Syndrome that you should really read up on. . ."

I stopped dead and grabbed her shoulders so we were face to face. "Listen to me. Nathan Miller never hurt me – not once. He may have stuffed up a bit and let other people hurt me more than he should, but he's paid for it. He really did save my life, Jo. I'd be dead if it weren't for him."

I itched to tell her the whole story, but I stood by my word as Nathan stood by his. Now, if only he'd stand by long enough to do this interview, I'd have the money to start a new life, far from here and the memories of pain.

She stared at me, as if trying to read my thoughts. I hoped she couldn't – my head held more darkness than she should see.

"I want to believe you," she said finally. "Before this, I'd swear you're telling the truth. Now, I feel like you're hiding something. Fine. Fine. But if I'm supposed to be nice to him as your boyfriend, I won't stand and watch if he hurts you. I'll break both his kneecaps if he so much as thinks about hurting you."

I smiled weakly. "Thanks, Jo. If he hurts me, you can get in line. I'll castrate him first and if I leave him alive, then it's your turn."

She laughed. "That I believe. Though I think you're too nice to kill him. I'll help you, if the time comes."

I forced a smile. Jo didn't know I was already a killer – and she didn't need to, either.

"So, how much are you selling your soul for?" she asked, bouncing back onto the bed.

"My story," I corrected, tapping the screen. "This one is offering two million for an exclusive interview with Nathan and I. Photos, recorded TV interview and all magazine coverage."

She whistled. "Seriously? Take it, take it! With that much money, you could finish your degree without having to work part-time, plus you could even record an album if you wanted to."

"If only Nathan will agree. . ." I mused.

"Test him. Tell him it's a test of his love or commitment or whatever," she suggested.

I shrugged. "I'll try. Hey, I've been working on some new songs while I've been stuck at home. Part of my physio exercise is daily piano practice and Nathan inspired this one. . ."

I led the way to the music room and lifted the lid on the piano. "It's called Necessary Evil."

A smile spread across her face, widening as I played the opening notes of what definitely wasn't a love song.

SEVENTY FOUR

**Beach − Ambulance − Sand − Shots − Surf − Road
− Nathan − Numb**

So cold. So tired.

He made me drink something, full of sugar and bubbles. He asked me irrelevant questions, but he wouldn't even tell me his name.

Shouts and lots of people on the beach. After so much darkness, their bright torches were more than my eyes could handle. Blindly, I clung to him.

Don't leave me, blind, alone and helpless with strangers. I've had more of that than I can take. My eyes filled with tears, the torch beams shimmering and fracturing through them, but I fought to stop them from falling.

I could feel him standing up, lifting me in his arms. I couldn't let go of him. He was the rock holding me steady in this universe of whirling, erratic stars.

I could feel his footsteps on the beach sand, then the sudden jarring of each step as we reached the bitumen.

After only a few steps on the road, bright light exploded overhead. I squinted, trying to adjust to this brightness that hurt my eyes, as Nathan gently set me down on something soft. The feeling of cool, crisp fabric on my exposed skin. I tried to look, but the white sheet blinded me, reflecting the beam from above.

Nathan's gentle hands helped me lie down. My vision blurred as I looked right at the fluorescent light on the ceiling. Then he leaned over me, his face mercifully blocking the worst of it, with the remainder haloing his head like my own personal guardian angel.

As if he took this role seriously, he told me, "You're going to be all right." His voice cracked as he said it, as if he was trying to convince himself.

I smiled at him. Of course I'm going to be all right. I wanted to hug him and tell him thank you, but he moved and the light blinded me again, my eyes watering. By the time I'd blinked the tears away, an ambulance officer had usurped his place.

"Where is he?" I asked this new stranger. He pulled on gloves. I shrank away from the very thought of him touching me, of anyone touching me.

His voice tried to soothe me, as he held his hands up in a gesture of polite surrender. "It's all right. The police have him now. They'll arrest him and lock him in a cell where he won't be able to hurt you. And when he goes to prison, do you know what happens to child molesters and rapists? The other prisoners think they're the lowest of the low. He'll get a bit of his own medicine, and if you're lucky he might not even make it out alive."

He sounded pleased at the thought of what

awaited the man who'd hurt me.

My response was angry. "No! He never hurt me. They can't send him to prison! HE NEVER HURT ME!"

SEVENTY FIVE

Let the world know he's the hero who saved my life. Whatever else he did doesn't matter now. I gave my word.

I focussed on slowing my breathing for the drive to the TV station. Nathan talked non-stop but I didn't listen to him. I had to try and keep the story straight in my head, without opening the dark cesspool of memories. Today I'd tell a story that was only based in truth – the story people wanted to hear.

Some of Nathan's words started to sink in. If you've had enough, end it. Remember what you're protecting him from. A small price to pay for his protection, as long as it's needed. If you've had enough, end it before you can say too much about how it ended.

I let Nathan guide me into the building, my thoughts so full I moved on autopilot.

"Can I help you?" a bored-looking receptionist asked when we stopped by her desk.

It's time. Realisation rocked me and I had to place both

hands on her desk to stay standing. She looked at my hands with disgust, as if they marred the marble with the slightest touch. She had no idea just how deep the taint ran. To the depths of my very soul, if I even had one.

"I'm Caitlin Lockyer," I said calmly. I waited for her eyes to widen as she realised I wasn't simply a child with dirty hands but a dark denizen of realms she could only imagine in her worst nightmares. She didn't disappoint.

"Ffffollow me, please," she stuttered, tottering forward on her impossibly high heels into the studio. "You'll need to go to makeup before your interview and wardrobe, too. . ." Her jerky movements betrayed her fear.

Nathan, I need your help today, more than ever. Don't let me out of your sight.

I took his proffered arm and hoped I wouldn't have to let go. Hope lasted less than a minute.

The round woman was only a tiny bit taller than me, but she looked twice my weight. She directed Nathan to a makeup artist, leaving me standing without support in the middle of the room.

A gleeful girl started working on him.

Wondering who would work on me, I was surprised to find that I had not one, but three. "Get her undressed," the woman in charge ordered.

Get her undressed and you know what to do next. . .

NO! A sob threatened to escape from my throat as I tried to focus on anything but the abyss of memory before me.

An unfamiliar hand with long nails touched my arm. "We're going to make you look absolutely beautiful for your interview, hon. New clothes, makeup and everything. But first, we have to get these clothes off you," she murmured.

We have to get these clothes off you. Then I have to. . .

Darkness and dreams. Stronger than me. Hands beneath my shirt that I was powerless to push away. Trust turned to panic but it was too late. No, please. . . please. . . don't. . .

Nathan.

His hands were warm around mine. His lips were warmer still as he kissed me softly. I swallowed my scream. Safe.

I froze as his fingers moved to unbutton my shirt, baring me to everyone. "You don't have to do this," he murmured.

You don't have to do this. . .

I do.

Yes, I fucking well do. Let them see my scars. They barely scratch the surface, for the damage runs deep.

I held still as Nathan took my shirt off. I stood rigid in the middle of the room and no one said a word. Nathan dropped his hands lower.

"No, I can do this," I warned him, stripping down to my underwear.

The horror on his face spun around the room, from one gasping girl to another.

Don't push me. You have no idea what I've been through.

A dress was passed from hand to hand until Nathan slipped it over my head. No one else wanted to touch me. I understood. Nathan would, because he had no choice.

The wrap dress was beyond him, but I didn't move to assist him. It hung half open when he threw his hands up in despair.

"May I?" one of the girls asked.

I nodded once and her deft hands quickly repaired the damage, tying the dress in a tight bow at my hip.

"Are you sure?" Nathan asked.

Shit, Nathan. It's hard enough telling myself I can do it, without you doubting me. I took a deep breath and let it out before I lost it. I told him I was. I told him I knew what I was doing. I told him to get ready for the interview. And then my courage failed. I couldn't do this alone. "I need you," I admitted.

I wasn't sure if he heard. Nathan turned away from me to return to his makeup artist.

My knees shook, as my legs started to ache from standing so long.

"Sit down, hon," one of the girls whispered, escorting me to the makeup chair beside Nathan.

He turned to me, excitement making his eyes shine beneath his light coat of eyeliner. I felt his fingers close over mine.

"Close your eyes, sweet. It's my turn to make you look even more beautiful than you do already." My grip tightened on Nathan's fingers as I obeyed her.

Nathan's hand slipped from mine and I heard the swish of fabric before he enveloped my hand in both of his. He kissed my fingers and started to apologise.

I cut him off, not wanting to cry with so much makeup on. I waited impatiently for the woman to finish painting me so I could get this over with. Finally, she told me she was done.

My eyes flew straight to Nathan. My reflection wasn't important – would he support me?

His smile said yes.

I managed to force out a smile of my own as I thanked him. I stood up unsteadily and one of the girls sprang to my assistance. I endured her touch but still I reached desperately for Nathan.

It wasn't until he took my arm, giving me the support I needed, that I followed a man in black into the studio.

SEVENTY SIX

I eyed off the armchairs, wanting to sag into one and knowing that I couldn't. I had to sit with perfect posture and poise, as if this was a job interview. In a way, perhaps it was.

"Grab a seat," our escort directed, listening to something over his headset. He waved at the chairs and walked away.

I carefully sat down in the middle chair, where I'd be facing front. The same girl who'd fixed my dress helped me smooth my skirt. "Good luck," she whispered. I managed to smile in response.

I glanced at Nathan to my right. His smile seemed as rigid as mine and his hand tightened over my fingers. Wonderful. My support was as scared as I was. We were screwed. They wouldn't believe a word of our story and a few well-placed questions would pick it apart like frayed hessian.

The interviewer gave a little cough to draw my attention from Nathan. I took a deep breath and turned my head toward her.

From start to finish, it was a carefully scripted exchange, though it followed my script more than the interviewer's one. I wondered if a soap opera like *Home and Away* was more realistic.

"What were you thinking most, in the pain and the dark?" she asked. Her fake sympathy set my teeth on edge.

I summoned a sad little smile. "I wanted to kill them all," I began. I felt considerable satisfaction at her shock. "But I knew I couldn't." I sighed deeply, as if it was my deepest regret.

She gaped for a few seconds, before moving on to the next question. I behaved myself this time, responding with the carefully crafted responses that turned me into a tragic heroine, rescued by Nathan, the big alpha-male hero, like they wanted. It was entertainment – not real.

Nathan stumbled a little over his responses to the first couple of questions, before he fell into his stride. I listened to every word, alert for the tiniest slip that I'd have to step in and correct. Even when he started describing the beach where he'd found me, his description sounded real. Real to everyone but me, for I remembered a clearer picture than he outlined. So did he, I was certain.

Nathan's eyes landed on me and I heard his paean of praise for his plucky little princess: "She's amazing. No matter how much pain she was in, she never stopped fighting to live, to get better. Anything else would mean they'd won."

One glance at the interviewer told me his words didn't help build my image as a fragile little fainting blossom.

Before he could say anything else he shouldn't or the

interviewer could open her mouth to ask another question, I chose to be cruel.

In the same voice I'd used when I'd uttered those fateful words on the beach, I whispered, "End it."

Nathan froze, silent and wide-eyed. I felt sorry for him, but it did the trick. He announced that the interview was over and helped me to my feet.

The black-clad man with the headset pursed his lips up in a kiss, his wide eyes fixed on me as he pointed at us.

I nodded and guided Nathan into a classic pose, seen in a million movies where the hero kisses the girl. And kiss me he did, until the cameraman told us he'd had enough.

Keeping with the fainting flower persona, I leaned heavily on Nathan as we were escorted back to makeup to dress in our own clothes again. I felt like I couldn't breathe freely until we left the TV studio and stood in the sun outside.

"You did it," he said in wonder.

"We did," I replied.

"Miss Lockyer! Miss Lockyer!" The receptionist ran out of the building. "You forgot this!" She handed me an envelope, smiling at me. "You were really brave in there. I hope you're happy together." She scurried back inside.

I ripped open the envelope, knowing what was inside, but needing to check. The first tear revealed the word "million" on the cheque. I didn't need to read the rest to know it was enough.

"What is it?" Nathan asked, curious.

"Our cheque from the TV station for the interview. Would you like to know how much heroism like yours is worth? Half of this is yours, Nathan."

He shook his head, waving the paper away. "No. All of it belongs to you. I did the interview to help you. I don't need any payment for it. It doesn't matter how much it is — it'll never be enough to pay for your pain." He looked like it pained him to say it.

Damn right. No amount of money can pay for pain. But it could help a tiny bit to take my mind off it. . .

SEVENTY SEVEN

Ambulance – Shots – Road – Police – Blood – Nathan – Numb

I pushed hard and sat up, sliding my numb legs to the end of the tiny stretcher, until they dangled out of the ambulance door.

"What are you doing? You need to rest!" The paramedic raised his voice, laying his hands on my shoulders, trying to make me lie down again.

I shook him off, shuddering at the touch of a stranger. Without him, I'd be surrounded by strangers again. Can't... Won't let them hurt me again.

I shoved the blankets away from me and dropped from the end of the stretcher to the road. I wore nothing but the huge, bloodstained shirt, but I didn't feel the cold now. My rage heated my blood to boiling in my chest. I couldn't feel my feet or my legs – it felt like they'd fallen asleep. I wobbled a little, but I took a shuffling step, my toes curling and dragging on the road. And another step...

I could see a police officer pushing him

into the back of a patrol car.

"NO!" I shouted. "Don't take him away from me!" I reached for him, even though he was on the other side off the road from where I stood.

Both he and the police officer heard and turned to look at me. There was a brief scuffle before Nathan pelted toward me.

I managed two more shambling steps before the prone police officer started shouting at Nathan, telling him to stop or he'd shoot. Not to touch me, or he'd shoot.

"NO!" I screamed out as I took one more step. This time I stumbled and fell to my knees.

Nathan was there. He dropped into a crouch to help me back up to my feet. I wobbled a little again, as the officer fired.

SEVENTY EIGHT

"This has got to be a joke." I threw the papers down on the table. "This isn't what we agreed. There aren't any conditions on it. And my new name? What in hell do you think you're doing?" I tried not to shout, but it came out louder than I'd intended. Fury does that to a girl.

"I'm running an anti-terrorism unit is what I'm fucking doing. And if you think this is how the negotiation is going to go, you can fucking leave." Beneath his dark hair, his dark eyes flashed, his face heating up.

I crossed my legs and sat up straighter in the visitor chair on the client's side of the desk. He hadn't even offered me a drink of water, the prick.

"Well, you're *fucking* incompetent, then." I smiled sweetly. "You sent an operative who's clearly suffering from insomnia and the worst case of post-traumatic stress I've ever seen into a dangerous undercover operation. And an innocent bystander gets beaten and raped almost to her death as a result."

"You're not innocent. You killed two people," he spat. "First the bloke on the beach and then his wife."

I'd have loved to chalk up a third right then and there.

I shrugged. "In self-defence. They wouldn't have died if YOU hadn't let them hurt me in the first place."

"Don't you pin Miller's incompetence on me. . ." he blustered.

"He reports to you. You signed off on his fucking competence for the operation. How much training has he had?"

Mott wouldn't meet my eyes.

"*How* much?"

"He's a contractor. He only needed a very basic orientation. . ." His voice was very quiet.

I knew it!

I shot to my feet. "You mean you sent an untrained civilian against the bastards who hurt me? And after he'd completely failed to stop my kidnapping, you assigned him to protect me? Where do you get off with this kind of incompetence? Seriously, if you're the best it has, ASIO is screwed. We should put up a sign – 'Terrorists welcome. Come rape our women and children and mess with the minds of our men.'"

His breathing was heavy and his eyes were on the desk. "I can have you charged for terrorist activity and you'll never go home again."

I snorted. "What will you charge me with? Calling you an incompetent wanker? I bet your staff do that on a daily basis."

"You killed two terror suspects who were wanted for interrogation. They must have known something you didn't want ASIO to hear," he replied weakly.

I leaned over the desk so I could meet his eyes. "Yeah, they knew what it felt like to rape me while I was helpless to stop them. That's something no one wants to hear, unless you get off on that sort of thing."

"You were part of Al Himar!" he insisted.

I stopped dead. "Where did you hear that name?" That was what Laura had called Nathan. He was as crooked as the rest of them. I wondered if it was just the sex or if she'd paid him in money, too. She can't have been that good in bed. It must have been a lot of money.

His grin was fierce. "That's the name of your terrorist group, isn't it? I'm onto you, you little bitch!"

I laughed. "No one calls a terrorist group Al Himar, least of all the people in it, unless they're a bunch of asses. Don't you have an Arabic translator? My Arabic's bad, but even I know what that means!"

He jumped to his feet. Now his face was red. "ASIO do NOT negotiate with terrorists! You can't blackmail me into a recording contract for you and your band! Public celebrity isn't part of witness protection! You'll go into witness protection quietly or I'll. . ."

"You'll what?" I asked. "I like my life as it is. The people who hurt and hunted me are all dead. I'm not at risk any more. If you want me to go into hiding as a favour to you, then you'll deliver the modest conditions I asked for. And a couple more." No normal ASIO staff member would agree to this. If he did, he had a hell of a lot to hide. Like Laura.

"What else do you want?" He looked ready to explode.

"You're going to arrange a television appearance for my band. Then you'll see if anyone notices it's the same girl in my exclusive interview and the music performance. Hell, make sure the band appearance is the same day they air my interview. I bet no one notices." I kept my eyes on him.

"You're not giving a television interview on a matter of national security! I won't let you, you little. . ."

I cleared my throat. "Little tragic heroine, little rape victim, little innocent who suffered as a result of your incompetence? It's not only bought and paid for, it's done. And Nathan sat beside me, answering questions, too."

"You little Arab bitch!"

"My mother was Persian. You want to get racist about this? I'll report you and get you dismissed. Maybe I should add that to what I tell the press. Racist ASIO staff, verbally abusing the tragic little heroine. . ." I watched the words sink in. "That's right."

He swallowed, sitting down heavily. "So you gave a fucking television interview? And he did, too? What did you say?"

"Nathan came out looking like a bigger hero than Superman. As for my interview questions. . ." I smiled. "I don't believe I have to tell you that."

"Like hell you don't!" he exploded. He rose to his feet and leaned over like he was trying to intimidate me.

Maybe before my abduction it might have worked. Somewhere along the line, my fear had died. Anger burned in its place. This bastard had sold both Nathan and I to Laura.

I regarded him calmly. "That's right, I don't. I don't work for you. I don't have to keep anything confidential because all of your so-called terrorists are dead." All but one, I thought but didn't say. "So you can make a deal with me for whatever I'm willing to tell you and my silence after that or you can find out from the front cover of tomorrow's *West*, the same as everyone else."

He thumped down in his chair, glowering as he picked up the pen. "Your. . . demands, then?"

I ticked them off my fingers as I recited them. "First, the contract and television appearance. For the band, of course, not me as an individual. Medical school and a new name. And then there's the matter of Nathan Miller."

"Nathan's our top undercover interrogator – he goes as deep as he needs to in order to get whatever we need. He's not going to take a bribe from you." He dismissed me with a flick of his fingers.

I frowned. "He was damaged when you took him on and he's worse after working for you. What about counselling, helping him find another job? He shouldn't be working on this case or any case like it."

"He took on the job knowing the risks. That's not my problem."

I smiled. "Did he really know the risks? Did he know you'd order him to do whatever it took, including making him hurt another girl the same way they killed his sister?"

His eyes held a touch of fear. "He knew when he took the job. He agreed to do anything he had to in order to save his sister. What are you complaining about? He got you out alive."

My words came out bitter. "You know what he did. He was acting under your orders."

"That's bullshit! He was supposed to watch them kidnap you and take them into custody! Instead, he disappeared. When he turned up three weeks later, it was in a police report with your half-dead body. We had to cover up the mess from whatever he'd done while he was AWOL," he insisted.

I shook my head. "Either he's obeying orders or he's a rogue. You can't have both. I was never the target – it was him they wanted. They set him up to take the blame for a hate crime – against a Persian girl. Me. He was always the target." I saw from the way his eyes flickered that he knew. "And you sent him to his death. Was he just bait to catch your suspects, or did they get to you and offer you something for him? They didn't want to kill him. They threatened his sister so he'd cooperate, but she was never really in any danger. They wanted to turn him into a racist rapist. Then they'd let him kill himself."

"That's not. . . she didn't. . . that's bullshit!" he stammered. He knew she was in charge. Fuck – he really was one of Laura's bastards. He sold Nathan to her. And me. He fucking sold us, like pieces of meat.

"They didn't even know my name," I said softly. "Nathan wasn't supposed to survive, was he? You know, deliberately sending one of your staff to die can land you in jail, under the occupational health and safety laws. I'd say negligence doesn't cut it here – in your case, it'd be murder. But all that goes away if you give him an office job, far from here and this case, like he should have been in the first place. He's so damaged he can't see you're responsible for the mess in his head – but I can. He needs intensive therapy because he's not safe the way he is. You need to reassign him to some other government department where the most traumatic thing he has to deal with is a paper jam in the printer."

I wanted to cross my fingers, knowing that his bigger crime was a matter of national security and nothing to do with safety laws at all. But I didn't dare say it. If he knew, he might risk killing me himself. I needed him angry enough not to think straight, but not angry enough to kill. A hell of a balance for a girl who struggled to walk straight.

He stared at me. "I can't. With his successes on this case, his application for operative training has been approved. Full training and a five-year contract. A television interview will seal the deal – making him a public hero and our best interrogator. There'll be girls paying to get into his pants. . . and they'll tell him anything, just like you did."

No! Not Nathan. He wouldn't make it through training and more of this work – it'd kill him or drive him mad. What would happen to him without me? "Nathan's in more danger than I am – you know he is. This bunch might be dead, but whoever hired them might hire more. He's the one you should send into witness protection – to protect him. Nathan is part of the deal or I'll have none of it."

"First you want your band and now you want to take Miller as your gigolo? Everyone knows you've been fucking him. No wonder he's the best undercover operative we have – he's been busy lubricating your cunt! Pumping you for information, the best way he knows how. He won't turn down the job he's always wanted just to keep fucking a damaged little slut like you. You can shove your deal where you let terrorists shove their. . ."

I stood calmly, wanting to gut the man but restraining myself. "I think you should apologise for that, as a very small beginning. Suggesting I asked to be raped will sink your career like a bad radio DJ. Especially if I leave here and ring the press with the other half of my story. ASIO agents deliberately letting me get hurt so they can catch their suspects, active participants in the abuse, callous about my injuries. . . Whether I have or haven't engaged in sexual intercourse with Nathan is none of anyone's business, least of all yours. But I will tell you for free that I'll never sleep with a man who raped me, no matter what his reasons were. You should check out your surveillance people if they tell you otherwise."

"You little bitch. . ."

I inclined my head. "That's what the so-called terrorists called me and they died for it."

"Are you threatening me?" he spat.

I smiled again. "Finally, you understand. Yes. Prison, losing your job, possible terror charges. . . and death. These are all very real threats and I don't have to be alive to carry them out. I've made some very detailed accounts, entrusting them to people who will release them to the media if I meet with a mishap." I slapped a CD case on the desk. "This is what I'll be giving to the police tomorrow. It's what you've been trying to get Nathan to find out from me, though it's not a complete account by any means. You'll find the dates and requirements for the TV appearance and recording contract on there, too. You have until close of business tomorrow to let me know the details. Or you get to find out what rape's like in prison, because I remember everything that happened. Plenty more that's not on that CD. And if Nathan raped me on your orders, I'll pay your cellmate to do the same to you ten times over for every time he did it to me." I glared at him, praying he wouldn't call my bluff. I knew Nathan had done no such thing, but I hoped Mott didn't.

"Fucking Miller. . . I knew he couldn't keep it in his pants." He swallowed and reached for the CD. "No, wait! Honestly, I can do all of it, except for the bits involving Miller. He'd have to give up his whole career. That's not my call to make. And he'll never do it – not for you. He won't give up everything he's worked so hard for to spend all his life with you and a shrink."

He didn't know Nathan.

I shook my head. "No deal."

"If he raped you, why in hell would you let him anywhere near you?" he asked suddenly.

I thought fast. "He did what he had to. No cruelty, no more pain than necessary. Always because of his orders. And the guilt of what he had to do on those orders eats him up inside, so he'd do anything for me to make up for it. Even kill for me." I gritted my teeth. "He knows he owes me. I want him to pay his debt. And just in case I'm wrong, I want to know where he is. I don't want to be looking over my shoulder, worrying where he might be." I held his gaze until he looked away.

He swallowed a couple of times. When he did speak, he sounded desperate. "All your other conditions, fine, but all I can do is present your offer to Miller. Whether he agrees to counselling and taking an office job near you or the successful career he's earned is up to him."

But I didn't have to ask him to do that. You're going to give him the ultimatum, you prick. I wished I could see his face. . .

I wet my lips. Slowly, I nodded. Nathan had a choice, after all, and forcing his boss to make my offer sounded like fun to me. Proper payback for being a prick. "Put it all in writing and I'll consider it." I stood up. "One thing, though. If Nathan's sister really was in danger, and you believed him when your top interrogator told you she was their next target, why didn't she have anyone guarding her? Why was I the one being babysat?" I didn't wait for an answer. Instead, I left, closing the door carefully behind me.

The walls weren't thick enough to prevent me from hearing his final word on the matter.

"FUUUUUUCK!"

I smiled.

I didn't think he'd keep his job long enough to follow through on all of it – but I was counting on the band arrangements and Nathan. After all, if he was stupid enough to leave evidence on Nathan's phone, surely ASIO could find enough to arrest him.

Navid drove me home from this meeting, too.

"Making him angry will only mean trouble," he said as soon as the building was out of sight.

I shrugged. "He called me a terrorist, an Arab bitch, a slut and damaged besides. He also suggested I'd invited rape. Before he accused me of being a member of a terrorist group called Al Himar."

Navid laughed. "He called you Al Himar? What an ass. We really need to get a translator. Oh, I'm sorry. The rest isn't funny, but that. . ." He collected himself. "For the rest, I'll report him. That's not acceptable. Don't give him any information – keep it to yourself until we get this sorted."

"I already gave him a copy of everything I remembered – what Nathan's been trying to get out of me," I admitted.

Navid shook his head. "You shouldn't have done that.

Several records of interrogations have disappeared in this case – including ones on Laura, the woman who. . ."

"Died," I supplied. "He knew things that he can only have heard from Laura. Someone needs to investigate him – I think he sold Nathan and I to her."

He looked grim. "I've told you before – that's a very strong accusation to make."

I glared at him. "Would you arrange a music recording contract and a TV appearance for someone you were forcing into witness protection?"

He laughed. "Shit, no! That'd be stupid. What's the point of witness protection if you're not going to hide the witness? It'd be like telling the people that want to kill you exactly where to find you. . ." He stared at me, realisation hitting hard. "Keep copies of everything. Get Nathan to do the same."

I took a deep breath. "I'll give Nathan a copy of everything I gave Mott, too. And other people have copies. Just in case. And then I'll go into witness protection and hope to hide." I paused, not wanting to consider that Mott was right about Nathan's feelings for me. "Is it true that Nathan's been offered full operative training and a five year contract? And he won't be able to contact me while he's working for ASIO?"

Navid shrugged. "I have no idea. Applications are handled in Canberra. If he has, and you disappear. . . it's true that we aren't permitted to consort with contacts, witnesses and suspects outside of standard work arrangements. You won't see or hear from him, especially if you're in witness protection." He glanced at me. "You should ask Nathan about that."

I shook my head. "No. Nathan has no idea I know who he works for and I think he prefers it that way. Mott's going to negotiate that with Nathan. He said. . . Nathan will take the job."

Navid snorted. "And you believed him?"

I didn't say anything. I wanted to believe that Mott was a blatant liar as well as a bastard, but I also wanted to believe that Nathan had been operating under his orders. . . until he disobeyed them to help me. Only Nathan could tell me the truth.

I wasn't sure I wanted to know.

SEVENTY NINE

As Navid pulled out of the driveway, I called Jo. Jason answered instead.

"Just who I wanted to speak to," he drawled, as I thought the opposite. "How long before you think you can play? We'll lose our Freo gig if you can't in two weeks. . ."

"A gig in Fremantle won't last long," I replied impatiently. "I've arranged us a recording contract and a live performance in Melbourne next Friday. I need to talk to Jo and we need to book flights, accommodation. . ."

"You got us a recording contract? How?" Jason shrieked.

"Give me that," Jo demanded and her voice grew louder. "Caitlin? Why does Jason seem to think we have a recording contract?"

"We don't yet, but we will by next week," I replied. "Part of. . . the interview that's airing next week. It's a long story, but it's true. We'll sort out the contract details next Friday morning and we have a live TV appearance scheduled for that evening in Melbourne. If all goes to plan, we'll spend the following week recording our first album."

"I. . . don't believe it," she admitted. "How?"

"I can't really say," I hedged. I wondered if my phone was tapped. "Come over and we can discuss the details. We also have to book the flights. . ."

"I'll be right over," she responded. "Bye."

Fifteen minutes later, she was indeed over and I was able to show her Mott's email, confirming what I'd told her, including the name of the label we were apparently signing with.

She reread the email twice, shaking her head. "I thought you'd have to sleep with, kill or blackmail someone to get a contract like this, but you. . ."

Did all three. I forced a smile. "I should have discussed the terms with you and Jason first, but this is a better contract than we'd get any other way. Do you think you'll be able to go to Melbourne next week?"

She laughed. "I've already rung work to take the time off. We need to get you some new clothes before we do anything else – Melbourne shopping is just what you need. I think we should leave tomorrow if we can."

The last bastard would have to wait. If he turned up at all – he might be sitting under a rock somewhere, where slimy things like him hide. "Okay," I replied, my heart feeling lighter.

"You're not bringing Nathan, are you? I'm not dragging him shopping," she said.

I hadn't even thought about Nathan. I tried to hide my shock. "I. . . haven't even mentioned it to him. It's not like I'll need him in Melbourne." I swallowed, suddenly feeling very alone. Witness protection might feel just as lonely, if Nathan chose his career over me and his own health.

"Cool. Let's head up to the travel agent's and sort out our flights and accommodation."

EIGHTY

Ambulance – Shots – Road – Police – Blood – Nathan – Numb

Blood blossomed on Nathan's shoulder, painting a red flower on the chest of his shirt. He looked horrified.

I threw myself on top of him, knocking him over, so both of us lay flat on the road.

My breath caught in my throat. Was he shot in the heart or lungs? I wanted to pull off his shirt and check the damage, but getting my weird, twisted, numb hands to grasp his shirt was hard to do.

"Don't leave me," I told him raggedly.

He gaped like a fish out of water. His mouth moved but no words came out.

Please, not his heart or lungs. Please don't let me watch this man die for helping me.

After a few moments, he made an effort to speak. "It's all right." He forced the words out. He said something else, but it was drowned out by the shouting behind him, between the police officer on the ground and two of his colleagues. They made him hand over his weapon, pinning him to the ground like some kind of criminal.

You shot the man who helped me, you bastard.

Nathan's shirt was saturated with blood. I'd never felt more helpless, unable to help myself or this wounded man. This man I desperately didn't want to die. I needed him alive.

My voice was hoarse, partly from emotion and partly from shouting earlier. "You said you'd never let them hurt me again. You promised."

He just stared back at me, agony on his face.

I tried to shift his shirt clear of the wound, so I could see where he'd been shot, but my hands wouldn't cooperate. He pulled my hand away from his shirt, looking sad.

"Please..." I began, shifting off him and back onto my knees. I touched my fingers to the road to steady myself, then realised that the road was wet and my hands were damaged, so I lifted my hand away, but it came away red. Fresh blood, pooling on the road. How could he lose so much blood and stay conscious?

The world slid sideways and went dark.

EIGHTY ONE

I debated whether to tell Nathan about the trip, the contract and the new life I'd be living in Melbourne, then realised I couldn't. His boss was supposed to make the offer to him and he might not have said anything yet. Part of witness protection was not telling anyone – I couldn't even tell Nathan.

Fate had other ideas. Detective McGuinness called, asking for both my memories and my ability to identify my attackers. Apparently someone had noticed suspicious activity near an old World War II bunker in some bushland down south. When the local police had gone in to investigate, they'd found dead bodies and evidence of someone being held captive in one of the bunker chambers, so they'd called him in.

He didn't need to say it. I already knew he'd found where they'd held me. A forgotten war bunker, which had probably seen no violence or action until my advent. Hopefully it never would again.

His voice went all funny as he said they'd had some help from ASIO in identifying what were apparently terror suspects. Did I still have that ASIO operative watching my every move?

I wondered how to tell him that Nathan was with me, without letting Nathan know I knew who he worked for.

"Just put me on speakerphone so he can hear me," the Detective said after a moment, probably guessing my dilemma.

I let him repeat a much abridged version of the story he'd told me, followed by an urgent entreaty to identify the bodies on Monday.

No, not Monday. I'd be in Melbourne.

I stammered an excuse, without saying where I'd be. "Tomorrow, maybe?" I suggested.

"We have a relative coming in at two, so maybe. . . at three? Would that be too late for you? It's probably best that you don't meet him, especially if you identify his son as one of the men who. . ."

My money was on Simon. The last remaining bastard. I swore to pack a knife. I'd stabbed him once and this time I'd make sure it was fatal. He'd feared me from the start and so he fucking should.

My eyes darted to Nathan, silently asking him if he'd help me tie up this one last loose end. He nodded, as if he understood completely. A man who'd kill for me. Could anyone ask for more?

I'd miss him in Melbourne – and every day if he chose to stay here instead of come with me. Could I blame him for choosing his career over me, a girl so damaged I didn't know if I'd ever be right again?

I held out hope, all the same. Life had been cruel enough to me lately – maybe I did deserve to have a heart and some kindness, after all that had come my way.

One more man to kill. . . and my bad luck would end.

EIGHTY TWO

I checked the CD before I gave it to Detective McGuinness. He shot strange glances at Nathan, like he suspected more than either of us told him, but he didn't say it outright. Then he pulled out pictures of the bastards – all of them taken in what I recognised as my house. I identified the pictures as best I could, but this was one time the perpetual darkness was far from my friend. I'd never seen some of their faces – Simon included. I knew their voices and hands in the dark, but dead men had neither voices nor sexual preferences.

I looked long and hard at the police officer who'd shot Nathan, who he said had also shot at me. I hoped he was the son Simon had spoken of – and I hoped that Simon was here. I wondered if he was one of the people I'd seen earlier, but I hadn't recognised any voices. I needed him to speak before I could kill him.

When we headed out into the car park, I despaired of seeing him. Maybe Simon was hiding, far from my reach. I'd brought the knife for nothing and I'd never be safe.

"Excuse me."

Two words that both froze me and made my day.

I saw the gun pointed at Nathan – he aimed it too high for me to be his target – as he said, "You killed my son. Give me the girl."

"I don't know what you're talking about. . ." Nathan protested.

"I do."

I slipped the knife from its sheath in my sleeve, feeling the hard handle in my palm.

He kept the gun aimed at Nathan as he repeated, "Give me the girl."

"Let me do this," I murmured to Nathan, hoping he'd pull out his weapon if I needed him to. I detached Nathan's arm from mine with some difficulty and strode forward.

It's not the girl you'll get, but what she wants to give you.

"No, don't hurt her. . ." Nathan sounded like Chris, all over again.

The idiot kept his gun pointed at Nathan over my shoulder.

"You killed my son," he whimpered.

I had no sympathy for him. This bastard had almost killed me and so had his prick of a son.

"No. Nathan killed him for me. And he'll kill you, too, if you so much as look at me wrong. But I owe you something. Something I promised, if you ever touched me again." I jabbed low and hard, putting my full weight behind the blow. I felt the blade sink deep into his groin. I yanked it out again. "Now, you dickless bastard, I can keep stabbing you until you die of your wounds or you can take the easy way out. You so much as touch me and Nathan will shoot you. For me."

I saw the fear in his eyes. Fear and pain. I almost felt pity, but then I remembered. He hadn't even had the guts to see the same in my eyes as he raped me in the dark.

I watched impassively as he stuck his gun in his own mouth and ended his misery.

"Good riddance, Simon," I spat. I turned to Nathan, more relieved than I could say. "Now it's over and I'm safe." I relaxed in his arms, before I realised what time it was. "I have to get to the airport, Nathan."

He looked from me to Simon's body and back to me, stammering the start of several sentences but not finishing a single one.

I didn't have time for him to make an excuse, or explain to me what he'd hidden. Wishing I didn't have to, I said gently, "You have friends to call, to clean this up. That's what they're good at, isn't it? Tell them you have the last one."

I wanted to kiss the shocked look from his face and tell him everything, but I didn't dare. When I got back from Melbourne — after Mott had made my offer. When maybe Nathan would agree to come with me. "I need to get to the airport. May I borrow your car? I'll leave it at my house, with the keys on the table inside the front door. You know where I keep the spare house keys. You can get a lift with your colleagues, right?"

He didn't want to stay and deal with the mess. He wanted to come with me, but he couldn't.

Not yet. Maybe. . . My heart hoped.

He gave me his keys and I remembered the CD I'd wrapped in the printout for him. On every page I hadn't given to the police, I'd written as much, so he'd know what I had and hadn't told anyone. I didn't tell him about the copy I'd given to Mott – if it still existed. Crooked Mott might have destroyed it already.

In the papers I'd told him how to meet me, too, if he wanted to see me again, one last time before I left for good. When he could tell me what his answer was to Mott's offer.

As I drove away, I couldn't take my eyes off his reflection in my rear-view mirror. I wanted him to choose me.

EIGHTY THREE

Our first morning in Melbourne, Jo told me, "I'm not sharing a room with you any more. You thrash around so much in your sleep. . . and you even screamed a couple of times. I'd rather share a room with Jason – and the last time I did that, I found another girl asleep in my bed one night. I'm sorry, but I just can't."

I nodded silently. I understood. I didn't know how Nathan had managed to stay in the same room as me when I had nightmares.

"Will talking about it help?" she asked timidly. "Can you tell me anything about your ordeal?"

I stared at my best friend. It'd never occurred to me to tell her about the horrors I'd seen – though I'd easily have told her anything before it. But I couldn't burden her with the knowledge no one should have. Nor did she need to know I'd killed people. Nathan knowing was bad enough. "No, Jo. They hurt me and. . . you don't want to know."

"Does Nathan know?" she demanded, snatching up the

room keycard as we headed downstairs for breakfast.

In the mirrored lift, it was hard to avoid her eyes. "Vague details of most of it, yes. There are some things I just can't tell anybody."

I found her staring at me. "He really didn't do it, did he? I mean, if he had, he'd know everything already. . ."

"Jo," I warned her.

Her hands flew up in surrender. "Fine. Forgive me for maligning your sleazy boyfriend. Jason's going to be heartbroken when he finds out you're sleeping with Nathan instead of him. You know he's had a crush on you since high school."

"Nathan's not so sleazy. I haven't. . . we haven't. . . I can't yet. One day, maybe. . ." I tried to keep my head down to hide my blush as we entered the hotel restaurant. Jo gave the waitress our room number and we followed her to a table.

I walked around the breakfast buffet, avoiding her, but I loaded my plate up quickly and had to return to the table.

"But you want to," she said, lifting her cup of coffee to her lips.

With my mouth full of strawberry yoghurt, I nodded emphatically.

After breakfast, we asked the hotel and managed to upgrade our room into an apartment, though we paid for the privilege. As we headed to the first shop on Jo's long list, she interrogated me on style.

"Are you trying to match the look from the TV interview or are you going for the complete opposite? Do you want people to recognise you? What did you wear for the interview?" she demanded.

I explained the minimal makeup and modest, mulberry-coloured dress I'd worn to the interview. "For the interview, they made me into a delicate little doll, someone to be rescued by a hero. If I'm trying to hide in plain sight, I need something completely different."

Jo laughed. "More realistic, you mean. If you're a doll, you're made of Kevlar."

I wished for my not-an-angel t-shirt that I'd worn the day they took me, but that was long gone. It did give me an idea, though. "Didn't the newspaper articles describe me as an angel?"

Jo snorted. "Yeah, the Absent Angel. Like you were just going to waltz back into life. Some really stupid journalist came up with that one."

I glanced around and there was no one within earshot. I still kept my voice low. "Did you know that all of my kidnappers have conveniently turned up dead?"

Jo glanced at me. "That hasn't made the news."

I gave a tight little smile. "No, nor will it. That's confidential – something ASIO and the police are keeping quiet."

Now she didn't look at me at all. "How do you know? Did you. . . ?"

"I've seen the bodies," I replied honestly, my tone flat.

"Well, I'd say the angel of death is really into you, too. Your Nathan had better watch out."

I laughed a little. "Consort to the angel of death, or the angel of death herself. Black's a good colour for a musician – I say we go with it."

"Caitlin, the angel of death? I'm not going to be able to keep a straight face!"

I shook my head slowly. "No. I'll have a new name. I won't be able to use mine any more." Hesitantly, I told her the new name I'd need to get used to.

"That sounds familiar, though. Isn't that. . . another girl who was in the news last year? The one who died?" she asked, worried.

"Spelled differently, but yes," I admitted. "Shouldn't the angel of death have the name of a dead girl?"

Jo lost it laughing. "A reincarnated dead girl, consort to the angel of death. She's going to have one hell of an afterlife. "

"Starting with a live TV performance of her band's song," I replied.

She laughed harder. "What if we hit it big? I mean, we won't. . . but we could! An afterlife as a rock star!"

I summoned a smile. "There are worse things." I tried not to think about such things, though. Today was not a time to be sad, when the future seemed so bright.

A new name and the prospect of a new life – new clothes seemed like very little in comparison. I hadn't counted on Jo's lust to replace my entire wardrobe, though.

The second night, after I'd closed the door of my lonely room, I slipped the sheathed, cleaned knife from my bag to beneath my pillow. I slept with the light on and wished Nathan was beside me.

The interview cheque had cleared, so I had more money than I was used to for clothes. I was glad we'd arranged extra luggage for the trip home – I had double my luggage allowance after three days of shopping. I hoped Jo would quit soon – I wanted to see more of Melbourne. I'd heard that they had a really good zoo, plus I wanted to practice for our Friday performance.

Jason flew in on Thursday morning, asking happily who he got to share a room with.

Jo sweetly told him he had the couch. I heard her pull him aside and warn him not to make the slightest come-on to me, for fear of his life.

The rest of the day we spent rehearsing Necessary Evil, my new song. Jo had insisted, I'd been pleased and Jason didn't dare argue. I caught him humming the quirky chorus a few times at dinner, which meant it was catchy enough to stick in his head. I hoped it'd have the same effect on other people when they saw our live TV appearance the following night. If not, we'd be wasting our time and my money in the recording studio next week.

That night, I locked my bedroom door and made sure the knife stayed under my pillow, in easy reach. Jason tried the door after Jo had gone to sleep, but the lock held.

Every night, I missed Nathan, counting the days 'til I could go home.

If he did his training in Canberra while I lived in Melbourne, surely I could still see him. It was only a few hours' drive. We'd make it work, if he wanted.

Please, Nathan. . . I want you to want me.

EIGHTY FOUR

"Can I call you Jay? Tell me a bit about your band. I've never heard of you before and this is my first interview. I used to do the weather for the news before *Today Tonight*," the girl positively gushed.

I touched up my dark lipstick, my equally dark smile keeping the makeup artists at bay. I was still getting used to the gothic style makeup, but it seemed to be effective. They'd been advertising my interview with Nathan all week, with shots of me smiling and looking scared. Some of the ads talked up the mystery man from the newspaper, a big question mark over Nathan's blurred photograph. If anyone was going to recognise me, surely it was the network's own staff.

"Miss?"

I regarded the wardrobe supervisor without speaking.

"Do you need any assistance with makeup or wardrobe? They're waiting for you in Studio 3."

I nodded. "This will be fine." I glanced at Jason, who

was still flirting with the anchor girl.

"I can't wait to hear it," she said with a giggle.

I wondered if there was an IQ test for news anchors. Surely the girl couldn't be as stupid as she sounded. No one could be. . .

With one final spritz of Jo's hair, her makeup artist smiled. "All ready to go."

A black-clad man gave me feelings of déjà vu as he gestured the way to the studio. I stalked forward, regretting the combat boots Jo had talked me into. They were a nightmare to walk in. I consoled myself with the thought that I could kick a hole in any man's groin while wearing the platform-soled, knee-high monstrosities.

Fuck YOU boots.

After so many hours of playing this song to heal my hands, I could barely wait for Jo to set the beat before I launched into the intro.

Jason sang better than he had in any of our rehearsals – only one tiny mistake, which even I barely noticed. Perhaps it was the little fangirl of a news anchor he kept winking at throughout the performance. She squealed as she applauded at the end.

I felt sick just watching her, but she completely ignored me. She had eyes and ears only for Jay – and for one more wink she'd probably give him the rest of her body, too.

Jo and I had a coffee in the green room afterwards, watching Jason's interview on the screens. The flirty bastard looked like he was ready to jump the poor girl on the interview couch, cameras rolling and all. He ended the interview with a showy kiss to her hand, like something out of a romance novel. She fanned herself with her other hand as if he gave her the vapours. She was too young for it to be hot flushes.

"Looks like you have competition," Jo said softly.

I looked at her in disbelief. "Jo, you know I don't want your brother."

She looked pained. "I know you keep saying that, but somehow I figured that one day you'd change your mind. He's not a bad person and he's been obsessed with you since he met you, back in primary school."

I shook my head. "Maybe that's the way it would've been, but things are different now. I'll never be the same and I'll never be happy with Jason." I looked at her sad expression and winked. "Come on, if I loved both Nathan and Jason, we'd have one of those fucked-up love triangle things that only happen in books. This is real life, not a story for teenagers."

"We're adults, but we're still teenagers," she pointed out.

I shifted uncomfortably. "Yeah, but. . ."

"Come on, you two, after all that playing I need a shower," Jason interrupted, a cheerful grin on his face as he hefted his guitar case. The rest of our gear was packed into the trolley he pushed in front of him.

"So, did you get her phone number?" I asked nastily.

Jason looked smug. "Yep. Phone number, a date for tonight and an offer to stay at her place when she heard you were making me sleep on a couch." He seemed uncertain at my shock. "I'll cancel if you promise to come instead." Jason's smile crept back. "Yeah, pun intended."

I considered the offer. I really did. He meant it. "No, Jason. You have a great night and we'll see you tomorrow some time." I meant it, too.

I didn't see him tomorrow. Neither Jo nor I saw him for three days – until we reached Tullamarine Airport, just before our flight home to Perth. He looked like he hadn't slept much, but he didn't look upset about it, either.

"The studio got thousands of messages after our performance," he told us as we lined up to check in.

They recognised me. I'd never play live again. Shit.

"Did people like our song that much?" Jo asked brightly.

"Ah, mostly they liked me," Jason admitted proudly. "The rest of them hated Paige. They said some really horrible stuff about her. And most of them were teenagers."

"Paige?"

"The girl I met at the TV studio. The one who interviewed us," Jason explained. He turned red.

The next One Direction. Oh, fuck.

I started to laugh. "Way to go, Jason! You're the cream of the jailbait fangirls, if they're sending death threats to your girlfriend!"

He didn't look so happy after that.

If life were like a book, I'd have felt jealous, surely. Instead, I simply shrugged. "As long as they buy the CD, the fangirls are all yours, Jason. We'll put a photo of you on the cover."

I'd had enough media exposure to last a lifetime. Jason was welcome to it – fans included.

EIGHTY FIVE

We arrived early, so we both took a seat in the back of the church to watch the wedding. All the family seemed to be the groom's and there were no bridesmaids – just a grumpy little flower girl, dressed up like a doll-sized version of her mother. I envied the bride her beauty and her breasts, her happiness and her loving husband.

"Those boobs are huge. I bet he can't wait to get her out of her wedding dress," Jason whispered loudly.

I glared at him, but didn't say anything.

"Please rise to welcome Mr and Mrs Fisher!" the priest called out and I rose along with the Fishers' invited guests.

As the couple passed out of the church, her eyes met mine. Hers held sympathy for my sadness, as if she knew me and she shared similar pain. She inclined her head to me and I responded in kind. Then she turned away, stepping into the sunlight outside with her new husband. I remained in the darkness, where I belonged.

I kept checking my watch as four thirty approached,

wondering if I should have told Nathan to meet me in the church instead of just giving him the address. A church on a Saturday afternoon meant weddings like the one I'd just witnessed – I didn't want to give him the wrong idea.

Marriage wasn't what I had in mind.

"Do you think the boobs were real?" Jason asked in a normal voice, now we were alone in the church.

"Weren't you going to go to reconciliation?" I replied, irritated. I should never have told him about my meeting with Nathan.

"What, and desert you before your boyfriend turns up to break up with you? I'm here to keep you company and be your moral support. A shoulder to cry on and all that shit." His wicked smile didn't charm me any more. He just wanted to see me say goodbye to Nathan, I was sure.

From the shadows, I could see the wedding party outside, taking photographs on the steps. Movement on the footpath drew my attention and I moved into the foyer for a closer look.

Nathan scanned the wedding guests, as if looking for me. The anguish on his face told me more than anything else he could say. He'd made his decision and he was going to hurt me for the first time. I froze, not wanting to move. I wanted to remain in the dark and not know the truth, if only for a few moments more.

He stepped inside, from daylight to darkness, and he didn't seem to see me standing at his side. I reached for his hand, hoping it wouldn't be the last time. He pulled back, as if the contact was unwelcome, splashing his hand into the holy water font. I helped him cross himself with the water, babbling about baptism and other things I'd learned in religious education at school. I wasn't sure I believed in any religion any more. Not my mother's Islam, nor Dad's Catholicism.

Feeling shaky already, I made some excuse to lead Nathan deeper into the church so I could sit down. Years of Catholic schooling had trained me well, though, and I dropped to my knees instead of sitting in the pew. Once down, I didn't want to rise. Eventually, my babbling died as I ran down.

I glanced at Jason. He bowed his head as if in prayer, letting his long hair fall forward to hide the gleeful smile on his face. His hair was longer than mine. He looked like a ranger out of a Tolkien novel, instead of my sleazy lead singer.

Fuck off, I mouthed at him. This conversation was hard enough without an audience.

Ceremoniously, he ascended from his genuflection to march down the aisle, piously keeping his eyes on the stained glass behind the altar. I didn't say a word until he'd closed the door of the confessional behind him.

Now alone with Nathan, I still couldn't bring myself to ask him – and start the conversation I dreaded would end in *goodbye*.

Once more, Nathan came to my rescue.

"Caitlin, I'm so sorry."

I turned to see he knelt beside me. "Chris..." I hadn't said the name aloud since that night in the toilet, but it held more meaning than any name should. I summoned all my courage. I needed to know. "Why did you do it, Nathan?"

"It was my job to watch them kidnap someone and get out with the witness. But I didn't – couldn't – *didn't* know what they'd done to you until that night on the beach. Then it was too late. I'd let them hurt you like that and I hadn't done a thing to stop them."

It was his job. He did it to protect his sister. He wasn't a bad person – he'd simply been ordered to let fucked-up things happen. But how far did orders go?

"Why did you kill him?" I asked next. Was that orders, too? Or was that when you decided to try and make up for what you'd done? I pressed my lips together so I didn't ask the other burning questions.

"I thought it was for Alanna, or even for me. Maybe it was for you. I... just... couldn't let him live... knowing... what he did... and what I didn't. How I'd failed."

You ended it for me and for your own conscience. Now for the general knowledge question. We both know the answer, but are you the super-sleazy interrogator or the honest man I trust? "Why me, Nathan? Why did they choose me?"

"I couldn't take my eyes off you," he whispered as he stared at the floor. "I couldn't stop them." He swayed, as if he was trying to rock away his pain.

I pitied him. I'd seen his anguish before, but it was worse now that he knew everything I'd been through. I never should have given him the account of what they did to me.

"You helped me recover from it. You even saved my life. Maybe one day..." I thought of the happy couple I'd seen earlier and hoped he couldn't see my blush. I tried to say something else, but I couldn't think of anything. "I'll be able to... I... forgive you for it." There. I'd said it.

Absolution, Nathan. Don't feel guilty about me. You've

paid for your sins against me and I forgive you. Now you can go and further your career like you want to without feeling you owe me anything, any more.

Oh, fuck, now I was going to cry...

I lurched to my feet and ran out of the church, furiously blinking the tears away.

I heard his footsteps behind me, but I didn't stop until I was certain I had my eyes under control.

"I'm sorry. I'm so sorry."

I knew he'd take the job. Even if he did care for me, he wouldn't put his life on hold for me any more. I reminded him too much of his mistakes. And when did he ever pay attention to his own health? It's not like he'd even mentioned the nightmares to me.

I looked up at him and permitted myself one last indulgence. I might never get to do this again. After today, I'd probably never see him again. I kissed him. The passion in that one kiss was more powerful than any I'd witnessed during the wedding this afternoon, but our only witness was Jason, rapidly walking away because he didn't want to watch.

I broke the kiss, forcing myself to step back. "Goodbye, Nathan." I turned and drove my feet away from him.

"I love you, Caitlin." His voice held desperation.

But not enough to stay with me. "I know." My voice died to a whisper and I couldn't turn to face him. "Under better circumstances, I think I could have loved you, too." Liar. It didn't matter what he'd done. I loved him and I wanted him to choose me. To fight for me, one more time.

I forced myself to keep walking, every step a necessary effort. Tears streamed down my cheeks, but I didn't dare stop. I made it to the side door of the pub before I gave in to them properly, sobbing my heart out for a few minutes where no one could see me. I couldn't face Jason right now.

Jo and Jason were waiting. It was time to go back to work, I told myself, straightening up and wiping the tears away with my hands. I slipped into the toilets out the back to wash and dry my face, hoping I looked normal. I locked myself in a toilet cubicle to get changed. I slid the white dress down to puddle at my feet and pulled on the tightly fitted black dress that I reminded myself was a work uniform. I kept the knife sheathed at my thigh, within easy reach yet still hidden from view. The boots were next — something Jo had gloatingly called New Rocks, all black leather and metal. Then I slid on the feathered black wings Jo had bought me in a costume store. The angel of death indeed.

I washed and dried my face again, just in case, and put on enough eye makeup to masquerade as a panda. Real cute, but one swipe and I'd take your head off. I carefully painted my lips the colour of venous blood. The effect was dark and disturbing. The girl in the mirror looked like a stranger to me. I smiled and my reflection looked sinister, like she was planning to kill me slowly or take off with the contents of my bank account.

Or tell the man who'd saved her life and killed for her that he didn't deserve her, so she could walk away from his rejection with her dignity intact. As if he hadn't smashed her heart.

The smile vanished. I stuffed my other clothes and makeup into my bag quickly, before I left the toilets and went in the pub's back door.

As I crossed the half-full pub, there was no sign of recognition from the beer-sipping denizens. Who would mistake the innocent little victim they'd seen on TV for the vengeful dark angel stalking across the room?

No one.

Jason had set up the equipment already when I reached the stage. He looked relieved to see me, his easy smile lifting his lips. "Damn, you look like the angel of death. You can fuck me to death any night you want to name."

"Fuck off, Jason. Find yourself a fangirl to fondle you after the gig."

"Caitlin." He grabbed my arm, his voice low and urgent. "I'd be good to you. I'd show you a heaps better time than that crazy, perverted prick. He was a necessary evil while you were recovering, but now I..." He stopped when he felt the cold, hard blade against his balls.

"... don't need your balls to sing?" I asked sweetly. "Just think of all the high notes you'll hit if you EVER touch me without my permission again. Or if you ever say another word about Nathan. As far as I'm concerned, the necessary evil in my life is you, for the duration of this recording contract." I hid the blade with my sleeve as I tucked it away again. He didn't need to know that he'd only felt the sheath and not the blade itself. "You won't be the first bloke I've castrated, either. And I sleep with that knife. Do your job and you can have all the fangirls you like afterwards."

His eyes widened in something like fear. Perhaps the gothic makeup had its uses, after all. Or maybe it was Laura's knife. My knife now.

"Let's kick off with a cover of *Nobody Sees*. The duet we practiced," I told him.

I sat behind the keyboard as he started with just his guitar, his solo of the first verse.

It was Jason's voice I heard, but my thoughts were of Nathan. My heart felt shattered at the thought of what I'd said and done today, however necessary.

I closed my eyes as I started singing the second verse.

"...*Who will be there at the end?*"

It's over. I heard the words he spoke in my memory as I realised it was over. This was the end of it. My voice failed and Jason sang the chorus alone.

He repeated it, drawing it out to give me a minute to get it together. I shook my head, put the pain into my voice and I found it helped.

"...*FALL DOWN at your feet?*"

He repeated the line until I remembered I was supposed to stand up. The final time he dropped to his knees in front of me, just vocals with no guitar for the last chorus.

I looked down at Jason for a second, before he stood up again and launched into another Powderfinger song, the upbeat one that we always followed this with.

Jo sat at her drums, smiling encouragingly at me. I hadn't seen her there until she started playing.

Nobody got to see my heart break. Damn right. I returned her smile.

This'd be our last gig in Fremantle. Next week we'd fly back to Melbourne and hope something would come out of the new contract.

Jo and Jason launched into Necessary Evil and I allowed myself to smile. I wasn't going to lose it on this one – I'd sing it the whole way through, my heart in every note.

For Nathan. For me. For the necessary evil and my hope that one day I'd truly be free.

EIGHTY SIX

I found the papers in my bag the next morning, under the clothes I'd stuffed into it when I got changed for the gig.

The writing on the first page was Nathan's and it was rough.

**I started writing down my nightmares, too.
I thought you should know.**

The pages beneath were all word processed, a printout of something he'd typed. I sat down and read it.

Normal nightmares are never this clear and constant. I only close my eyes and I'm there again, so real it's heartbreaking. And I can never change what happens, no matter how much I want to.

Mike found me first. "Here," he said as he threw something to me.

I caught it without thinking. I recognised

the keys to my car and looked at him, wanting to ask why he'd given me the keys back, when I was on my way to see her.

"You'll need the car to dump the body when you're done with her. One more fuck and you'll wear her out." He grinned. "Don't let that stop you. She's better alive than dead."

I didn't bother to reply.

It was late at night and without the moon it would've been pitch-black outside the house. I wondered if she was awake yet. I walked faster through the bush than usual, taking the steps into the old underground bunker two at a time. I crossed what I thought was the weapon storage room and slowly opened the door to the sleep quarters, not bothering to shut it behind me.

I could hear her laboured breathing, telling me where she was, but I couldn't see her in the gloom. My toes brushed something and I fell to my knees, feeling for her with my hands. My hands touched bare skin – she was so cold! She moaned at my touch, then started coughing.

I tried to find her a blanket in the dark, but I couldn't. Even the mattress was gone. While she still slept, I wanted to go get her another blanket from the house. Maybe a quilt, too, I decided. After all, it wasn't like I couldn't spare mine.

Quickly and quietly, I made my way back to the house, grabbed the quilt, then headed to the cupboard where the extra blankets were kept. I bundled the quilt into my arms and grabbed the top two blankets.

I detoured by the kitchen on the way back, switching on the light. I opened the fridge and wished I'd asked them to pick up some extra food for Caitlin. I grabbed a can of Coke from the box on the bench and raised my hand to turn off the light.

There was a smear of blood on the light switch. I looked down, to see two bloody handprints on my quilt. I turned my hands over, dreading what I knew I'd find.

Traces of her blood stained my hands.

NOOOO! I screamed in my head, knowing that my mouth was open, but I couldn't make a sound. Can't let her die. Have to help her. To hell with everything else.

I shoved the Coke in my pocket, tightening my arms around the blankets and quilt. I ran all the way back to her.

I set the quilt down beside her and she barely stirred. She was cold and asleep, which gave me the idea of trying to smuggle her out as a corpse as she slept. After all, Mike expected me to kill her tonight.

I gave her the last pills I had left, to make sure she'd sleep until I could get her to hospital. Desperately, I prayed my crazy plan would work, so I could save both her and Chris.

Then I tried to wrap her in the quilt, thinking to cover her face as if she really was a corpse. The quilt almost smothered her, so I took it off her and wrapped her in the blankets instead. Focussing on her even breathing on my shoulder, reminding myself with every step that I had to keep her alive, keep her breathing, I cradled her blanket-wrapped body and carried her to the car. I laid her carefully across the back seat, closing the door as quietly as I could, before I slid in behind the steering wheel.

I drove to the beach, to the spot I always drove to. Where they'd found Alanna and I'd never find peace. I knew she had to get to hospital as soon as possible, but this was my only chance at pulling this off. Protecting her and my sister.

Once I'd failed to obey my orders and stop them from taking her, Mott's next orders were clear. Tail them until they dumped the body and catch them on the way out.

Catch them, keep Chris safe... and keep Caitlin alive. I didn't think I could succeed in all three, but I had to try. I'd take two out of three - the most important two. To hell with the rest.

I forced myself to park the car and take the keys out of the ignition. I clenched my hands on the steering wheel and took a deep breath. When my exhalation emptied my lungs, I shoved the door open and stood up.

I slammed my door shut and opened the one behind it. She looked as if she hadn't moved at all during the short drive. I leaned over to check on her before I touched her. I could hear her breathing, which sounded wheezy, as if she had a cough or worse.

I remember desperately wanting to take her to hospital NOW, to shut the door, get back in the car and drive as quickly as I could.

I lifted her out of the car and carried her to the beach. I laid her on the sand, still wrapped in the blankets.

I realised that I'd left my phone in the car, so I went back to get it, bringing back the first aid kit from the car, too, little good though it might be. I switched the phone on for the first time in weeks and rang an ambulance, telling them I'd found a girl lying unconscious on the beach. Then I rang the police and told them the same thing. Only I told the police it was my fault.

I took the scissors from the first aid kit

and tried to cut through the rope around her wrists, but they were too caked in dried blood. I looked for something to wipe it away with and came up with a bottle of disinfectant, a couple of vials of saline and some gauze. Dousing the gauze in the disinfectant, I hesitated. "I'm sorry, Caitlin, this will hurt, but I need to do it to free your hands," I told her, wincing as I touched the gauze to her wrist. She didn't react, even when I poured the remaining disinfectant over her hands and wrists, and I realised why. She couldn't feel her hands - the rope was cutting off her circulation, or she was too cold.

I hacked at the rope with the scissors again and I felt the strands part. When I pulled the rope away, her hands stayed in the twisted position they'd been tied in. I tried to massage some blood back into her poor hands, but I stopped as I realised that her hands were twisted because her fingers were broken.

Shaken, I sat back for a second, trying to work out what to do next. It was too dark to see clearly, the crescent moon visible between clouds, then hidden again. I needed to wake her up, I decided, so that she could tell me where she was injured. Why there was so much blood... No, first I needed to cut her free. I sawed at the rope around her legs. This was cleaner, without the blood coating, so it was the work of barely a moment to free her completely.

"Wake up, angel. Now you're free." I'm not sure if I just thought it or if I said it aloud.

I poured the contents of the bottle of saline onto a bandage and started washing her face, willing her to wake up. She stirred at the cold touch and I tried to reassure her.

I thought I heard a car door slam, back on the road. I left her to walk back to the road, to see if the ambulance had arrived, but there was no one there, just my car. I walked up and down the road a bit, looking, but saw nothing and no one.

So I headed back to her. Too late.

I could see their silhouettes in the moonlight, her lying on the sand, him crouching next to her or on top of her, I couldn't say. By the time I was close enough to tell, he'd stood up and started walking to meet me. She just lay there not moving and I could feel my heart freeze as I wondered if she was already dead. "She can't be, she can't be..." I mumbled to myself, forcing my legs to keep trudging toward them.

"Are you listening?" he hissed. I knew he'd been speaking already, but I never heard it, so I can't remember it. "I said if you want her, now's your last chance. She doesn't fight as much any more. May as well do her before you kill her."

Some ancient instinct stirred at the thought, I'm ashamed to admit, and more besides. Traitor, I thought, willing it to go down, as I trudged across the beach to where she lay, naked on the sand.

Mike tossed me his gun and I almost missed it. My palms were sweaty and the gun threatened to slip out of my hand onto the sand, though I clutched at it like a lifeline. "You can do this," I muttered aloud to myself.

As though he'd heard, Mike called out, "Go on, Chris. Oh, and give her a little kiss to wake her up, before you stick it in her."

My eyes on her, I registered dully that, shining in the moonlight, there was a slick of fresh blood on her thighs from what he'd done to her before I got here.

I'd reached her by then. There was no need to wake her up - her eyes stared blankly at the sky. I fell to my knees beside her and still she didn't move. The ice in my heart spread throughout my body as I thought, Oh my God, she's already dead. I leaned over, cupped her cheek in my free hand, closed my eyes and kissed her cold lips. I was so stunned I barely felt her icy fingers on the gun in my hand, forcing it slowly up. I sat up, jolted by the thought that she was still alive, barely registering that she'd made me bring the gun up to her face, where she held the barrel to her forehead.

"Do it," she rasped, holding the barrel firmly in her twisted fingers. Her eyes still stared up at the sky, not at me. No longer blank, now they were full of pain and anguish and... defeat? "I've had enough pain. Give me death. Please. Before the pain comes back." Her eyes begged me now, dark pools in her face that seemed to drag me in, eyes that I wanted to see laughing, defiant, even crying, ANYTHING but this, like twin black holes pulling on my heart. "End it." Her fingers crept up the gun, but she didn't have the strength to move the trigger.

My heart dropped to new depths of despair. I'd promised her I wouldn't let them hurt her again, yet it had happened twice. I owed her more than I could ever repay. I couldn't let her die - by his hand or hers. Or mine.

Mike's voice came from behind me, coming closer. "Want me to show you how to do it? Sure, this one's even better than your sister was. I wonder how good the other one will be..."

If her eyes were black holes, I felt like a sun about to go nova. My eyes held hers as I rose to my feet, wrenching the gun from her fingers. I heard the snap of bone as she cried out in pain. A heart-wrenching sound that would haunt me later, but I felt almost numb to it at the time. End it, I thought.

I swung around and shot him, point blank in the chest, where his heart should have been. Then again, in the head, over and over, 'til the gun was empty and he had to be dead, as he slumped onto the sand. I lowered the gun and walked over to him. I pulled his shirt over his head, though it was already covered in blood and gained more in the process, and checked for a pulse. Dead, after all this time, finally DEAD. I spat on his corpse and carried the shirt he didn't need any more back to her.

She was barely conscious and so cold she wasn't even shivering, as I struggled to put the bloody shirt on her. It might have reached her knees, had she the strength to stand, but I doubted she'd manage that tonight.

I opened my jacket, then slid an arm under her shoulders to help her sit up. I held a blanket against her back as I wrapped my arms around her, trying to share my body warmth. She slumped against me as I called her name over and over, urging her to wake up.

"Why? The nightmares aren't as bad," she grumbled finally, her eyes still closed. I could have cried, I could have kissed her, I could have danced with her all along the beach, because in my head I was almost singing, She's conscious, and if I can keep her that way 'til she's warm she's going to live and I won't have killed her, I won't...

One less crime on my conscience tonight.

Instead, I replied, "It's over. They're not going to hurt you again."

She gave a breathy snort of laughter. "Promise?" Her tone was wistful, though she also sounded resigned to hearing a no.

The only way I could make sure I hadn't killed her was to keep her alive. "I swear I'll never let them hurt you, ever again."

"Then you'll have to kill them all," she said. "Because they won't let me live. Or you, either. We can identify them."

"It doesn't matter," I replied. "We'll say I did it. I hurt you. You'll go to hospital and my sister will be safe. I'll... get arrested. Go to prison. And it'll be okay."

I became aware of something in my pocket. Reaching in, I pulled out the forgotten can of Coke. I cracked it open and took a mouthful, before I pushed the can to her lips. "Drink this. It's Coke. The sugar'll give you some energy."

She opened her eyes, looking bewildered, before she took a sip. I held the can for her – gun in one hand, can in the other – as she drank, until she'd finished it. When it was empty, I dropped it on the sand, not caring about anything but her.

"You need to warm up. You're too cold," I told her, wrapping the blanket tighter around her, pulling her closer to me. "Stay with me, angel. You need to stay awake 'til you're warm. Tell me about your family."

"Caitlin," she mumbled.

She was still sleepy from the pills. Pills I shouldn't have given her, I realised now, too late. "Hmmm?"

"Caitlin. My name is Caitlin."

"I know," I replied softly. "You didn't want me to..."

"My friend. You... saved my life. That makes you my friend. You can... call me by my name." She coughed violently and rested her head against me.

"Sure, angel. Caitlin," I corrected. "It'll take some getting used to. Is it okay if I occasionally call you angel, too?"

She nodded slowly, her body growing heavier as she drowsed. But I couldn't let her sleep. Not yet.

I repeated my question. "Tell me about your family. The people who'll be really relieved to see you very soon." I was patient. What else did I have to do but keep her awake and help her get warm until the ambulance came?

"I don't have much family. My mother died when I was very little - I don't remember her. There's just my father and he works away so much, on contracts, that I don't know if he'll even know I've been gone..." Her voice faded and I tried to think of something else to ask her, to keep her talking, but my mind was blank when she suddenly asked, "What day is it? I mean, the date?"

I had to think a moment, then checked my watch. "It's the 31st of July."

She let out a wordless exclamation, then swallowed. After a few moments, she spoke again. "Then the semester's started. I'll be so behind."

I fought down a laugh. Just like Alanna, her first thoughts were to her studies. Not how long those bastards had her, not how many days 'til her birthday... how many days she was into the semester.

My blank mind coalesced into a question.

"What are you studying?"

"Medicine." She started coughing.

I automatically tried to pull the blanket tighter around her, my mind suddenly anything but blank. Full of questions, I didn't know which one to ask first.

How old are you?

Did you know Alanna?

Why did I never see you there?

What would a normal person ask first?

"How long have you been studying that?" I tried to ask casually, but I found I was gritting my teeth.

"One semester," she croaked, her throat still sounding raw from all the coughing.

So she started after... I took a year off. She couldn't have known Alanna. I wouldn't have seen her. That'd make her around eighteen.

"What made you choose medicine?" I asked.

She cleared her throat twice before the words came out in her voice. "Someone told me once that it helped them feel better just because I was there. I remember feeling useless and wishing I knew enough to be able to do something more material to help them. I went and got my first aid certificate, but it wasn't enough. I wanted to be a doctor because... one day I could save someone's life and that makes it all worth it..."

She continued speaking, but I didn't hear it. The voice I heard was Alanna's. "What if after all my study I could save someone's life? How could you want to do anything less, if it meant someone could die if you didn't do everything you could?"

Don't let her die. Keep her alive.

I became aware of the faint sound of sirens, coming closer, as I realised Caitlin had fallen silent, her head coming to rest on my chest.

"Stay with me, Caitlin. You can't sleep yet," I warned her.

She raised her head. "Tell me about you, instead," she mumbled. "I don't know anything about you, not even your real name, nothing, except that you finally want to help me. Pity you're not a doctor..."

That night I wished I was a doctor - how much she'd never know.

I tried to laugh it off. "I'm dull and boring. If I tell you about me, I'll put you to sleep. Maybe later, when you're warm and having trouble getting to sleep."

"So tired." She yawned. "It's hard to imagine having trouble getting to sleep. It's too hard trying to stay awake... Tell me something interesting about you, something that will help me stay awake."

I hesitated, opened my mouth to say something even as I didn't know what to say. "I'll tell you my real name when you're safe in hospital," I lied. "Hang on until then and I swear I'll tell you anything you want to know." I wouldn't be allowed to go with her to hospital - I was about to be arrested.

"Okay..." she began grudgingly, "but..."

Red and blue flashing lights lit up the beach. People in police uniform came spilling out of the dunes, shouting incoherently, as I strained to hear her finish what she'd tried to say.

"It's all right, angel," I said softly. "The police are here. They'll take the vicious, raping bastard away and you'll be safe."

Her reaction was the opposite of what I'd expected. She clutched at me, her arms suddenly around me under my jacket. "No. They'll find a way to kill us. If you leave me alone, they'll hurt me again. They won't want to leave witnesses. Don't leave me. You promised!"

Fuck. My whole plan lay in tatters. She was right, of course. They'd kill us. Maybe if I killed myself they'd leave her alone and... no. The only way to keep her alive was to stay with her. Oh God, I called the fucking police. In a move that could get her killed.

I pulled her closer, unconsciously tightening my grip on the gun as they fanned out to encircle us, stopping several metres away.

"Great. Now, thanks to the sirens, he's got a gun and a hostage. Now what?" a voice lamented.

Her raspy breathing became more rapid. I had no hostage - she couldn't feel her legs, let alone walk - and the gun was useless empty. My brain raced her breathing, the gun by her throat. I lifted the gun into the air and started to pull back the trigger, to show them that it wasn't loaded, and they backed away a bit.

"Don't kill her," one of them breathed, more in disbelief than to me.

Kill her? I couldn't do it, not even when she begged me to.

I stood up slowly, cradling her body in my arms, trying to keep the blankets around her.

This gave one of them the cue he needed to start giving orders. "Put the girl down and step away from her, hands in the air."

"No," she whimpered, her face white with pain and effort as she wrapped her arms clumsily around my neck. The blankets slid away from her chest, exposing her blood-soaked shirt.

I only held her tighter. "Get her an ambulance. She needs help. She's badly hurt - I'll put her down only in an ambulance."

I could hear one hiss to the other, "She's bleeding badly - look at her shirt! Let him get her back to the road, then..." He lowered his voice so I couldn't hear the rest, but I could guess... then we get him. I was beyond caring.

"I want to get her to hospital. She needs help - there's so much blood," I repeated, much louder.

"There's an ambulance back at the road. You can take her there," a voice called back.

I took a step forward and they took more steps back.

One step forward, two steps back, like some kind of deadly dance, through sand dunes that shifted and presented a pale backdrop to the real drama, like unwilling spectators. To say nothing of the unwilling participants.

Back on the road, bathed in the blinking red-blue-purple light from the patrol cars, was the promised ambulance, glowing like a beacon in the weird light show. It had one door open and ambulance officers standing by - like a chauffeured limousine, ready to take care of her every need.

I laid her carefully on the stretcher. In the bright, harsh light of the ambulance, I saw for the first time what they'd done to her - what I'd done to her, in letting them hurt her. Every bit of her skin that I could see was a mess of bruises and fresh and dried blood. Mike's bloodied shirt hardly helped matters, but it probably hid far worse injuries than those I could already see.

You let them do this, I told myself, trying to hide my horror as I covered her up with a hospital-issue blanket. Scared to do anything that might hurt her further, I forced myself to reassure her as she looked at me pleadingly. I touched her hair, briefly, and smiled as best I could as I voiced my desperate hope. "You're going to be all right."

And, with an effort, she smiled back.

I drank in the sight of her. Surely saving this amazing girl's life counted for something in the overall scheme of things. Deep in my gut, I dreaded she was right and I was going to die soon. I wished I'd left some bullets in the gun - I could've used one to end the uncertainty.

Somebody behind me roughly took my arm, saying something about a few questions, and started pulling me back out of the ambulance. I stared at her in shock as she reached out for me with a hand on which all of the fingers were definitely broken, bones protruding through her skin in ways that were far from normal. Just like Alanna's had been. As I focussed on her hand, for a moment it wasn't her face I saw behind it, but Alanna's. Not alive, but as dead as she'd been when I identified her in the mortuary. Like a zombie, risen from the dead to make me pay for my negligence.

You don't get to die today. You still have work to do.

I was too stunned to resist as I followed my arm out of the ambulance and back onto the road.

An ambulance officer climbed in then and hid her from sight.

Reluctantly, I turned away.

"You're in no shape to drive. I'll give you a lift to the hospital." The sympathetic voice belonged to a police officer who looked almost thirty – Senior Constable Nick Dennis, his uniform said. He gestured toward one of the patrol cars.

"Aren't you going to arrest me?" I asked dully.

"Just get in the car," he said. "As long as you cooperate, I won't need to yet." He opened the rear door.

My bum had barely touched the seat before I heard raised voices. I jumped up, trying to see what was happening.

He turned his head toward the noise, his body blocking the doorway as he started to close the door. "You should have shot her while you had the chance."

I froze with one leg sticking out of the car.

No. No... not Caitlin... they paid off a police officer... and he'd shoot me as soon as we got on the road. Caitlin... her time would come later. The ambulance officers? The nurses? The doctor? Oh God...

I threw my weight against the door. It flew open, knocking the crooked cop aside for a second, and I saw.

Caitlin crouched at the door of the ambulance, where she wasn't supposed to be.

He took advantage of my distraction, trying to push me back inside his car, but the crack as my fist met his jaw sent him to the ground. Once he was out my way, I ran to her.

She'd climbed out of the ambulance and started staggering toward me, arms outstretched. The image of a zombie, a walking corpse – an image I'd never get out of my mind.

I swore softly under my breath – she had a death wish, this girl I had to keep alive. And I couldn't live with myself if I let her die the way Alanna had.

I could hear the police officer on the ground shouting something at me, but I wasn't paying attention, so I didn't turn around to look, just kept running toward her.

"NO!" she screamed as, sickeningly, she stumbled, and her legs gave way beneath her. She fell to her knees in the gravel. She would have pitched forward face-first had I not dived forward to reach her before the rest of her body hit the ground. Her weight pushed me down onto the road. Pain burned across my shoulder as she screamed again and more blood flowed down her leg. The echo of the shots resounded in the cold air.

I opened my mouth to tell her how stupid... but those tortured eyes could have shut up even the most garrulous politician.

She sobbed helplessly, drenched in tears, shaking so violently she had trouble getting the words out. "Don't... leave me."

She's been shot. The cop was aiming for me but shot her instead. It's my fault she's been shot. The thought registered and I forgot anything else. "It's all right. I wasn't leaving you." I tried to stem the stream of blood with my hands.

The torment and the pain in her eyes! Under that lurked raw terror. "Never... hurt... again. You... promised!"

God, she'd been right. Her terror at being alone and helpless again had driven her to find me. She barely had the strength to stand and it had almost killed her. I knew she'd kill herself before she'd let them hurt her again, if I wasn't there to stop her. And I'd let her get shot.

Her twisted fingers clutched at my shirt,

scrabbling at the gun in my pocket. Oh God, she was going to try and shoot herself again.

"Chris. Please." Her eyes were on fire in pain. Still she didn't let go.

"I'll never let them hurt you again. If I have to stay with you every waking moment until you recover. You'll never have to remind me again. And I won't let you hurt yourself, either." I peeled her fingers from my shirt. She gasped, squeezing her eyes shut, and her body went limp.

Her blood tainted my hands once more, but she was only unconscious. I carried her back to the ambulance and laid her down again, dimly aware of the other police officers pushing the handcuffed Senior Constable Dennis into the back seat of his own patrol car. The car he'd almost killed me in.

I sat beside her in the ambulance this time, as the paramedic returned to take care of her. Squeezing past me, he didn't spare me a glance as he sat beside me.

He pulled out a stack of dressing packs from the cupboard above her and tossed one to me. "Here, press down hard with that. It should slow the bleeding."

I stared at the dressing in my hands, confused. "You need me to help you?"

"No, but it'd be nice if you didn't bleed to death while I'm taking care of her. She's lost too much blood already."

I looked at him, more puzzled than ever, and he took pity on me. "You've been shot, Rambo. There's blood all down your arm."

At the bottom of the last typed page, Nathan's handwriting was almost illegible, but the words were carved deep into the paper and underlined:

<u>I'm sorry.</u>

I ripped the pages into pieces and dropped them into the kitchen bin, on top of the mushy, mouldy remains of some tomatoes I'd left in the fridge before I went to Melbourne. As I carried the rubbish bag to the wheelie bin outside, I wondered at his stupidity in writing it all down. What if someone had found it? After all the trouble I took – we both took – to hide the truth from the police and everyone else, as I'd promised I would. . . did he think I'd forgotten? Horrible memories, carved into my mind deeper than any knife could?

I dragged the wheelie bin to the kerb, hoping the rubbish truck wouldn't be too long. I needed Nathan's compromising evidence to disappear as quickly as possible.

Then I went to my bedroom and started packing my things, so I could fly away and leave all this behind to start my new life with a new name.

There could be no looking back.

After all, however sorry he might be, he didn't want me.

The story concludes with

Afterlife of Alanna Miller

the third book in the Nightmares Trilogy

ABOUT THE AUTHOR

Demelza Carlton has always loved the ocean, but on her first snorkelling trip she found she was afraid of fish.

She has since swum with sea lions, sharks and sea cucumbers and stood on spray drenched cliffs over a seething sea as a seven-metre cyclonic swell surged in, shattering a shipwreck below.

Demelza now lives in Perth, Western Australia, the shark attack capital of the world.

The *Ocean's Gift* series was her first foray into fiction, followed by her suspense thriller *Nightmares* trilogy. She swears the Mel Goes to Hell series ambushed her on a crowded train and wouldn't leave her alone.

Want to know more? You can follow Demelza on Facebook, Twitter, YouTube or her website, Demelza Carlton's Place at:

www.demelzacarlton.com

Books by Demelza Carlton

Ocean's Gift
Ocean's Gift (#1)
Ocean's Infiltrator (#2)
Ocean's Depths (#3)
Water and Fire

Turbulence and Triumph sub-series
Ocean's Justice (#1)
Ocean's Trial (#2)
Ocean's Triumph (#3)

Nightmares Trilogy
Nightmares of Caitlin Lockyer (#1)
Necessary Evil of Nathan Miller (#2)
Afterlife of Alana Miller (#3)

Mel Goes to Hell
Welcome to Hell (#1)
See You in Hell (#2)
Mel Goes to Hell (#3)
To Hell and Back (#4)
The Holiday From Hell (#5)
All Hell Breaks Loose (#6)